The Corioli Affair

The Corioli Affair

by
MARY DEASY

An Atlantic Monthly Press Book
Little, Brown and Company • Boston

ATLANTIC—LITTLE, BROWN BOOKS
ARE PUBLISHED BY
LITTLE, BROWN AND COMPANY
IN ASSOCIATION WITH
THE ATLANTIC MONTHLY PRESS

Published simultaneously in Canada
by Little, Brown & Company (Canada) Limited

PRINTED IN THE UNITED STATES OF AMERICA

The Corioli Affair

Among the documents in the possession of the Historical Society of the city of Corioli is a thick green copybook containing the following record of the events surrounding the Dayton trial, which took place in Corioli in the year 1884. The writer was Lacey Dereen, a young Irish girl who was involved in the case and who later, under the name of Moira Barry, became one of the best-known actresses on the New York and London stage. In 1896, at the height of her career, she retired to the small river town of Le Jeune, in the Upper South, where she bought the house once occupied by Captain Jed Dayton and wrote this account.

On the first page of the copybook there are written only four words: "Jed darling, how long — ?"

CHAPTER I   THAT WINTER I LIVED IN CORIOLI, IN A red-brick house on Longmill Street. There was a little shop on the ground floor where Nora Casey sold notions and candy, and above it a floor that was let to a family named Maher. Nora and I lived behind the shop. She was my father's cousin, and she had been kind enough to me when I had come, and had said she was happy to have me for the company, but I knew she had managed the shop alone before that, and that she would be even happier if I married someone or went off somewhere and found myself work. My father had left me very little money, and the trip to America had taken much of that. It had been a long, difficult journey, but Nora said it was nothing to the way it had been when she had come over, in '49. She said they had been over a month on the sea and that three people had died on the way. They had finally landed at New Orleans. That had been more than thirty years before, but she still remembered the wrought-iron balconies on the houses and the black people on the docks. She had never seen colored people before that time.

It was very exciting at first to be in a new country. In the evenings I walked down to the river and watched the great white steamboats lying at the foot of the public landing. The river was larger than the rivers in Ireland, broad and brown, with much queer debris floating lazily on its surface. Nora said it wasn't safe for me to go alone there, but there were splendid sunsets, cold and magnificent and leaving at the end only a faint stain of color over the black horizon, and no one ever spoke to me except a policeman who saw me crying one evening. He was from Galway too, and he had heard of my father, and for a long time we stood there and talked about Irish politics. He had great faith in Parnell, and said he would do what no man in the history of Ireland had ever been able to do before. He was very confident. Listening to him, I could almost believe I was hearing my father speak again.

Later, when I went back to the shop, Conn Mulranny was sitting in the little parlor behind it, drinking a whisky toddy that Nora had made for him.

"Did you bring anybody home with you?" he asked me.

His knees were doubled up before him like two great knobbed tree trunks as he sat in Nora's low rocker. I looked at him. His face looked happy. He was a little drunk.

"Why should I bring anybody?" I said.

"A nice young lad? Did you see never a nice young lad on the way, sighing for a snug room and a bit of your company?"

"Leave the girl alone, Mulranny," Nora said.

Conn grinned. "That's for the lads outside to do," he said. "She'll have the girls from every kip on Diamond Street after her with their nails for interfering with business if she goes on walking out that way. Setting a poor example, it is. A man'll be afraid to pass a word with a woman walking the streets alone for fear she'd turn out to be as respectable as the statue of the Holy Virgin on the altar of a church."

"And serve them right, too," Nora said. "The mucky creatures they are."

She sipped genteelly at her own glass. She was almost twenty years older than Conn, and her hair had gone completely gray, but she looked at him the way a young girl looks at a lover she knows she has in the palm of her hand. She had a bit of money, and the house and shop, and Conn had nothing but his own two hands.

"Unless she's practicing up to enter the profession herself," Conn said. "She'd be a lovely piece of goods for a cold night — ah, the two of you, don't mistake me," he included Nora gallantly.

Nora shrieked and bowed her head into her apron to hide her laughter.

"You're a divil out of hell, Conn Mulranny," she said. "You are and that's the truth."

"Did I ever tell you the story of how Mag Kenelly came to enter a bawdyhouse instead of a convent?" Conn said. "Straight off the boat she was, and walking along Diamond Street to see would the holy nuns take her in for a novice. Who should she ask the way of but Red Bess Scully? It's God's truth, and you can believe it or not. And Bess says to her, 'Ah, you wouldn't want to be wearing black now, would you, all the days of your life? A fine young girl like you? In this country there's barrels of opportunity for the like of you, and silk to wear along with it, from the skin out. And if you want to sing hymns for a side line, that's nothing to me. I've eight daughters at home myself, and all of them sing hymns whenever they've a mind to.' Begod, she had the girl safe in the house in forty seconds. They used to call her the Bride of the Holy Ghost."

He was very pleased with himself. Nora had flung her apron over her face and was leaning back in her chair, laughing in shocked terror and pleasure at his irreverence. She was like a young country girl who does not know how to stop her lover. It was queer to see a woman who was nearly at her sixty-mark, and sharp and experienced in business, behaving like a boisterous, frightened girl.

I stood up to go out of the room.

"Where are you going?" Nora asked me.

"To bed."

"Find yourself a nice young man to keep you warm," Conn shouted.

"Good night."

"Good night," Nora said.

She had been very good about saying nothing to me about the money. For a while after I had come to Corioli I had not wanted to see anybody because of the way I felt about my father, and she had understood that, and had not

minded that I had not gone out at once to find work for myself. I thought about that, not sleeping as I lay in bed, listening to her voice and Conn's from the parlor.

Afterward she came into the bedroom, sighing guiltily
and beginning to say her prayers half-aloud as she undressed in the dark. In the middle of them she suddenly
stopped.

"Lacey," she said cautiously.

"I'm not asleep."

"I wouldn't want to wake you," she said, "but if I don't
tell someone the tongue'll jump out of my head with keeping it." She came over and sat down on the edge of the bed.
"Didn't that divil of a Mulranny ask me to marry him tonight?" she said.

"And will you?"

"Ah, have sense, girl — at my age! What would people be
saying of me?" She waited for me to speak. "And he's ten
years younger than myself, it may be," she went on at last,
a little more doubtfully.

"It may be."

"Still, he's a grand man to have about the house. You
wouldn't deny that. Six feet of him, and the shoulders on
him as broad as an ox." She was braiding her hair; I could
just see her hands moving swiftly in the dark. "And he
isn't the first to tell me I'm a fine decent figure of a woman
still myself," she complained.

I knew what she wanted me to say.

"Are you very fond of him?" I asked.

She shrieked again. "Ah, go to God! Fond of that great
omadhaun!" She was embarrassed. She got up from the bed
and I heard her moving about in the dark, adding a drop
of oil to the little light that was burning before the picture
of the Virgin on the wall. "It's the way I should be asking
that class of question of you, a young girl," she said, "not
you of me." She paused. "Isn't there ever one of the lads
around here you have a fancy for?" she asked hopefully.
"Sure you might catch any one of them if you tried."

"No," I said.

"There's Bartley Lynch. He has a fine job now with the railroad, they say."

"No."

"Would there be somebody in Galway, then?"

"Can't you have your love affair without trying to make one up for me too?"

I knew she had it in her mind to marry Conn Mulranny. She had me on her hands now, and that complicated matters a bit. I wanted to tell her I would not be a complication, but I thought I might hurt her feelings if I did.

After she had come to bed and fallen asleep I lay awake thinking what I would do. I had traveled all over Ireland with my father, and kept the two of us in clothes and food on little enough money, and for six months I had lived in London when my father had gone there as an Irish Nationalist Member of Parliament; but none of that seemed a very good recommendation for any sort of work I was likely to get in Corioli. There was only one person I knew of who might help me. Her name was Margaret Dandy and she was a relative of my mother's. I knew very little about her except that she had quarreled with my father and that she lived in a big cut-stone house on Sevier Street with her nephew, who was an attorney. I made up my mind that I would go to see her the next day. It was a long time now since I had found out that it is very easy to be brave when there is nothing else for you to do.

CHAPTER II   IN THE MORNING IT WAS FINE, AND I walked over to Sevier Street about eleven. The red-brick-and-stone fronts of the houses looked very cheerful in the morning sun. There had been snow in the night but it had melted quickly, and now there were only rivulets of water across the walks where the last of the snow had lain. The air was cold and felt like spring.

Miss Dandy's house was set far back, with an iron fence shutting it off from the street. Behind the fence there were trees and a long brick walk that led up to the house past a silent cast-iron dog on the lawn. The houses around were built directly on the street, so that the bare shrubs and trees before Miss Dandy's house looked queer and rather out of place. I went up the walk and up the steps and rang the bell. I had no idea what was going to happen.

A conscientious-looking country girl in a blue cap and apron opened the door for me. She seemed to be new in the house, and when I asked to see Miss Dandy she did not ask my name, but went off into another room where she began talking excitedly to someone. In a few moments she came back.

"Are you the young lady about the bazaar?" she asked.

"I'm afraid I'm not," I said. She looked more confused than ever. "I'm a relative of Miss Dandy's," I said.

"Oh, you'd better come in so," she said recklessly. She threw the door open and pointed me the way to the parlor on the right.

I went to the parlor door and stood there waiting. Miss Dandy was sitting at the other end of the room, playing with an old white cat that was lying in her lap. She held a spool suspended by a cord for him to tap at. The cat was very lazy and looked bored with the game.

Miss Dandy glanced up as I came to the door. I saw that she was a formidable-looking woman with a long alert ugly face. She wore a dark iridescent silk dress that changed color like the feathers on a pigeon's breast in the bars of sunlight coming through the blinds.

"You're not about the bazaar," she said.

"No," I said. "I'm Lacey Dereen."

"Are you indeed?" She stopped dangling the spool before the cat and looked directly at me. Her eyes were like marbles, very dark and clear and unreadable. "Fair," she said.

"Blue eyes. Quite a nice little face if it weren't for that determined chin. You don't resemble your mother; I remember her as a very beautiful girl."

She had not asked me to sit down. I stood there waiting.

"You took your own time about coming to see me," she said. "If you'd had any proper sense, you'd have come to me in the first place instead of to Nora Casey. Or did your father warn you against your mother's relatives?"

"He told me you would probably have no use for me, as you hadn't for him."

"Nonsense. Of course I was angry with your mother when she married him. She was brought up right here on Sevier Street, you know; I thought as much of her as if she'd been my own daughter. And she might have married very well — something better than a man out of a thatched cottage who thought he'd been sent by God or Saint Patrick to deliver Ireland. The only saving part of the business is that she didn't live to see him die in Kilmainham Jail."

"He died in Kilmainham Jail because he loved Ireland more than he cared for his own safety," I said.

I turned toward the door.

"Where are you going?" she called after me. She sounded astonished.

"I'm sorry. If I spoke badly of your father, would you stand listening to it?"

"My father was a bad husband and a poor father and I say it myself," she said. "I'm a realist; I've learned how to face facts." She lifted the white cat and set him on the floor. He was heavy; his hind legs dangled stiffly as she put him down. "Come over here and sit down," she said. "I suppose you came to me for a reason."

I had known before I came that I would have to swallow my pride, but now it was not pleasant to turn again and walk slowly across the room and sit down on the chair before her. It was a fine room, a long double parlor with two marble fireplaces and a pair of tall windows at each end.

There was a chandelier in the center that hung from a large white-painted medallion of twisted vines and grapes on the ceiling.

Miss Dandy sat looking at me, waiting for me to begin.

"I'd like to find some work to do," I said. "I thought you might be able to help me."

"Is that all?"

"Yes."

"Have you any money?"

"No. A little. Not much."

"And no young man who wants to marry you?"

"No."

She lifted her shoulders. "Why don't you stay where you are and wait? There will be one. Even if I am not married myself, I know it isn't hard for a young woman to find a man who will marry her. If she isn't too particular, of course."

I did not say anything.

"Nora wants to be rid of you — is that it?" she asked.

"No." I didn't know how much I ought to tell her. "She'll probably be marrying soon herself," I said.

"Marrying? Nora Casey?" She sat back in surprise. "The woman's older than I am. I never heard anything so ridiculous in my life. Is she going into her second childhood?"

"She's lonely, I suppose," I said.

"So am I lonely, but I don't make a fool of myself because of it. I don't believe in giving in to emotion. When I was a girl I saw my older brother and his wife lying dead in that room upstairs" — she raised her eyes briefly to the ceiling — "a murder and a suicide, for nothing but unbridled emotion. I made up my mind then that that would never happen to me. If I want to make a fool of myself, it won't be over anything more dangerous than an old white cat."

I sat waiting. I was sorry that I had come. It seemed that I would not gain anything by it after all, and it made me feel very depressed to listen to her. I sat there trying to think of an excuse to leave.

Somebody turned a key in the lock of the front door and came into the house.

"That will be my nephew," Miss Dandy said. "You had better talk to him. He may be able to do something for you." She raised her voice slightly and called, "Thomas."

A man of about forty, rather stocky, with very blue eyes and thinning hair, came into the room. He looked much more Irish than Miss Dandy. He was the sort of man you can see in every little town in Ireland, gregarious and persuasive and full of easy flattery that he will use on you across the counter of his shop or from behind the desk in his law office.

"This is John Dereen's daughter," Miss Dandy said to him. "She wants to find some work to do."

He stood there looking from one to the other of us, smiling a little, his eyes very bright and clever in his round florid face.

"I'm very glad to meet you, my dear," he said. "And what sort of work would it be, now?"

He came over and sat down. I felt at home with him. I knew the look in his eyes, the queer bright light you see in the eyes of men who live by their wits, whether it is keeping a little shop together that ought rightly to have gone down long before, or wheedling a prisoner's neck out of a jury with nothing more than a few flimsy tatters of evidence.

"I'm not sure," I said. "I thought I might be able to teach in a school. Only the little children, of course. I'm afraid I'm not very thoroughly educated."

"You sound very thoroughly educated to me," Thomas Dandy said. "You wouldn't have to teach them geometry, you know. We go very fast here in America, but we still haven't managed to bring philosophy and Greek into the third grade."

"She would have to have a certificate," Miss Dandy said. "Of course she hasn't got a certificate."

She did not seem interested in me any longer. She had picked up the cat and was playing with it again.

"We'll get her a certificate," Thomas Dandy said. "There'll be no difficulty at all. Of course it may be easier if we try to find a place for her across the river. They're not so particular down there." He looked at me. He was adding me up behind his intent, encouraging smile. "All you'll need to do is to study up on our American currency," he said. "I don't know about your Irish schoolbooks, but our American ones are full of examples about A buying so many apples for ten cents, and B so many for fifteen, and then the two of them going into some complicated financial transactions with each other."

He seemed to think it was all settled. He stopped talking about the schoolteaching and began asking me questions about my father. He said he had never known my father, but that he had admired him very much.

"He was a man of principles," he said. "I'm afraid I haven't any principles."

I did not know what to say to that. I thought he and Miss Dandy were both very queer people, the one saying she had no emotions and the other saying he had no principles.

"I'm sure you have lovely principles," I said. I was trying to make a joke out of it.

"No, I haven't. I haven't any principles at all. That's why I'm so successful."

I couldn't tell if he was joking or not. He sat there smiling at me.

"You're very much like the pictures I've seen of your father," he said. "I'd have known you anywhere: all that fair hair, and those blue eyes that look straight at you and straight through you — A very poetical gentleman told me once that John Dereen carried his innocence and his courage in his eyes like a flower."

He broke off then and asked me to stay to lunch, but I said Nora didn't know where I was and I would have to go back to the shop.

"I'll get in touch with you then," he said. "Are you sure you won't stay?"

"I really shouldn't."

I said good-by to Miss Dandy and he brought me to the door.

"I'll find you a fine job," he promised me. "It's a poor time of year to be trying, but I'll do my best."

I did not think he was really much more interested in me than Miss Dandy was. He seemed very good-natured, and he probably did things for people automatically, knowing besides that a favor is never wasted to a man who is in a profession where he may have to ask many favors of other people. Still I liked him very much. It was impossible not to like him.

That evening I told Nora I had gone to see the Dandys about a job. She was hurt and a little upset; without my saying it she knew that I had gone because of what she had told me about herself and Conn.

"Ah well, then, it's only natural you'd want to take up with them," she said. She was rather stiff about it, trying not to let me see how she felt. "They've a good deal more money than I'll ever have, with only my bit of a shop here."

We were sitting at supper in the kitchen behind the shop. The door opened and Conn Mulranny came in. He looked at us both, seeing that something was wrong.

"Quarreling, is it?" he said.

"It's not that at all," Nora said. "Where would you get such an idea?" Without asking him if he would stay, she got up and set another place. "It's only this girl here," she said, "has gone waltzing off to the Dandys asking them to find her a job because I gave her a whisper of what you said to me last evening."

"What did I say to you, acushla?" Conn reached his great

arms around her from behind and kissed her on the cheek. "Somehow it doesn't come back to me at all. You'd best be reminding me what it was."

"Ah, you divil, you!" Nora pulled herself free of him, blushing and bridling. "As if you'd forget a thing like that —"

"I might, I might now. Oh, it'd make a great difference, sure, if I'd got a plain answer out of you, but I never had the head for this flithering and flathering."

I got up to leave them alone. Nora was having a fine time. She had forgotten all about the Dandys already. Conn looked around at me over his shoulder.

"Tell Tommy Dandy he's the greatest rogue and whore's son alive in this town," he said. "Tell him I told you."

I did not say anything.

"Gallows-snatcher," he said. "Tell him they call him that on every street corner in this town. Tell him the day will come when it'll be his own neck he'll be wheedling and bribing and conniving for, instead of some jailbird's who can pay him a fat fee."

I went out of the room. He was a little drunk, as usual. It seemed foolish to worry about what he had said.

CHAPTER III   IN MARCH THE DAYS WERE LONGER. The buds thickened on the few small trees that grew crowded in the narrow spaces between the houses on Longmill Street, and children began to play in the cobblestoned street outside the shop till long after dusk. While I waited to hear from the Dandys I kept the shop for Nora or helped her with the sewing for her wedding. She was going to marry Conn at the end of the month, and she was fitting herself out in a green silk dress that needed more stays than she had worn in twenty years to be able to reach around her.

She and Conn were very skeptical about the Dandys, and I began to wonder too as the days went by and I did not hear from them. Finally one morning there was a note from Miss Dandy, asking me to come and see her that day at four. She did not mention anything about a school. Nora said she would probably give me tea and as a special privilege allow me the favor of holding her cat.

"I know that dirty white cat," she said.

"He's beautifully clean," I said. "I've never seen such a clean cat in my life."

"Much good that will do you. Bartley Lynch was nosing around here last evening. You'd best stay at home and put a curl in your front hair so you'd look nice for him if he comes around again tonight."

I laughed and said I would do that the next day. She was very anxious to have me safely married.

When I arrived at Miss Dandy's house that afternoon there was someone with her in the parlor. It was raining, and there was a pearl-handled umbrella in the stand in the hall and a green Ottoman-silk dolman hanging on the hall-tree. From the parlor I could hear a light girlish voice talking very quickly. The maid said please would I go right in, Miss Dandy was expecting me.

Miss Dandy was sitting in the same chair that I had seen her in first, pouring tea with the white cat on her lap, the cat arching its neck to peer greedily over the urn at the cream pitcher on the tray. Opposite her there was a pretty young woman with dark chestnut hair and very large, intense hazel eyes.

"Come in," Miss Dandy said. She did not stop pouring the tea to look up at me. "Did you walk in this rain? Are your feet wet? I made Sallie take her shoes off. Any woman who wears such ridiculously thin shoes in March in the rain deserves to be introduced to someone in her stocking feet. Mrs. Dayton—Miss Dereen."

"How do you do?" Mrs. Dayton said. She did not look old enough to be married. Then I noticed the line between her eyes. She was probably several years older than I was—twenty-four or twenty-five. It was her manner that made her seem like a young girl. "I don't know what they'll say when I bring back such a pretty teacher to Le Jeune," she said.

She had a lovely voice. I was beginning to recognize a Southern accent when I heard one. Corioli, they told me, was the gateway to the South, but it was not strictly speaking a Southern city, though it had many of the characteristics of one. Across the river it was legitimately the South. I did not think Mrs. Dayton came from Corioli, and later I learned that she had been brought up in La Fayette, which is ninety miles south of Corioli and as legitimately Southern as anything west of the Alleghenies. Miss Dandy said she lived now in a small down-river town called Le Jeune.

"Their school has just lost its teacher," she said to me. "You needn't look sympathetic; it was marriage, not death. Thomas knows a good many people down there, and he's pulled some wires, so you're to have the place. Fortunately Sallie is leaving tomorrow; you'll be able to travel with her. She's promised to see to everything for you. The school board has already arranged matters with some very respectable people who will be glad to give you a room."

She poured some cream into a saucer and set it on the floor for the cat. He stood up in her lap, waved his tail cautiously once or twice, and jumped down. I looked at Mrs. Dayton.

"Tomorrow?" I said.

"Yes. At five. My husband is the master of the *Fair Maid;* we're going on her. Have you ever been on a river packet? The *Maid* is a beautiful boat; my husband thinks she's the most beautiful boat on the river. He has another boat named the *Sallie Dayton,* and it's not nearly so beautiful."

"The *Sallie Dayton* is a very serviceable boat," Miss Dandy said. "I expect it will be making its regular trips down to Memphis long after the *Fair Maid* is at the bottom of the river. I've noticed that the more magnificent a steamboat is, the more likely it is to have an idiot for an engineer and a madman for a master."

"Oh, no," Mrs. Dayton said. "Jed never takes chances; he's very careful. He'd as soon take chances with Lorna or me as with the *Fair Maid.* Sooner, I reckon."

"How is Lorna?" Miss Dandy asked.

"She's very well. She's a wonderful child. She's never ill." She looked over at me brightly. "She'll be one of your pupils," she said. "It's her first year at school; I'm afraid she doesn't like it very much."

I said something polite. Miss Dandy handed me a cup of tea; I was glad of the excuse it gave me to seem to fasten my attention on it for a moment. I did not know how I felt. I was glad for the school, but it is not pleasant to be taken up and set down somewhere else as if you had no mind or will of your own.

Mrs. Dayton got up and said that, really, she had to leave.

"Are you at the St. Victor?" Miss Dandy asked her.

"Yes. I wanted to go to the Phoenix; Jed always stays there when he comes to Corioli alone. It's so much more picturesque down there on the river."

"And so much less respectable," Miss Dandy said. "You ought to get rid of those romantic ideas. At your age it's positively disgraceful." She looked down. "Where are your shoes? Or is that another of your romantic notions — to go walking around Corioli in your stocking feet?"

"Oh, dear," Mrs. Dayton said. "I suppose I did forget."

She stooped quickly, found the shoes under her chair, and sat down again to put them on. They were made of bronze leather, fastened with many little straps across the open front. I noticed that they were very small and fitted beautifully.

"I don't know what your poor mother would say if she could see the way you go on," Miss Dandy said. "Does she ever come to Le Jeune?"

Mrs. Dayton shook her head. "You know she and Jed don't agree. I sent Lorna to her while I came on this trip. She's very fond of Lorna."

"She's very fond of *you*. I don't know what she would say. Those ridiculous shoes in weather like this, and that disgracefully expensive hat."

Mrs. Dayton turned to me and began talking quickly about the trip the next day. I was to meet her at the St. Victor Hotel at a quarter past four. She said we would be in Le Jeune in the morning. She told me also that she was going to be very fond of me, and that she was sure they would not keep me long at the school because somebody would certainly make off with me and marry me. I began to think that everybody I met in America was only interested in finding someone to marry me.

After she had gone I sat down again. I did not know how long I was expected to stay, but I supposed I should at least finish my tea.

"She's a foolish young woman," Miss Dandy said. I thought she had probably spoken of me in just that practical tone to Mrs. Dayton before I had come in. It was not a pleasant thought. "She comes from a very good family, and she married very young and very badly, and now she's paying the consequences. Everyone knows her husband married her for her money except her. Of course she may know it too, but she won't admit it."

I did not say anything. I liked Mrs. Dayton, or I was sorry for her because she looked so bright and vulnerable and determined to be happy, and I did not want to talk about her. I sat there knowing I would have to thank Miss Dandy, and wishing Thomas Dandy were there so I could thank him instead. Miss Dandy said he would be home shortly, but she did not ask me to stay until he came.

CHAPTER IV   NORA AND CONN WENT WITH ME TO the St. Victor Hotel the next afternoon. The rain had cleared off and it was a fine early spring day, the right kind of day to walk into a splendid hotel lobby filled with the warm green smell of potted palms, and the mingled odor of many perfumes, and furs and silks of ladies, and bright buttons and neat red jackets of darting bellboys. Nora was impressed and Conn rather flustered; he stood there looking around and twisting his hat uneasily in his enormous hands. Finally he said he'd best go back and mind the shop, because there was only that Slade kid in it now that would give six pennies in change for a five-cent piece any time and congratulate herself on having the best of the bargain.

"Oh, Sacred Heart!" Nora said. "Sure you wouldn't leave me to get home alone?"

She clutched his arm anxiously. I knew she wanted to go too.

"Why don't you both go along now?" I said. "I'll be all right. I'll just sit here and wait for Mrs. Dayton."

"In a hotel lobby, alone? They'd put the detectives on you, girl," Nora said.

"No, they wouldn't. I'm a very respectable-looking young woman." I looked over at the elevator and saw the door opening and Mrs. Dayton getting out. "There she is now," I said. "Do you want to stay and meet her?"

Nora started to say yes, but then she looked at Conn and changed her mind and said they would best be getting along.

"God and all the saints keep you safe," she said.

She kissed me. I felt lonesome, watching her go out the door with Conn. She looked very queer in that place with her old cloak and hat and her run-over shoes. She had never paid any attention to her clothes till she had begun to get serious about Conn, and even now she was afraid to spend money on them. I knew that she had been very poor when she was a girl, and that all her life she had been afraid there would not be enough money to keep her when she was old.

When she had gone I turned and went across the lobby to Mrs. Dayton. She was talking to a bellboy about her bags. I had mine with me, and she told the boy to bring it out with hers to a carriage. I had thought her husband would be with her, but she said he was already down on the *Fair Maid*.

"He sent Captain Dix to look after me, but I'm afraid he's gone off somewhere," she said. She turned to another bellboy. "*Would* you go and try to find him? Captain Dix Menary — "

She was having a fine time managing it all, like a little girl sent on a trip alone. The bellboy went off, and in a minute or two came back with a tall thin man of about fifty. He had a hawklike, humorous face and a self-confident smile that faded to a complete impassivity as he stopped before Mrs. Dayton.

"All ready, ma'am?"

"Yes, we're ready to leave now, Captain Dix." She spoke too gaily; it wasn't hard to see that he made her uncomfortable. "And this is our new schoolteacher, Miss Dereen — Captain Dix Menary. Captain Dix is pilot on the *Fair Maid*."

I looked at Captain Dix and he smiled. I liked to see him smile. When he did, he looked — as Conn would have put it — as if he had just knocked out John L. Sullivan himself with one hand tied behind his back. He was really very sure of himself.

"You're a great improvement, ma'am," he said. "There hasn't been a good-looking schoolteacher in Le Jeune since one of John Morgan's men ran off with Lucy Battle in '63."

"I ought to warn you that Captain Dix is a terrible flatterer," Mrs. Dayton said.

She spoke as if he were someone who had just brought her an ice at a party and was holding her fan. The smile disappeared from his face again, and he stood looking at her with his eyebrows very high and a long-suffering expression somewhere behind his cynical blue eyes.

The carriage was ready with our bags and we went outside. It was only a short drive to the landing, the streets looking very gay and busy in the spring sunlight and the horse going briskly. When the carriage drew up at one of the wharfboats Mrs. Dayton pointed to a big white steamboat lying alongside.

"That's the *Fair Maid*," she said. "Isn't she lovely?"

We got out of the carriage. I could not see the *Maid* well because of the wharfboat. The whole levee was a confusion of drays, baggage, boxes and barrels of every description, chanting Negroes, and hurrying passengers. The river looked broad and calm and green. Across on the other side the shadows of the greening hills were lengthening as the sun began to fall in a clear late-afternoon sky.

We went through the echoing wooden wharfboat, which smelled of molasses and dried apples and spices, and up the gangplank to the main deck of the *Fair Maid*. There was a broad stairway leading up to the passenger quarters. We went up at once. Mrs. Dayton said I must register at the office, but she would not allow me to pay the fare for my trip. The clerk was very respectful to her, and gave me the stateroom she said I must have, but I noticed that on board the boat she seemed even more unsure of her position as Mrs. Captain Dayton than she had on land.

As soon as I had looked at my stateroom she took me to see the rest of the boat. First we went through the ladies' cabin, which was very elegant, with much gilt and white paint, and glittering chandeliers and mirrors. Then she took me outside again and up the stairs to the hurricane deck. There was a long narrow cabin above us, which she said was

the texas, where the officers had their quarters. Above that
was the pilothouse. I looked up at it. It was like a summer
pavilion, glass all around, and painted white, with a grace-
ful railing of wooden lacework above it.

"Do you want to go up?" Mrs. Dayton asked me.

There was a sign at the foot of the steps leading up to
it — *No Passengers Permitted Beyond This Point.* She saw
me looking at it.

"Will it be all right?" I asked.

"Of course." She took hold of my hand. "I'm going to
call you Lacey," she said. "I'm sure we're going to be great
friends."

We started up the stairs. There was someone in the pilothouse — Captain Dix, talking to a Negro in a white coat.
The Negro looked apologetic and upset. Mrs. Dayton reached
the top step and turned the knob of the door, but the
door stayed shut. She pushed against it, and the Negro
came and opened it for us; as soon as we had got inside he
flew out and down the stairs without another word.

"I've brought Miss Dereen to see the pilothouse," Mrs.
Dayton said to Captain Dix. She sounded very gay and
nervous.

Captain Dix looked noncommittal. I was sure we ought
not to have come up. Mrs. Dayton moved about, talking
very quickly and showing me the big pilotwheel and the
braided bell cords with which the pilot signaled the engineer
below. Captain Dix remained expressively silent.

Someone was coming up the steps behind us. I turned
around. A tall man of about thirty, in a blue-serge uniform
and cap, came into the pilothouse. He had light-brown hair
and very steady dark hazel eyes. His face was rather broad
over the cheekbones, not handsome, the mouth too wide
and all the bones too prominent under the tightly drawn
tanned skin. He stood there and looked at us. Captain Dix
took a discreet interest in the sunset. Mrs. Dayton looked
guilty.

"Oh — Jed dear," she said. "I was just showing Miss De-

reen around the boat. She's going to be our new schoolteacher and a very dear friend of mine. This is my husband,
Captain Dayton," she said to me.

"How do you do?" I said. "It's a lovely boat. We were
just going."

I started toward the door. He smiled a little — it seemed
he could smile, even if it was more a grudging acknowledg-
ment than a sign of civility — and said without conviction
that he was glad to know me.

"Thank you," I said. "I'm sure you're very busy."

I tried the door, but it fitted tightly and again would not
open. I looked around at Captain Dix and he came and
opened it for me. It was a ridiculous situation. Mrs. Dayton
was trying to talk to her husband about some things she had
bought in Corioli for their little girl, but he did not en-
courage her, and after a few sentences she said brightly that
she would see him at dinner and followed me down the
steps to the hurricane deck. I was angry with her for having
brought me up there. Then I saw her biting her lips and
staring off fixedly into the sun, and I could not help feeling
sorry for her as I would have felt sorry for a child who
had done something forbidden but not really wrong and
been punished for it too severely.

"Why do you call him Captain Dix if he's not the master
of the boat?" I said. I wanted to say something.

She drew a deep breath. "Oh, Captain Dix has been
master of a lot of boats," she said; "he had both Jed's other
packets, the *Sallie Dayton* and the *John D. Prescott,* at one
time or another. But he says he'd rather be a pilot, now
that he's in the gold-braid trade; he says pilots are licensed
to be rude to passengers and masters condemned to be polite.
He's known Jed for ever so long, you know. Jed says he
taught him everything he knows about the river."

By the time she had got that far her voice was almost
normal again. We went over to the guardrail together.
From there we could look down at the river that seemed far
below now and watch the last-minute confusion on the

wharf. The roof-bell on the *Maid* had begun to ring, and the Negro roustabouts were dragging over the side the wooden walkways over which they had been carrying freight into the boat. They fell with a great clatter somewhere below us. Then the gangplank was raised, there was a long blast of the whistle, and the *Maid* began to move slowly away from the wharfboat. For a moment, as the green water widened below us, it seemed that we and the boat were still motionless and the shore was receding steadily from us. It was a strange feeling, as if the world were slipping away and leaving you nothing but the deck of a boat and the water all around, the shore still there where you could see it, but not so near that it could ever touch you or mean anything to you.

After a little the sun set and it began to grow dusk and it was time to go below to dinner. It was a lovely sunset on the river and I did not want to leave the deck, but I went down with Mrs. Dayton. She was very disappointed because Captain Dayton did not come to dinner.

CHAPTER V   IN THE MORNING I WOKE EARLY. THE boat was making a landing; I heard the long, deep, sad note of the whistle and from the land the sound of voices and the rattle of wheels on a cobblestoned wharf. I dressed and went out to the deck. By the time I left my stateroom the *Fair Maid* was already under way again. I looked back and saw on the south bank of the river the red roofs and white courthouse dome of a little town, hardly visible through the morning mist.

I went on up to the hurricane deck. It was a lovely silent spring morning, the light just coming, no one about, the *Fair Maid* gliding through the low fog that covered the river and lay in long wavering clouds up the valleys she passed. I stood at the bow and watched the hills dropping slowly behind us and the little creeks coming in, shrouded in the trailing fog. The black smoke from the two huge stacks above drifted and hung over my head in the quiet air. After a while I heard footsteps coming up behind me. I turned around. It was Captain Dayton. I said good morning and turned back again to the rail.

"You're up early," he said. He came over to the rail. "Wasn't your stateroom comfortable?"

"Very comfortable, thank you."

He looked the same as he had the day before, not so much without civility as with a civility in which he did not believe. He stood at the rail beside me and looked down at the white fog ahead.

"It'll clear soon," he said.

"Will it?" I wondered why he bothered to stop to talk to me. "I've never been on the river before. I've only watched the steamboats from the landing."

"But you like it now?"

"Yes." I turned my head toward him and smiled a little. "Please don't think you have to stand here talking to me," I said. "You had a perfect right not to like it when you walked into your pilothouse yesterday and found me there. The sign was very explicit."

"You think I'm apologizing now?"

"I don't really know. I'm not very good yet at American manners. But Mrs. Dayton told me yesterday that the captain of a packet is 'condemned' to be polite to his passengers."

"How long have you known my wife?"

"Only since yesterday. She's a friend of my relatives, the Dandys."

"They must be fine relatives if they let you go all this way off alone to a strange town to teach school."

"They're not very close relatives," I said. "It was really very kind of them to find me this place."

He did not seem much interested in our conversation. He

was leaning on the rail, looking down at the water. I thought
he would go away now, but he did not.

"I'm told it's a very nice town," I said.

He glanced up at me for a moment, did not say anything,
and then looked down at the river again.

"But you prefer the river?" I said. I suppose I was a little angry.

"I prefer the river."

"Of course. With three beautiful boats like this. The
Fair Maid, the *Sallie Dayton,* and the *John D. Prescott.*
The *John D. Prescott* sounds very impressive. Who was
John D. Prescott? One of your American statesmen?"

"He was my father."

He glanced at me again. I did not know what to say; I
suppose I looked very foolish.

"I was born in Dayton, Tennessee," he said. "That's
where the Dayton comes from. You haven't known the
Dandys very long or they'd have told you all about that."

"I don't see why they should have told me anything at
all about it," I said.

"They would have. Anybody would have. A thing like
that is supposed to be very interesting. Or very funny. It's
all according to your point of view."

I thought it was a strange sort of conversation that we
were having. The fog was breaking up now into long thin
luminous trails of vapor that showed the water beneath. I
could see some queer-looking boats, like houses on rafts, off
in a little cove to the right, their outlines ghostly and uncertain in the fog.

"What are the boats?" I asked.

"Shantyboats. There are people who live on them. They
move up and down the river as it suits them." He looked
at me, leaning against the rail and watching me. "You're a
fine girl," he said unexpectedly, after a moment.

I smiled. "Yes, I'm a fine girl. And you know nothing at
all about me, so you can speak with authority. Is that it?"

I smiled, but I did not feel like smiling. All at once it

seemed very strange to be standing there alone with him on the quiet deck in the early morning on the river. It was one of those things you do for the first time that you are quite sure you have done before or that you will do some day again.

The Negro in the white coat whom I had seen the day before came up the steps to the deck, carrying a coffeepot on a tray, and went on up to the pilothouse.

"Will we come to Le Jeune soon?" I asked.

"In another hour."

"I think I should go down then. Mrs. Dayton said she was going to stop in at my stateroom before breakfast."

I turned and walked over to the stairs. Below, in the ladies' cabin, I found Mrs. Dayton. She said she had just been going to look for me.

"I've been up watching the river," I said. "It's a lovely morning. And I had quite a conversation with Captain Dayton."

"I told him he was very rude to you yesterday." She looked bright and fresh this morning, full of the excitement of coming home from a trip. "I told him he ought to be more agreeable to you. Was he agreeable?"

"Very agreeable."

"I'm so glad," she said.

We sat down to breakfast together. It was a very elaborate meal — bacon, sausages, hominy, creamed potatoes, eggs, hot biscuits, fried apples, jam and honey, and milk and coffee. Mrs. Dayton took an egg and a biscuit that she hardly touched. There was a little cut-glass dish of strawberry jam on the table before her, and she would put a spoonful of the jam on her plate and nibble at it till she had finished it, then look around gaily to see if anyone was watching her and take another.

"I'm not allowed to do that when I'm at home," she said. "Barbara would never let me. She's a wonderful house-keeper, and so good with Lorna, but she treats me as if I were Lorna's age too. Down home in La Fayette we always had nothing but colored help, but I just gave up in despair after my third girl left me, the year I was first married. Then Ailie McLean found Barbara for me, and she's been with us ever since. Ailie's Mrs. Orrin McLean, you know; they're the family you're going to board with. They've had hard times; Orrin had his own store, but he's had to sell out and now he only clerks at Mr. Moffat's."

She talked all the while we ate, glancing around over her shoulder every now and then toward the doorway as if she were looking for someone to come in. Finally she stopped the colored boy who was waiting on our table.

"Has Captain Dayton had breakfast yet?" she asked.

"Ma'am?" He looked confused. "I don't know. Shall I find out?"

"Please."

He went away, and in a little while came back and said Captain Jed had had his breakfast. Mrs. Dayton looked disappointed.

"I'd better go and say good-by then," she said. "Do you want to come too?"

I said I thought she would rather go alone.

"Oh, no. I want you to come too. I want Jed to like you; he never likes any of the people I like. We're an old married couple, you know; we won't embarrass you. He'll give me a peck on the cheek and we'll say good-by, and that will be all there is to it."

I did not want to go, but she was standing there waiting for me, so I got up and went outside with her. While we had been eating breakfast it had cleared, as Captain Dayton had predicted; I saw the river sweeping around a bend of the hills like a wide sheet of pure, glancing light, with the long lines of our wake drawn out behind us. We met Captain Dayton at the top of the stairs leading to the hurricane deck. He said he had been coming down to see that we were all right to leave the *Fair Maid* at Le Jeune.

"We're fine," Mrs. Dayton said. "Mr. Fraser — is that

your clerk's name? — said he would take care of everything; he's been very helpful. We came to say good-by.
I made Lacey come too. I think she's a little afraid of
you."

It was no use wishing she would not say things like that.
I said, "No, really. I've enjoyed my trip very much." When
I looked at Captain Dayton I knew he understood that he
was not to take what his wife said seriously. It was a little
embarrassing to know that he did understand. It seemed to
put us on a footing of intimacy where Mrs. Dayton could
not join us.

"I'm sorry Lorna won't be back home from Mama's yet,"
she was going on. "Barbara could have brought her down
to the boat. You see so little of her, and she's growing so
fast. Even if you'll only be here half an hour, you could
at least set eyes on her."

"Tell her I'll bring her a present from New Orleans,"
Captain Dayton said.

"You always bring her presents from New Orleans. I
declare I never saw a child have so many things. She has
everything, but she hasn't got her father. You ought to quit
this old river and stay at home with us. We could all move
to Corioli, and you could take care of the business end of
the Dayton Line on shore, and let somebody else go on
the *Fair Maid*."

He did not bother to answer her. I could imagine that he
had heard all that many times before. He glanced forward
at the wide sparkling curve of the river. The roof tops of
another little town were just coming into view on the
south side. Mrs. Dayton saw them too.

"Are we almost there?" she said. "Shall I say good-by
now?"

She stood on her tiptoes and put her hands on his shoulders and kissed him quickly.

"Good-by, dear," she said. "You will take care of yourself? All those awful steamboat accidents in the papers —
I wouldn't want any of them to happen to you."

"Nothing is going to happen to me."

"You oughtn't to say that. It's bad luck. I'll never forget the night the *Indian Queen* almost ran aground in that dreadful storm — the night I met you —"

"Nobody was in any danger that night."

"I know better. I was never so frightened in my life. I thought we were all going to be drowned that minute."

Captain Dayton looked at the river again, and then at me.

"Good-by, Miss Dereen," he said. "I hope you like it in Le Jeune."

"She will," Mrs. Dayton said. "I'll see to it. We're going to be great friends."

"Good-by," I said.

I followed Mrs. Dayton down to the ladies' cabin. Half-way down the stairs she stopped and turned around, and I glanced back too and saw Captain Dayton looking after us. When he saw us looking back he turned and walked away.

Mrs. Dayton went on down the stairs.

"I was seventeen years old when I met Jed," she said. "Mama and I were going down to Memphis on the *Indian Queen* to visit my aunt Callie Perkins, after Papa died, and he was the pilot on the *Queen*. I fell in love with him the first time I saw him. Do you believe in love at first sight?"

I said I had never thought very much about it.

CHAPTER VI   LE JEUNE WAS A FINE SMALL TOWN that looked down on the river from a low plateau, with hills behind and other hills across on the other side of the river. The main street faced the levee and the river, and at the end of it was the house where the McLeans lived. It was an old house, with a passage straight through from the front to the back and a room on either side and the kitchen built on in a lean-to behind. It needed paint very badly but it was a lovely house. I liked the house and the town and the bright spring morning and the river flowing past so close that you could always see it when you turned a corner or looked out of a window.

Mrs. McLean met us at the door. She was a small quick pretty woman in an old percale dress, with her light-brown hair untidy and her hands full of flour.

"I'm just in the middle of my baking," she said. "Do you-all mind coming in the kitchen?" She looked at me, smiling, as Mrs. Dayton introduced us. "Lacey Dereen. What a pretty name. It'd be a pity to change it; you'll get something like Pickenpepper; I just know you will."

"I can't stay," Mrs. Dayton said. "I only wanted to bring Lacey over. How are Orrin and Davie?"

"Just elegant, thank you. You look so splendid, Sallie; isn't that a new hat?"

"I bought it in Corioli. I shopped like mad; I've got all sorts of things." She bent forward and kissed Mrs. McLean lightly on the cheek. "Good-by, Ailie; now I really can't stay. You take good care of Lacey."

We said good-by, and Mrs. McLean took me into the house and back into the kitchen.

"I'm going to tell you straight off to call me Ailie," she said. "If you're going to live here, you may as well be one of the family. There's only Orrin and Davie and me, you know. Davie's going on twelve, and I *hope* he's going to be one of your good scholars, but I ought to warn you that he's never been before."

She kept on talking while she kneaded her bread deftly and then shaped it into loaves and put it into the pans. I sat on a splint-bottom chair listening to her, and looking at the strange room around me with the strange cups and saucers on the dresser and the strange clock on the shelf behind the stove. When she had finished she turned around and looked at me.

"You poor child," she said. "You look tired to death. I'll

take you up to your room. I expect you didn't sleep last night. I'm always too excited myself to get any sleep on a steamboat."

I followed her out of the kitchen and up the stairs.

"No," I said. "I had a splendid trip. I'd never been on a river packet before."

"The *Fair Maid* isn't just a packet, you know. She's the most beautiful thing on the river. I remember the first morning Jed brought her in here. He had her built in Corioli, and they say she cost a hundred and eighty thousand dollars. There isn't another boat like her from Pittsburgh to New Orleans."

She opened the door of the room I was to have. It was a nice room, and had a big bed with a red-and-green quilt on it and a rag carpet on the floor. I went over to the window and looked out and saw the river off through the trees. I could see the levee, but the *Fair Maid* was gone.

"Sallie always declares on her soul she's as jealous of that boat as she would be of another woman," Ailie McLean said. "She's not river-folks herself, so she can't understand how Jed feels. I remember when he was only a little shaver, growing up here, he always said he'd have the finest boat on the river some day. And the Mackenzies were *poor*, you know; everybody'd just laugh and say, 'Oh Lordy, hold your breath and wait for the day —'"

"The Mackenzies?" I said.

"Jed's folks. His mother's daddy and mother. Didn't you know — ?" She stopped suddenly and looked at me.

"I know a little," I said. I wanted her to go on. "Who was John D. Prescott?" I asked.

I was sitting on the bed. She made a little distracted gesture, bit her lip, and then began to smile again.

"I know I talk too much," she said. "Orrin's always telling me. But it's not as if it was any secret; everybody in town knew, years ago, about Jennie Mackenzie and John Prescott. She went down to Tennessee to have the baby, and the Mackenzies always gave out, when they brought it

back, that it was a niece's child that had been left an or-
phan — but that didn't stop any of the talk." She sat down
on the bed beside me. "Oh, that's only old gossip now,"
she said. "Nobody cares about that any more. Of course
John Prescott couldn't marry her; he was married already,
and president of the Diamond Line, and I don't know
what-all besides. And Jennie never did come back to Le
Jeune — went out West somewhere and married, we *heard*,
but nobody ever knew for sure. Then John Prescott was
drowned on the *Laura Franklin* when Jed wasn't any more
than a year old, and so the whole thing was over and done
with."

"Except for Captain Dayton," I said.

"Oh yes, except for Jed. It wasn't easy for him; people
can be awfully cruel about something like that. Even the
children. If I'd been the Mackenzies, I'd have packed right
up and gone somewhere else where nobody knew anything about Jennie and John Prescott. It just isn't fair to a
child to let him have to grow up living with a thing like
that."

"He doesn't seem to mind it now," I said. "Not naming
that boat the way he has."

She laughed. "Oh, that's only Jed's way of telling us all to
go to the devil," she said. "I always liked Jed; people used
to say he had the stubborn Prescott streak in him, but he
was an awfully dependable boy. When he went on the
river I knew he'd make good. Of course I didn't expect
him to marry anybody like Sallie Denslow. He met her
when he was on the *Indian Queen;* she was going down to
Memphis with her mama, and at the end of the trip she
and Jed just walked off the boat and got married. They say
her folks made a terrible fuss, but it didn't do a bit of
good. Jed's doing awfully well now with the Dayton Line.
It was all Sallie's money, you know, but they can't say he's
invested it in something that doesn't pay."

I sat on the bed listening to her. It was a common enough
story, and I had heard it before, with other names and

other circumstances in it but still the same story; but I
could not fit Captain Dayton into it. He seemed much too
sure of himself ever to have needed to take advantage of
the foolish infatuation of a young girl to make himself important in the eyes of people who had slighted him. Still
he did not care for his wife; that was plain enough for anyone to see. He might have been in love with her once. He
was not so old that he would not have been at an age to do
something foolish himself seven or eight years before. I was
trying to find excuses for him, it seemed. It was none of my
business, and it had nothing at all to do with me, but I was
trying to find excuses for him. I got up from the bed and
unfastened the clasp of my bag and began to take out the
clothes I had brought with me from Corioli.

"What lovely linen," Ailie McLean said. "Is it Irish? It
looks as if it would wear forever. You have a very small
waist, haven't you? I'm smaller than you are, but I could
never get that petticoat around me. Of course you haven't
had three children, the way I have. I had three little boys,
you know — Little Orrin and Davie and James Donald.
Little Orrin died of typhoid when he was ten, and James
Donald died of croup when he was only fifteen months old.
They both died in the same year, and that's the year I
turned into an old woman. A nice old woman, I hope, but
an old woman just the same. I'm thirty-eight years old, and
I haven't cared about pretty things for three years now. I
don't care about anything any more; I just pray to God to
leave me Davie. Do I look like a sight now? I reckon I
frightened you, coming to the door like this."

She tucked back a flying wisp of hair. She was talking
very fast and I knew she was trying not to cry. She was one
of the nicest people I had met for a long time. I pretended
not to notice that she was going to cry, and after a
little she was all right again, and we went downstairs
together.

CHAPTER VII   IN THE EVENING THE MCLEANS
walked over to the schoolhouse with me. It was a fine night,
and I liked the way the town looked with the lights on inside the houses and the river off below as we walked, very
black and quiet and with only a few lights making moving
gleams on it; but I could not really enjoy it. I was a little
worried because I was to meet Mr. Moffat, the district director, at the schoolhouse. I had never taught school before,
and I was afraid of what he might think of me as a teacher.
Orrin McLean worked for him, and he had a high opinion
of him.

"He's an educated man," he said, "and that's more than
you can say for most of the people in this town. People here
'learn' the river; they don't put much stock in learning
things out of books."

I was walking along beside Ailie, and I felt her squeeze
my hand.

"Orrin's from up north in Indiana," she said. "He doesn't
think much of us river-folks. I guess if it wasn't for Papa's
leaving me the store here in Le Jeune, we never in the
world would have settled down here." She shook her head.
"I can't help it," she said; "I like it just the way it is. When
I was a little bit of a girl I used to walk down to the landing with Papa and watch the steamboats coming in. Papa
knew every one of the pilots; he was on the river himself
till he got his bad leg, and then he kept a steamboat store
so he could keep up with all his old friends even if he was
ashore."

She saw her husband looking at her and stopped talking
suddenly. He had a way of looking at her as if he had hoped
for something better from her but realized now that he
had been setting his hopes too high. He was a tall man in

his early forties, rather impressive-looking in a common-place way, and she was very respectful of him, but she had a little wild demon of fun in her too, and she was always saying things that shocked or vexed him. He made me very uncomfortable, with his habit of discussing any subject at all as if it was as important as the Ten Commandments.

When we came to the schoolhouse I understood why he approved of Mr. Moffat. Mr. Moffat was older and sharper and more positive than Orrin McLean, but he had the same solemn way of talking. The two of them could not have been more serious if they had been a pair of prime ministers discussing a matter that would mean peace or war between their countries. I realized at once that Ailie and I were to be the audience and nothing more. I did not mind that; it made it a good deal easier for me. As long as Mr. Moffat had come there to impress me with his knowledge instead of expecting me to impress him with mine, I had nothing to be afraid of except that I might smile at the wrong place in the conversation. As a matter of fact, it might be better if I did not smile at all. I sat on one of the children's benches with Ailie and took advantage of the conversation to look around at my new school. There was only one room, with a blackboard and a desk, and before them the smaller desks and benches where the children would sit. At the top of the blackboard was an ornately printed text, surrounded with scrollwork in colored chalk — *Little strokes fell great oaks*. Mr. Moffat saw me looking at it.

"A beautiful piece of work, Miss Dereen," he said. "Miss Partington was very artistic. It's a great pity she took it into her head to marry at her time of life. People used to come from miles around when she had exhibition night just to see her blackboards. I hope you are artistic, Miss Dereen."

I looked at the vines and curlicues twining out in a tropical profusion from *Little strokes fell great oaks*, and said I did not believe I could ever equal that. Mr. Moffat looked disappointed and went back to his conversation with Orrin McLean. I whispered to Ailie what was exhibition night?

"Exactly what it says — a night to exhibit your pupils' accomplishments," she said. "The parents all come, and of course every last one of them whose pride and joy doesn't do well holds you personally responsible. All you have to do is smile, and listen to their criticisms, and keep order, and be polite to everybody at once — and then go home and wonder where in the world you ever got that splitting headache."

"It sounds splendid. Must I have the headache, though?"

"It's absolutely necessary. It's what we're paying your salary for. Miss Partington was very satisfactory. Last year after exhibition night she even fainted dead away. Everybody considered she took her responsibilities very seriously."

Orrin glanced around at her and she looked guilty and we both stopped whispering. I felt very young sitting there on the bench beside her, as if I were back in my own school days and had just been chided by the teacher for whispering in class. It was hard for me to realize that the next morning I would be the teacher myself.

Mr. Moffat was getting ready to leave.

"You come to us very highly recommended, Miss Dereen," he said. "Very highly recommended, indeed. I hope you will live up to those recommendations in every way."

I said I hoped I would too. It sounded like the proper thing to say, and he seemed satisfied with it, and put on his hat and went away. I was glad it was over. If the school was no worse the next day I thought I might get on very well.

The next day the school was a good deal worse. I had a classful of children of all ages who knew much more than I did about the school routine and the books they studied from and the places where things were kept. Also I had what my pupils called a "queer" accent, which did not do anything either to improve my standing with them.

"If a clerk sells three apples for five cents —" I began that morning.

A subdued stir and titter over the room. Davie McLean, a bright-looking, freckled boy with dark hair, who probably felt he had to dispel at once any idea that he was going to be "teacher's pet," remarked boldly: "We don't say *clark*, Miss Dereen; we say *clurk*."

"That's not the point here, Davie. People from different countries sometimes speak differently, but the arithmetic in this example is the same everywhere. Do you know the answer?"

A pause.

"Miss Partington always had the reading lesson before arithmetic."

"Well, we're going to do it differently now. Do you know the answer?"

"It isn't Davie's turn" — from a fair-haired, snub-nosed little girl. "Miss Partington heard us alphabletically."

"Alpha*bet*ically, Susan."

"Yes. And it's Joey Levett's turn. Miss Partington marked it all down in a book."

A sudden room-wide conference as to where Miss Partington had left the book.

"I have the book, children." I did not tell them that trying to unravel the meaning of the cryptic markings in it after each name was something I had given up shortly after midnight the night before. "But Miss Partington isn't your teacher any more, and we're going to do things a new way now."

Distrustful silence; then a hand shot up.

"Martha?"

"My name isn't Martha. It's Helen Jane Cooper. Martha is my sister" — pointing to a serious six-year-old. "*Her* name's Martha Ginevra Cooper."

"Well, Helen Jane?"

Renewed tittering.

"Her name's Nellie" — at last, explanatorily, from Susan. "Nobody calls her Helen Jane. She's putting on airs."

"If her name is Helen Jane, I suppose she can call her-

self Helen Jane if she likes. Now, Nellie, or Helen Jane —
what is it?"

"Please, Miss Dereen, Davie McLean isn't sitting in the
right place. Miss Partington said he had to sit in the front
of the room where she could watch him, and he isn't sitting there now."

"Davie —" I said.

Davie got up reluctantly and came forward to take a seat
on the front bench.

An excited buzz.

"Lorna Dayton isn't s-s-sitting in *her* right seat, either"
— this from an earnest little redhead with pigtails. "Miss
Partington said she couldn't sit next to Cynthy Snow because she and Cynthy whispered all day. She's supposed to
sit next to me."

"You're a tattletale, Stella Gibbs" — in supreme scorn,
from Lorna Dayton. She was only six years old but, plump,
fair, phlegmatic, in her fine blue dress and tasseled boots
and ribbons, she looked like a miniature Queen Victoria.

"Lorna Dayton, will you please sit in your proper place?"

Lorna sat still; finally, as I continued to face her, she rose
majestically and moved across to sit beside the redhead.

"I'm going to tell my mother," she announced. "She said
you'd be nicer than Miss Partington, and you aren't."

"That will do, Lorna. If you have any more remarks to
make, perhaps you'd like to sit on that stool in the corner
and make them."

By this time the problem of the clerk and the three
apples had receded so far into the background that it was
a major tactical operation to bring my attention or the
class's back to it again. No doubt that was what they had
been hoping for. They were very disappointed when I
turned back to Davie and asked him again about the apples.
He had to admit that he didn't know, and I tried to explain
the problem to him, but he was very foggy about fractions
and after a while I began to suspect that Miss Partington's
talents had run more to art than to arithmetic. It was a

rather discouraging day. By the end of it I did not think either the class or I had done any more than develop a mutual respect for each other's persistence.

At closing time Sallie Dayton came to take Lorna home. She sent Barbara for her usually, she said; she did not like Lorna walking around the streets alone. She came in to talk to me for a moment before she left.

"How did it go today?" she asked.

"Very well." I could hardly tell her the truth with Lorna there.

"That's lovely. I'm so glad you liked it."

"I don't like school," Lorna said. "I don't like Miss Dereen."

She was arranging the ribbons of her hat under her chin. She did not bother to look at us.

Sallie looked down at her and smiled. "Of course you do, honey. You mustn't hurt Miss Dereen's feelings."

"She won't let me sit next to Cynthia. I have to sit next to Stella Gibbs, and she has things in her hair."

Sallie looked at me in alarm.

"Really, Lacey —" she said. "Is that true?"

"I haven't the slightest idea. I didn't examine them, you know; I only tried to teach them."

The frowning line deepened between Sallie's brows.

"Well, honestly, I *don't* expect Lorna ought to have to sit next to a child like that," she said. "Those Gibbses are plain tacky people, if I do have to say it. You'll just have to do something, Lacey. Can't you let Lorna sit next to Cynthia Snow?"

"First I'll find out whether it's true about Stella."

"Of course it's true. Didn't you hear Lorna say it?"

She was beginning to get excited about it. I thought it was too unimportant to quarrel about, and I said I would see that Lorna did not have to sit beside Stella Gibbs.

The next day I found out that it was not true about Stella, but I knew there was nothing to do about it unless I wanted an unpleasantness with Sallie. She was like a child herself; you could not try to reason with her. I was discovering already that it was very difficult to be her friend unless you were willing to think of her that way.

CHAPTER VIII   THE DAYS WENT BY LIKE THAT. THE spring came fully, and the children were more restless, and along the river the reflections of the tall white sycamores rippled in new leaf on the water. Sallie asked me to visit several times, and the faces I saw on the streets began to be less strange to me and to have names attached to them. I thought it would have been a fine life if I had really belonged there. I was only the schoolteacher, and that was not the same thing. Ailie McLean tried to make me feel at home, but I knew that it bothered Orrin to have me in his house, and I was never really comfortable when he was there.

I used to go off by myself when school was out and take long walks along the river. The river looked different in different lights and at different times of the year. Now in the early morning there was no color at all, only pure light reflecting the light of the sky. Later it would be a clear green-brown, darkening at twilight. The sunsets were incredible, opalescent mauve and pink flung over the dark moving water like a fairyland. I was used to the sea, but I had not known before that a river could be so beautiful.

One Sunday morning when I was leaving the house for a walk I saw the *Fair Maid* lying at the landing. Church services were going on in town, and I thought she had probably stopped, as packets usually did on Sunday at some town along their way, to let her passengers attend them. I walked along the main street toward the levee. As I passed it I saw Captain Dayton and Captain Dix coming up the hill from the river. Captain Dix waved to me.

"How's the prettiest girl in Le Jeune?" he said. "Isn't there a sixteen-year-old in that school of yours man enough to have marched you up in front of a preacher and put a ring on your finger yet?"

He was in a very good humor. He came up and drew himself up and saluted me smartly.

"That's the way they do it in the Navy," he said. "Thank God I am not in the Navy."

I laughed and said good morning to him. I had seen him several times when the *Fair Maid* had stopped at Le Jeune on her way up- or down-river, and we had become good friends. With Captain Dayton I was still on much more formal terms. He said good morning to me now, and I said:

"Are you going home? I'm afraid everybody is at church."

"I haven't got a home," Captain Dix said. "I've got a room on the second floor of the Jenkins Hotel. At the present moment I'm going to investigate a certain stone jug I left there the last time I was in Le Jeune. I have a slight suspicion it may not be quite as full now as it was the last time I saw it. Mrs. Jenkins is a very untrustworthy character with a stone jug."

I laughed again. "I'm sure you're maligning poor Mrs. Jenkins."

"A woman who decorates a ham with carpet tacks instead of cloves lays herself open to suspicions like that." He raised one hand solemnly. "So help me, last New Year's Day I saw it myself. She'd have murdered the whole set of us if we'd been as far gone as she was herself." He nodded to Captain Dayton. "Give my respects to Mrs. Dayton," he said. "Miss Dereen, my compliments."

He took off his cap to me and went off down the street. I looked at Captain Dayton, expecting that he would go too. Or it was not expecting; it was knowing that he ought to go and that I did not want him to, and knowing at the same time that he did not want to go either, and that with him it was different from the way it was with me, because he was used to making things happen instead of only letting them happen to him.

"Where are you going now?" he said.

"Only for a walk. It's such a splendid morning."

"I'll walk along with you. They won't be out of church for another hour."

I hesitated.

"What's the matter?"

"Nothing is the matter."

I began to walk on with him, past the row of shops, closed and shuttered now in a Sunday-morning quietness. All at once I felt happy. It was really a splendid morning. I had had the kind of moment of warning that comes to you when you are going to do something important that later you will never be able to change, but it had gone quickly, and now there was only the happiness. I looked over at Captain Dayton. If he had felt the warning too it made no difference to him. He had waited very civilly for me to make up my mind, but I knew it was the same kind of civility that I had seen in him before. He did not really believe in it. All it meant to him was that he was pretending to defer to someone else's will when in fact he would live and act only by his own.

"How does it happen you're not at church with the others?" he asked me after a little, as we walked along.

"There isn't a Catholic church in town, you know. I go over to Feliciana when I can."

He looked at me. "Yes," he said. "You're Irish, aren't you? You're not my idea of an Irish girl."

"What is your idea of an Irish girl?"

"I don't know. Red hair and a temper, I suppose. Yours is more the color of a stubble field in autumn, and you don't look as if you would have the temper."

"That's for children, isn't it? I had mine all taken out of me long ago."

"It can't have been very long ago."

"Oh yes, it was. I was fourteen. My father was speaking

at a public meeting and the police came and when he tried
to go on speaking one of them struck him. I fought the man,
and afterward my father told me I must never do that
again because it would do no good and would get both him
and me into serious trouble. I learned to be quiet after
that."

"What is your father?"

"He was one of the leaders of the Irish Nationalist Party.
He died last year."

We were walking along past the row of shops. He looked
down at me.

"You're a fine brave girl," he said.

"No, I'm not. I only know how to get through things.
Things happen to you, and if you don't show it outside it's
a little better inside too."

"And when your father died you came to America?"

"Yes."

"You have a fine life, don't you?"

I did not say anything. We came to the edge of town and
the walk ended and we went down the slope to the narrow
strip of beach along the river. The river was high and green.
Across on the north bank the leaves on the lowest branches
of the willows hung in the water. On our side a faded red
rowboat was drawn up on the beach. Two dogs were hunt-
ing through the long grass on the slope. They came bound-
ing down past us to the water, splashed in for a few steps,
and then came out, shaking themselves and paying no attention to us. They were a young hound and an older black
curly-haired mongrel.

"The black one looks like a dog I used to have," Captain
Dayton said.

"Maybe it's one of his descendants."

"It could be. He had that kind of black curly coat. His
name was Spy." He called, "Here, Spy!" suddenly, and the
black dog lifted his head and looked around, but then went
loping off down the beach on his own business again.

"He doesn't recognize the family name," I said.

"No." We were walking along the river's edge. "That's the only trouble with dogs," he said. "They don't live long enough."

"Nobody lives long enough."

I said it before I thought. We were having a fine morning and I did not want to spoil it by talking any more about things that were over and done with. He looked at me and saw how I felt and did not say anything. After a little I forgot about the past and the happiness came back again.

"It's a lovely morning," I said. "I've never seen an American spring before, you know. It gets lovelier every day."

"How is it different from the others?"

"It's so much bigger. Everything is bigger, even the sky and the river. I feel lost and drunk when I get out in it — the way a bee would feel in a field of clover where every flower was as big as a beehive."

"It's the best time of year here. The summers are too hot."

"Even on the river?"

"Sometimes."

I looked at the river. It was almost blue now, with the sun going higher. I could hear the little lapping sound it made flowing past the shore.

"Did you always want to go on the river?" I said.

"Most kids do, in river towns."

He was looking out over the water, his eyes narrowed a little against the sun. He had taken off his cap, and I saw that his sun-bleached hair was almost the same color as the tanned skin drawn tightly over the cheekbones. Out here he seemed much younger and less formidable than he had on the *Fair Maid*. When he was with other people he always seemed to be alone inside himself, not because it was necessary, but because he wanted it that way. I had been alone inside very often in my life, but except for a short time after my father had died it had never been because I had wanted it. Then I had felt that if people were as cruel and as stupid as I had seen they could be, it would be better to have nothing to do with them. I had been badly hurt, and I had been afraid of what had hurt me. I did not think Captain Dayton was afraid. He was stronger than most people, and so he would not have to be afraid of them, but he would have no use for them. I thought it would be a very strange way to live.

We went on walking along the river. Upstream a ferry-boat was moving slowly across toward the north bank. In the sunlight we could see the little figures on board. It looked like a child's boat with little mechanical figures on it.

"That's the *Martha Ellis*," Captain Dayton said. "I had my first job on the river on her."

"Really?"

"I must have been a lot of use on her. I spent most of my time trying to persuade the mate of every packet that went up or down the river to take me on."

"And you finally succeeded."

"Yes. That's how I met Captain Dix. He was on the old *Day Star* then."

"He's a wonderful person. I like him so much. Have you been together ever since?"

"More or less."

The ferry reached the opposite shore. Up ahead of us we could see the dogs again. There were a few white clouds in the sky, high and moving fast, and I saw their shadows falling first on the shore ahead of us, then on the river, and finally on the hills across the river.

"We'll have to go back soon," I said. "We can't go too far."

"It's early still. Walk on a little farther."

"You might miss Sallie and Lorna at the church. You'll have only a few minutes with them as it is."

"I won't miss them."

I did not want to go back. It had been a long time since I had felt so happy. I had been alone for a long while and now I was not alone, and I did not want to go back to it again. I knew we had to go back. I stopped and Captain Dayton stopped too and looked at me. The young hound came tearing down the hill behind us. He came over to us and I reached down and patted him.

"I think we'd really better go back," I said.

I turned and started back the way we had come. We walked on with the dog trotting at our heels. When he passed anything that interested him he would drop behind for a few moments and then run to catch up with us again.

"Has he a home, do you think?" I asked.

"Probably. He looks pretty well fed."

"I thought perhaps he hadn't anybody. He made friends with us so quickly."

"He just wanted some company. He'll forget all about us as soon as he gets home."

"I hope not. If we had a few more hours we might manage to make it a permanent friendship."

"In a few more hours I'll be on my way down to the Mississippi," Captain Dayton said. He did not look happy about it when he said it.

"I've never seen the Mississippi. Is it as beautiful as the river here?"

"It's different. You lose the hills."

"Then I wouldn't like it so well. But I'd like to see it."

We could see the town off ahead of us, and the *Fair Maid* at the landing. She looked big and white and lovely lying there on the water with her curving decks and glass-enclosed pilothouse and the twin stacks with a lazy curl of smoke floating in the calm air above them.

"You're very lucky," I said. "It's a splendid day to be going on a trip. I wish I were going too."

"Why don't you?"

"Oh, no. I have to stay here and teach the little Gibbses and Collinses the difference between *i* and *e*."

I was joking about it but I wanted to go very badly. I saw him looking at me.

"You don't like it here, do you?" he said.

"It isn't the town. But I feel shut up in the school."

"I know how you feel."

"I'm not used to it, I suppose. You see, I never taught in a school before."

"What did you do before?"

"I lived with my father. My mother died when I was twelve, and after that I went wherever Da did and looked after him. He used to say it was a queer old life for me, but I liked it as long as he was all right."

We came to the town and the church bells began to ring for the end of the service. I stopped. My way to the McLeans' was straight ahead, but the church was off to the left.

"You'll have to hurry," I said. "I'd better say good-by."

I put out my hand and he took it. He did not say good-by.

"I'm glad we had the walk," I said.

I did not want him to go. He stood there holding my hand and I drew it away quickly and walked on up the street. I did not look back. The young hound, puzzled as to which of us to follow, came running after me.

"Go home," I said to him. "Haven't you got a home? You can't come with me."

I walked on fast to the McLeans'. They were all at church and I let myself in and went up to my own room. I looked out the window at the *Fair Maid* still lying at the levee. In a little while I heard the McLeans come in downstairs.

"Lacey," Ailie called.

I went down. She was standing in the parlor taking off her hat. Orrin was over at the mantel, winding the clock. There were three clocks in the house, and he wound them all every Sunday morning when he came home from church.

"Lacey," Ailie said, "what's this terrible story we hear about your keeping Jed Dayton so busy squiring you around this morning he couldn't take time out to go to church?"

She was talking too gaily and quickly; she sounded nervous. I glanced over at Orrin. He had finished winding the clock and was standing there looking at me with a solemn expression on his face.

"Old Mrs. Capper called us in on our way home from church to tell us all about it," Ailie went on. "She saw you from her window. She didn't get to church this morning; her rheumatism's been troubling her again."

"I met Captain Dayton and Captain Menary coming up from the levee when I was going for a walk," I said. I was angry, and I spoke very carefully not to show it. "Captain Dayton didn't want to go into church in the middle of the service, so he walked on with me for half an hour before he went back to meet Sallie and Lorna when church was over. Is there anything strange about that?"

"Oh dear, Lacey," Ailie said, "you know how people talk. Of course there's nothing strange. Old Mrs. Capper is a terrible gossip."

"Apparently she was only telling us the truth about what she had seen," Orrin said. He looked at me. "You ought to remember that you are in a position of public responsibility," he said. "Surely it wasn't necessary for you to walk out publicly with Captain Dayton like a hired girl entertaining her young man."

"Orrin — !" Ailie said.

"It's all right," I said.

I did not want to quarrel with them. I would not quarrel with Ailie, but she would be upset too if I quarreled with Orrin. I had told Captain Dayton I had learned how to be quiet, and now was a fine time for me to prove it. I went upstairs without saying any more. When I came down to dinner a little later I tried to act as if nothing at all had happened, but it was a very uncomfortable meal. All the happiness had gone out of the day.

CHAPTER IX   THE DAY AFTER THAT WHEN I CAME
from the school Sallie Dayton was sitting in Ailie's kitchen,
watching her make johnnycake for supper. Sallie had on
one of her elegant hats and a prune-and-cream-striped surah
dress; she looked out of place in the kitchen with the old
wooden dresser and the painted clock and the table with
its checkered cloth. She glanced over at me when I came
in.

"Hello, Lacey," she said. "We've been talking about you.
Haven't we, Ailie?"

"We've been talking about everybody in town," Ailie
said. She seemed a little upset. "There's a letter for you on
the table, Lacey," she said. "I brought it along from the
post office with ours."

I thought she was trying to change the subject. I picked
up the letter. It was from Nora. I was going to open it, but
Sallie reached up and snatched it out of my hand and held
it away from me, behind her back.

"You can't read it now," she said. "I want to talk to you
first. Promise you won't read it till I've talked to you."

"All right," I said.

I did not know what it was all about. Ailie was mixing
her batter quickly, not looking at either Sallie or me. Sallie
was a little too bright. I was beginning to know what that
special brightness meant. It came when she was doing something she knew people would try to stop her from doing.
She had many reckless impulses, which was queer, because
she was really a rather timid person.

"I wanted Ailie to tell you," she said, "but she wouldn't.
She said she'd make out somehow. I'd like to be told how,
in a little old house like this. And it isn't as if you wouldn't
have somewhere else to go. You know how lonesome I get

in that big house with Jed away most of the time. You'd honestly be doing me a favor by coming."

I looked at Ailie.

"Oh, it's Orrin's sister, up in Indiana," she said. She said it fast; I could see that she was exasperated. "She's just lost her husband, and I had a letter from her today; she wants to come down here and stay with us for a while, till she's had time to get over her grief. I never heard her say a kind word to the poor man when he was alive, but she's Orrin's sister, so if she says it's grief I'm bound to take her word for it. Anyway, I reckon she won't get over it any slower if she has to do it in that little cubbyhole of Davie's instead of in your nice room that she's probably counting on having to herself."

I did not say anything. I knew she did not want me to go, but I did not think Orrin would feel the same way about it. Sallie was talking to me again.

"I'd love having you, Lacey," she said. "Really I would. And there's all the room in the world; you know that. Now you've just got to say you'll come."

"When is she coming?" I said to Ailie.

"The end of the week. But it doesn't make any difference. I won't just put you out —"

"You're not putting me out. I'm going to Sallie's for a visit. It's all right."

"It's not all right. I'd like to tell that woman to stay at home where she belongs."

"You've got to think of Orrin," Sallie said. She looked triumphant. "You see, it's all working out splendidly," she said. "Lacey wants to come, and we're going to have a wonderful time. I hope you'll go over and tell Mrs. Capper all about it right away."

"Mrs. Capper?" I said.

Ailie looked at Sallie. "Sallie Dayton," she said.

She was really angry. Sallie colored a little, guiltily.

"What is it about Mrs. Capper?" I said.

"It's nothing," Sallie said. She was afraid of Ailie.

"Tell me."

"It's only what I told you yesterday," Ailie answered for her. "She told Sallie about Jed going walking with you while church was going on."

"She warned me," Sallie said. "It was so funny, Lacey; I could hardly keep from laughing. She said she never did trust Jed."

I did not know what she really felt about it, but I knew it did not amuse her. I understood now why Ailie had not wanted me to go and stay at her house. It was too late to say I would not go. If I did not go now, it would make things worse than before.

"I told her if I ever had any call to be jealous of Jed, it would be over a steamboat and not over another woman," Sallie said. "I told her I know all about Jed. After all, I've been married to him for seven years."

"She's nothing but a miserable old gossip," Ailie said. "You oughtn't to have listened to her, Sallie."

"I couldn't help it. She called me in and gave me a glass of blackberry wine before she even started on it. I had to finish the wine." Her eyes were very bright; she was talking fast. "I told her you were a very dear friend of mine, Lacey," she said. "I wanted to be angry, but it was so funny."

"It isn't funny at all," Ailie said.

She put the johnnycake in the oven.

"I don't think Lacey even likes Jed," Sallie said. "Do you, Lacey?"

"I hardly know him well enough to like him or dislike him."

Sallie laughed. "Oh dear, Lacey," she said, "you're so polite. I'd have come straight out and said I didn't. You wouldn't have hurt my feelings; a lot of people don't like Jed. It's because they don't understand him as well as I do." She stood up and said she had to go. "Why don't you come tomorrow?" she said. "I'll send Hendry over for your bag."

"I'll come at the end of the week."

"No. Come tomorrow. I want to see Mrs. Capper's face

when she finds out. I'll go over tomorrow and tell her myself."

"You won't do anything of the sort," Ailie said. "You stay
away from her."

"I'll send Hendry for your things right after school lets
out tomorrow," Sallie said to me.

She kissed me good-by, then Ailie, and left. Ailie stood
there in the middle of the kitchen looking at me.

"Well," she said. "If you're going tomorrow, you'd better
get your things together tonight."

She was vexed, but I knew it wasn't with me. I picked
up Nora's letter and went upstairs to my room. Standing
at the window I could look out and see the levee and
the river flowing past the town in the late spring sunlight.
I wondered where the *Fair Maid* was now. Somewhere
down on the Mississippi probably, on her way to New Orleans. It was easy to leave difficulties behind by walking on
board a steamboat and going more than a thousand miles
away down-river. I was not going a thousand miles or even
a hundred miles away. I had to stay right where I was
and teach school. I opened Nora's letter and started to
read it. If I had to stay where I was, at least I did not have
to think about it any more.

I went on reading Nora's letter. I had had only one letter
from her since I had come to Le Jeune, full of the trip she
and Conn had taken to Niagara Falls after their wedding.
She had still been in a whirl then with the grandeur of the
wedding and the trip on the railway train and Conn's masterful way with money: "Never mind what it costs, as long as it's
for my darlin' Nora!" Now it seemed that things were a little
different. I gathered that Conn still had his masterful way
with money, but that it had begun to worry Nora. She
sounded unhappy and frightened. I could guess what kind of
scenes were taking place in the rooms behind the little shop.
She said she would be glad to have me with her for the summer; there was the little room on the third floor that it would
be no trouble at all to fix up for me. I had not thought about

the summer, and I did not want to think about it. There were getting to be a good many things that I did not want to think about. I took out my bag and began to get my clothes together to put into it so that I would not have to think about anything at all.

The next afternoon I went over to the Daytons' to stay. They lived in the biggest house in town; it was painted white, and had stained-glass windows in the hall and a gallery around three sides with a railing that was fretted like the guardrail of a steamboat. Sallie took me upstairs with her and showed me through all the rooms, her room with the closets and drawers full of pretty clothes and ornaments, and Lorna's room where there were life-size dolls sitting in little chairs with a tea set on a little table before them. The room I was to have was large and cheerful in the afternoon sunlight and much finer than any I had ever lived in before. There was a four-poster bed, and on the dressing table a silver toilet set with the initials S. D. on it. Sallie saw me looking at it.

"Mama gave it to me for my birthday the year before I was married," she said. "I never liked it; you could have it, Lacey, if it weren't for the initials." She came closer and looked down at it. "The S looks a little like an L," she said. "Don't you think so? If this curve came down a little straighter — And your last initial is D too. Wouldn't you like to keep it, Lacey?"

"I couldn't possibly."

"Yes, you could. Now it's settled; I won't hear another word."

"It isn't settled at all."

She was very anxious to put me under obligation to her. I was uncomfortable already, before I had been in the house for half an hour, and I knew it would get worse instead of better.

Barbara Mason came to the door of the room carrying a cut-glass carafe of water. She was a quiet young woman in her early thirties with red-brown hair and a healthy, broad-cheekboned face. Lorna was with her. Barbara came over and put the carafe down on the table beside the bed.

"I think that's everything now, Mrs. Dayton," she said.

She behaved toward Sallie as if she were an indulgent older sister instead of a servant. I thought she was a little jealous of Sallie's sudden intimacy with me. At any rate, she was always very polite and silent and reserved with me.

Lorna was standing in the doorway, looking at my things on the bed. She was holding a doll dressed in a pink frock and striped stockings.

"This is Celinda's room," she said. "She's come to visit me from Memphis and this is where she sleeps."

"Who is Celinda?"

"It's one of her dolls," Barbara said. She smiled, at Lorna, not at me. "She's been putting her to bed in this room at night, pretending she was here on a visit."

"We'll pretend she's gone home now," Sallie said to Lorna. "We'll pretend she went Sunday on the *Fair Maid*."

"No," Lorna said.

"Why not, honey?"

Lorna stood there stubbornly. When she did not like something she did not cry or go into a temper as other children did; she simply retreated into an offended silence.

"We'll put Celinda to sleep in the little doll-bed Daddy brought you from New Orleans," Sallie offered.

"No."

"Only while Miss Dereen is here."

"When is she going away?"

"Honey, that's not polite."

"It's not polite either for her to take Celinda's bed." Lorna looked straight at me out of her stubborn round blue eyes.

"She didn't take it, dear. I gave it to her."

"You said Celinda could sleep here as long as Daddy

wasn't here. Where is Daddy going to sleep if he comes and Miss Dereen is sleeping in his bed?"

Sallie flushed absolutely scarlet. "What a naughty thing to say! You know Daddy only sleeps here when Mummy isn't feeling well. Now you take Celinda back to your own room and not another word — not another *word!* Barbara, I do think you could keep her from being underfoot at the *most* inconvenient —"

Barbara said, "I'm sorry, Mrs. Dayton," and took Lorna's hand and brought her out of the room. Sallie looked as if she were going to cry with vexation. She began moving quickly about the room, adjusting the curtains and pushing things about on the dressing table.

"I hope you're not angry, Lacey," she said. "She's only a child, and children pick up such fantastic ideas. I only hope she hasn't hurt your feelings."

"Of course she hasn't," I said. I knew she was not worrying about my feelings.

"Barbara shouldn't have brought her in here," she said. "She's a very imaginative child, and she really says such absurd things sometimes."

"Yes," I said.

"That silly old doll of hers —"

I knew it was not the doll she was so excited about. I said I would unpack my things later, to get her out of the room, and we went downstairs together to the big pink parlor. She had furnished it, like all the rest of the house, as if it were a child's queer pretty dollhouse, only on a larger scale. After we had sat there for a little while she got back her good humor again and gossiped with me quite happily till it was time for dinner.

CHAPTER X   THE NEXT FEW WEEKS WENT BETTER
than I had expected. Sallie liked having somebody in the
house she could chatter to and show off her pretty things to,
and after a day or two she seemed to have forgotten that
there was a reason for any unpleasantness between us. The
Fair Maid stopped at Le Jeune on her up-river run from
New Orleans, but I was at the school all the while she was
lying at the landing, and when I came back to the house
Sallie had a new cameo brooch and was in a fine humor.
She wore the brooch to dinner and I admired it, and that
evening she asked me to stay on at the house till the early
part of July, when she was going up to Corioli for another
visit. I said I thought it would be better if I left as soon as
school was out for the summer.

"I must be a mighty poor hostess if you're so anxious to
leave," she said.

"You're a splendid hostess. But you've done enough for
me as it is, having me here all this time."

"It's been no time at all. Now honestly, Lacey, I'll think
you don't like it here if you don't stay."

She really wanted me to stay. She lived a strange life
there in that house with everything she could possibly want
in the way of material comforts and the little luxuries she
was so fond of, but with no husband and very few friends.
The women of the town were respectful but they did not
like her. She was too irresponsible and too used to having
her own way.

I said I would think about staying, but I hoped something
would come up so I could go as soon as school was out. Just
then, though, I did not have much time to worry about it.
I had to get the pupils ready for the exhibition night at
the end of the term. Ailie McLean said if I wanted to be
asked back for the next term I would have to make a good

impression on the parents and the board. She advised me to have all the bright children learn speeches or poems that they could recite, and to make sure all the dull ones knew the answers to the questions I intended to ask them.

The afternoon of the exhibition night, when I came home from decorating the schoolhouse for the evening, Captain Dayton was at the house. The *Fair Maid* was laid up for a minor repair over at Feliciana and he had come down to stay overnight at Le Jeune. I said good afternoon to him and was going on upstairs to my room, but Sallie stopped me.

"Aren't you going to sit down and talk for a while?" she said. "I declare, Jed'll think you're trying to avoid him. I'm trying to persuade him to come along to the school tonight so he can see how beautifully Lorna's doing in her studies."

Captain Dayton was standing beside the table with Lorna, showing her how to wind up a little mechanical dancing doll that he had brought her. He looked up at Sallie briefly.

"I told you I'd go," he said.

"You said you weren't sure. I thought Lacey might be able to persuade you if she told you all the clever things she's going to have tonight."

Captain Dayton looked at me and I looked away. When I looked at him there was no one else in the room, and I knew I must not do anything foolish now. I could feel Sallie's eyes on me as she sat fanning herself quickly with a little Japanese fan. It was a hot day and the windows were all open. There were bees outside in the honeysuckle that climbed over the gallery rail.

"Tell Daddy what you're going to do tonight," Sallie said to Lorna.

"I'm going to recite a piece and be in a spelling match," Lorna said. She was bored with the doll on the table and went over and picked up Celinda and stood leaning against Sallie's knee. "I'm going to win a prize."

"Of course you are, honey. Mummy donated the prize herself. We're going to be terribly proud of you."

I said I really had to go up to my room if I wanted to be ready for dinner. I went out into the hall and up the stairs. It was very quiet up there. The shutters in my room were half-closed against the late afternoon sun and there were bars of sunlight laid serenely across the carpet. I stood there in the middle of the room listening to the murmur of voices from below. I felt as if I were standing in a trap.

At dinner that evening Sallie talked a good deal and Captain Dayton and I exchanged polite conversation about the weather. The sun was going down but it was not any cooler, and Hendry's little boy sat in one corner of the room, pulling the cord that made the big ceiling fan move slowly back and forth above our heads. Lorna sat eating calmly, paying no attention to her father. She had on a new muslin dress with a blue sash and a big blue ribbon in her hair.

"You ought to have a new dress too, Lacey," Sallie said. "I wonder if my yellow muslin would fit you. I'm an old married woman and it doesn't matter what I wear, but you ought to look nice tonight. Isn't that true, Jed?"

"You both look nice enough to me," he said.

"I'm not worried about how I look tonight," I said. "All I have to worry about is how well those children do."

"That's a very shortsighted way to look at it," Sallie said. "My goodness, Lacey, a pretty girl like you — you don't want to be a schoolteacher all your life. There are some nice young men right here in Le Jeune that you ought to be setting your cap for. I noticed Randy Chambers was mighty attentive to you at the May Day picnic last month."

She wanted me to go upstairs and try on the yellow muslin, but I said I had to get on to the schoolhouse. I wanted to leave early so I would not have to go with them. Sallie said they would see me at the school and at least we could all walk home together. Her cheeks were flushed with heat and excitement and she was talking too much. I saw Captain

Dayton looking at her as if she were somebody acting in a play he had seen before.

I went on to the schoolhouse. It looked unfamiliar with the lights shining out from the windows in the deep summer dusk, and when I went inside with the flowers and paper streamers decorating it and the extra benches crowded along the walls. After the children had come I stood at the door and greeted the parents and the other visitors. Ailie McLean came in and squeezed my hand.

"Good luck," she said.

She and Orrin were with Mr. Moffat. Mr. Moffat shook my hand formally and said he understood I had quite a treat in store for them this evening. He looked at the blackboard. There was only a map of the United States on it that I had drawn to use with the geography questions. Mr. Moffat looked resigned and went on to his place of honor on the platform at the front of the room.

Later, after the program had begun, Sallie and Captain Dayton came in. There were no more places, and there was a little commotion as people squeezed together on the front bench to make room for Sallie to sit down. Captain Dayton stood near her, leaning against the wall. It was not a conspicuous position but people turned their heads to look at him, and when they smiled and nodded to him he returned their greetings without pleasure and with a slightly angry and embarrassed air, as if he wished he were somewhere else.

The program was very long and very dull. The children stumbled through their recitations, the parents sat fanning themselves slowly in the hot silent room, and the June beetles and small green night-insects circled busily about the lighted lamps. There was a spelling match for the older children, with Mr. Moffat holding the book, and then one for the beginners, which I conducted. I knew Sallie would be upset if Lorna did not win, and I was coward enough to give her the easiest words to spell when her turn came. Finally she and Stella Gibbs had spelled down all the rest. I asked Lorna to spell *country* and she thought for a moment and said, "C-u-n-t-r-y."

"C-o-u-n-t-r-y," Stella said.

I began to say that Stella had won the match, but Lorna interrupted me.

"That's what *I* said," she said positively. "C-o-u-n-t-r-y."

She looked me straight in the face. There was a sudden silence. The fans stopped.

"I'm sorry, Lorna," I said. "Perhaps that was what you wanted to say. But you did say c-u-n-t-r-y, and I'm afraid that will have to stand as your answer."

I picked up the prize from the desk to give to Stella. It was a small square package wrapped in tissue paper. Lorna did not move to sit down.

"I want my prize," she said. "I said c-o-u-n-t-r-y and I want my prize."

Sallie stood up. "I must say, Lacey," she said, "you needn't act as if the child would lie about it. If she says she spelled the word correctly she did spell it correctly. You simply must have misunderstood her. Mr. Moffat, didn't *you* hear her — ?"

Mr. Moffat said prudently that he wasn't sure; he was sorry to say his attention had wandered for a moment. Two or three voices from the audience volunteered that they had heard the incorrect version. The children, who were restless from sitting quietly all this time, welcomed the dispute and began arguing about it among themselves. I knew I had to act promptly or there would be bedlam in a moment. I handed the prize to Stella and told Lorna to sit down.

Sallie came up and took Lorna's hand.

"Indeed she will not sit down," she said. Her voice sounded furious but her face looked excited and almost happy. I realized all at once that she had been miserable with tension ever since Captain Dayton had come that afternoon, and that it was a relief to her now to have a pretext to release it. "I have no intention of letting the child stay here to be branded publicly as a liar," she said.

She held Lorna by the hand and turned with her toward the door.

"Sallie, please — " I said. "I didn't imply she was deliberately lying. She was mistaken."

"*You* were mistaken," Sallie said. Now that she had begun to create a scene, she could not stop herself. I had seen women like that before. They seemed to feel a kind of exhilaration in doing things that at ordinary times they would have been too afraid or too ashamed to do. "And you're mistaken too in thinking you're welcome in my house if this is the way you repay my kindness," she said.

She started toward the door with Lorna. I saw Captain Dayton stop her and say something to her quickly in a low voice. There was no expression on his face that I could read. She listened to him only for a moment and then brushed past him, pulling Lorna toward the door. He followed her outside. As the door closed behind them the people who had turned their heads to watch them go turned again to look at me. There was an embarrassed, excited, disapproving silence in the room. I spoke to Stella Gibbs.

"You may sit down, Stella," I said. The room was so silent that the creak of her shoes as she walked across the platform sounded very loud. "We'll have the geography exhibition now," I said.

I turned to the blackboard and picked up the pointer and began asking the children questions about the map I had drawn. I could feel the pointer shaking a little in my hand as I pointed from one place to another on the map.

The exercises came to an end. There was some polite applause and then confusion as the visitors got up and the children went to rejoin their parents. Ailie McLean came up to me.

"You're coming home with me, Lacey," she said. "Now I won't hear any arguments. Sophie's gone and you can have your old room. I declare I'm so mad at Sallie Dayton I could shake her. The idea of going on like that about a little old prize."

"It was very unfortunate," Mr. Moffat said. "A very unfortunate incident."

He stood there shaking his head and looking at me with an expression on his face as if he had tasted something sour. Orrin McLean came up and began to talk to him. Some of the visitors were going. I said good night to them and they answered me, the men a little embarrassed, the women cool. I saw Captain Dayton come in the door. The people who were leaving stopped and looked around to see what would happen. He came directly up to the front of the room where I was standing with Mr. Moffat and the McLeans.

"Miss Dereen," he said. "You too, Mr. Moffat. I want to apologize for my wife's behavior tonight. I'm afraid she wasn't feeling very well."

There was a moment's silence; then Ailie said quickly, "The heat, I reckon." She looked helpfully at Orrin and Mr. Moffat. "Sallie's always been so sensitive to the heat."

"She sent me back to make her excuses," Captain Dayton said. He looked at me. "She was afraid you might take it seriously, what she said about your not being welcome in our house."

"Ailie's asked me to go home with her, Captain Dayton," I said. "It might be better if I did."

"I hope you won't do that. Sallie is badly upset about what happened, and she'll feel even worse if you decide you won't stay at the house because of it."

He was very formal about the whole thing. I could see it was having a reassuring effect on Mr. Moffat.

"Captain Dayton is right," he said. "I'm sure we're all anxious to forget this regrettable incident."

"You go along, Lacey," Ailie said to me.

I knew what she was thinking. She did not want me to go to Sallie's, but it would look better for me to patch up some kind of peace with her than to let the matter stand at the fact that she had turned me out of her house, for whatever reason.

"I'll get my hat," I said to Captain Dayton.

The others were all going. I put on my hat and came back and went outside with Captain Dayton. There were many people on the street and we walked along quietly, not saying anything except when we spoke to say good night to someone passing by. After a while I said: "I hope Sallie isn't really ill."

"No. She has a headache and she's gone to bed. She wants to see you, though, when you come in."

"She doesn't have to say anything. I know how she felt. She was anxious for Lorna to win."

He did not answer me at once. We were passing people on the street. The Daytons lived off at the end of town, at the top of a lane leading up a hill that overlooked the river. We turned into the lane.

"She didn't give a damn about Lorna," he said then. "All she wanted to do was to make trouble for you."

"Oh, no. Why should she want to make trouble for me?"

"You know why." I saw him looking at me through the darkness. "I didn't have to be back in town five minutes last trip before I'd heard all about that half hour I spent walking along the river with you."

"That was only gossip," I said. "She knew it wasn't anything but gossip. If she'd thought anything about that, why should she have asked me to stay with her?"

He did not say anything. We came to the gate of the Daytons' house. He stopped and stood there looking at me. It was a fine night; there was the scent of honeysuckle in the air.

"Walk on a little farther," he said.

"No. Sallie will be expecting us back. She might worry if we're late."

"She won't worry."

I did not want to go in. I put my hand on the gate and I could feel it move a little under my hand holding it tight.

"Yes," I said. "She might. If you don't want to go in

now, I'll say good night. I hope you have a fine trip tomorrow."

"You're very polite, aren't you?" he said. He was a little
angry.

"No. I'm not polite. But you ought to go in."

"Because Sallie will worry?"

"Yes."

"She'd be just as happy if I never came in."

"No, she wouldn't. You know she wouldn't."

His face changed a little and he moved slightly and
brought his hands down hard on the gate. He was very
quiet ordinarily, and when he made a sudden sharp gesture
like that it seemed more violent than it would have if anyone else had made it.

"You don't know anything about it," he said. "That's all
Sallie needs to really set her up — for me to do something
to prove to her that she made a fine mistake when she married me."

I shook my head. "No," I said. "You don't believe that.
She's very fond of you, and if it comes to that, she's very
loyal to you too."

"She's loyal to me because that's the part she's playing
now. A few years ago it was the child-bride, and after that
it was the devoted mother, and after that it was the fash-
ionable young matron. She's been working up to the neg-
lected wife for quite a while now; it's going to be a big dis-
appointment to her if she doesn't get a chance to do that
one too."

He did not say it as if it had anything to do with him.
I stood there looking at him. I knew he ought not to be telling me those things and I knew they were true. The way he
told them I could see that they did not mean anything to
him. He was finished with them. Or he thought he was finished with them, which was not the same thing, but could
be even more final than the other.

"Sallie's a child," I said. "You can't judge her the way
you'd judge anyone else."

"I'm not judging her. She can live her own life the way she pleases, and I'll live mine the way I please."

"You make it sound so easy. It's not so easy as all that."

"You know all about it."

"No," I said. "I don't know anything about it. But I know about easy ways. They're never really very easy."

"And that's what you're afraid of?"

"Yes."

I knew when I said it that it was true. Before my father had died I had never really been afraid of anything because nothing irrevocable had ever happened to me. If there had been bad luck before that, the luck could always change. It was only after he had died that I had learned there was bad luck that nothing could change.

"There's nothing to be afraid of," Captain Dayton said. "As long as you know what you want and are willing to pay for it. It doesn't make any difference if it's the easy way or the hard way; you have to pay for it either way, but you can always have something if you want it enough."

"There's nothing I want now," I said, "but to live quietly. I've had enough troubles in my time."

He stood there looking at me steadily.

"Is that the truth?" he said.

"Yes, it's the truth."

It was not the truth, but it seemed necessary to say it, and after I had said it I walked on quickly to the house. He came behind me and opened the door and we went inside. There was a light in the hall; Sallie was coming down the stairs. She had on a pink negligee and her hair was down on her shoulders. She had lovely hair, a dark chestnut-brown, very thick and a little wavy.

"Oh — Lacey," she said. She looked tense and guilty and a little frightened. "I thought it was you. I'm so glad Jed made you come back. Wasn't that silly of me this evening? I declare I don't know what got into me."

"It's all right," I said.

"No, it isn't all right. I feel downright terrible about it."

She was looking from me to Captain Dayton, uneasily. I was glad there was only a dim light in the hall. "Now you've got to promise you won't let this make any difference between us," she said. "You're going to stay here and go on up to Corioli with me?"

"We'll talk about it in the morning," I said.

I had to get away. I said good night without looking at Captain Dayton and went upstairs to my room. As I went up the stairs I could hear him telling Sallie that he would not be able to stay in Le Jeune overnight because he had to go back to Feliciana and rejoin the *Fair Maid* at once.

CHAPTER XI

IN THE MORNING WHEN I CAME DOWN-stairs Sallie acted as if nothing had happened. She asked me if I wanted eggs for breakfast, and marmalade or jam on my toast, and when I said I was leaving for Corioli that afternoon she said I wasn't to talk nonsense, because of course I had promised to stay and go with her.

"I didn't promise," I said. "I said we'd talk about it in the morning."

"It's the same thing. You knew if we talked about it I wouldn't let you go. Why should you want to go? We've made up, haven't we?"

"Of course. But it will be better if I go."

"It won't be better at all. Not in a little town like this. Everyone will say we've quarreled, and it will be uncomfortable for both of us."

I didn't know whether she was threatening me or trying to make me sorry for her. She looked tense and excited and as if she had not slept. She sat there looking at me, and all at once I realized that if I did not want any trouble I had better stay.

"All right," I said. "I'll wait and go with you."

"That's fine," she said. "That's much better."

I did not know why she wanted me to stay, but I did not think it was because she was really sorry about what had happened the night before. Whatever it was, though, I knew I had to act as if everything was fine between us.

It was a very strange time for me after that. We were together all day long, walking or driving or visiting or shopping, or only sitting with Lorna on the gallery in the long summer evenings, and almost every day she talked to me about Captain Dayton and then watched to see what I would say and how I would look. There were times when I did not think I could get through it. I even thought about trying to get a new school somewhere else for the next term. I had seen Mr. Moffat, and he said the board had agreed to keep me on if I wanted to come back to Le Jeune in the fall, but I told him I would have to think about it before I gave him a definite answer. I could not afford to turn the offer down as long as I did not have another school, but I thought that during the summer I might be able to find one through Thomas Dandy.

Sallie and I left for Corioli in July. The *Fair Maid* came in early in the morning, and we went down to the landing together and went on board. It was a lovely day, hot and clear and with a breeze on the river. Sallie was keyed up and happy about the trip. She made a point of taking me with her when she went to find Captain Dayton.

"Do you like my hat?" she said to him. "It's not a new hat, but you've never seen me wear it before. I'm going to buy half a dozen new hats in Corioli and wear them one on top of the other; then maybe you'll notice that I have on something new. Aren't you going to kiss me? And you might say good morning to Miss Dereen."

Captain Dayton looked at me. He did not say anything.

"Good morning," I said. "I'm just going to take a turn around the boat. It's such a lovely day."

I knew I could not stay there. All the while in Le Jeune I

had been telling myself that I could see him without its
really mattering to me, and now that I saw him again I
knew I had been lying to myself. I walked along the deck
to the stairs and down to the deck below where the staterooms were and stood there looking over the rail at the
water. Captain Dix came up to me. He was off watch
and was smoking a cigar.

"You don't look very happy for a schoolteacher with
school out for the summer," he said.

I smiled at him. "Must I look happy?"

"It might be safer. There are a couple of enterprising
young fellows on board who specialize in consoling females
in distress. Up to now they haven't had anything better to
practice on than a brace of widows and an elderly young
lady who lost her sweetheart at the first battle of Manassas."

"I'm afraid I was too young to have a sweetheart at the
first battle of Manassas," I said. "Were you in the war, Captain Dix?"

"I won the battle of Gettysburg."

"Really? I thought that was General Meade."

"That's what they tell you. He never could have done it
without me."

"I should have thought you'd have been on the other
side."

"I was. That's how he won it."

"Seriously."

"I was on a gunboat on the Yazoo. We got blown to hell."

"It sounds impressive."

"It wasn't. We swam ashore and sat down in the bushes
and waited for somebody to rescue us."

"Why did you have to be rescued?"

"It's a long sad story. We'd lost some articles of clothing
that are considered essential in polite society."

I laughed. "And after that you won the battle of Gettysburg," I said.

"Absolutely. I have an idea you don't believe me."

"I believe every word," I said.

It made me feel better to talk to him. I stood there leaning on the rail and looking out over the water. We were
moving upstream so close to the shore that I could hear
the cicadas and smell the sweet clover from the fields. It
was a fine day on the river. We passed another packet,
headed downstream. I saw the name *Sallie Dayton* on the
paddle box. The whistles of both boats blew and the pilot
on the *Sallie Dayton* waved to Captain Dix.

"Where is she bound for?" I said.

"Down to Memphis. Jed's thinking of putting her into the
Pittsburgh-Corioli trade next season; she and the *Fair Maid*
are cutting into each other's business down here. Steamboat-
ing isn't what it used to be before the railroads came in."

I looked at the *Sallie Dayton* slowly drawing away from
us behind the wide glittering rollers of her wake.

"It must be a fine life," I said.

"You sound like Jed. He's the only riverman I know of
who isn't happiest when he's going ashore."

"Why is he different?" I asked. I wanted to talk about
Captain Dayton.

"He's crazy. He was probably born steamboat-crazy and
he'll die steamboat-crazy. It's a kind of softening of the
brain."

"And he's always had it?"

"As long as I've known him. That's since he was a skinny
sixteen-year-old kid with enough persistence to talk me into
making a cub pilot out of him. Before that he might have
been normal, for all I know."

"And now he has everything he wants," I said. I did not
look at him when I said it.

"Yes. On the river, anyway. That's probably why he
doesn't care about going ashore."

"He has his home there."

"It isn't his home. You've lived there long enough to have
found that out by this time."

"Yes." I knew I ought not to be talking to him about it,

but I could not help it now that I had started, and I did
not think it would be dangerous. "Why did he marry her?"
I said.

"Why does any man marry any good-looking female who
goes after him with everything she's got?"

I looked down at the river. "You don't like her," I said.

"I know a spoiled brat when I see one. That's more than
Jed did. He never had a chance. He'd never been close
enough to a girl like that before to see the whites of her
eyes. All that lace and starch and silk, and throwing herself right at his head."

"Was he in love with her?"

He spat over the rail. "Hell, you could call it love. She
never gave him a chance to find out. She had a ring on her
finger before he came to."

"She can't have been much more than a child," I said.
"You make her sound dreadful."

"She wasn't. She was very stylish about it. She was just
used to having her own way. I've seen five-year-olds who
were pretty expert at that, and I reckon the system is still
the same, whether you're after a new doll or a husband."

I stood there looking across the water at the willows along
the shore. There was a light breeze blowing that turned
the silvery undersides of the leaves to the sun.

"Anyway," I said, "it was a fair bargain, wasn't it? He has
the *Fair Maid* now. He has everything he wants on the river."

"Yes."

"What would happen if he should lose it?"

"Lose it?" He did not understand me.

"All of it. The *Fair Maid*, the Dayton Line, all of it."

"He won't lose it."

"Or give it up?"

"He won't give it up either," he said.

I didn't say anything. I stood there waiting.

"Listen," he said. He looked serious. I had never seen him
really serious before. "It isn't the money."

"No."

"It isn't even the boats. It's something else."

"What is it?"

"I can't tell you. It wouldn't sound like the way it is."

"Tell me."

He looked at his cigar and then threw it suddenly in a long arc into the river.

"You wouldn't understand," he said. "You're a woman, and women don't mind being second in command. Or at least, if they do, they get used to it. Jed's never going to get used to it. And his own packet is one place where he can be master and President of the United States and maybe even God Almighty, if you're not looking for any miracles." He looked at me. "I told you it wouldn't sound right the way it came out."

"Yes," I said. "Why is he that way?"

"I don't know. You get a rotten enough deal when you start out in life and it either scares hell out of you, or turns you mean, or you make up your mind you don't need anybody else anyway and you can go it alone."

"He doesn't necessarily want to be alone because he's had to," I said.

"No."

"But you think he can't change now?"

He shrugged his shoulders.

I turned away from the railing. Sallie was coming along the deck, looking for me. She said good morning to Captain Dix and then told me to come along with her. She had met some people she knew from down in La Fayette, and we sat on deck and talked and afterwards had lunch with them. We all had a very pleasant time.

         ·

CHAPTER XII   LATER, AFTER IT WAS DARK THAT evening, Sallie said we must all go up to the hurricane deck

and look at the stars. We were a very gay party by that
time. There were two older men and one young man who
had been visiting the bar all afternoon, and Sallie had had
a glass of wine at dinner that had made her even giddier
than usual. We went up to the hurricane deck and she said
if we could find the North Star we wouldn't need a pilot
because we could bring the *Fair Maid* in to Corioli ourselves just by following the star.

"Like the three wise men," one of the ladies said.

The young man denied this. The river changed its direction so much, he said, that at times we were actually
headed south.

"I want to go south," Sallie said. "I'll tell Jed to turn the
boat around and take us all south."

"Spoken like a true Southern lady," one of the older men
said. His name was Mr. Courtney. "There are no Infant
Saviours in Corioli."

"Don't be irreverent," Sallie said.

"Dear lady, forgive me, I'm merely stating a fact. I appeal
to Mrs. Baker."

"I adore Corioli," Mrs. Baker said.

"It's a statistical fact," Mr. Courtney said, "that there have
been nine murders in Corioli in the past nine days."

"They have an interesting system there," the young man
said. "I read in the newspaper the other day that, of the
last fifty murderers caught in the city, they have managed
to hang four."

"The others probably had Tommy Dandy to defend
them," Mr. Courtney said.

"I adore murders," Sallie said. "I want to live in Corioli."

"You ought to live on the *Fair Maid*," the other older
man said.

"I would if Jed would let me."

"Why won't he let you?"

"I wish you'd ask him," Sallie said. "Please do ask him. I
want to go up and down the river between two lovely
wicked cities."

"That's just it," Mr. Courtney said.

"What is?"

"The two wicked cities. What would he do there with a wife on his arm?"

"Steamboat captains have a girl in every port," Mrs. Baker said.

"Jed hasn't," Sallie said. "He's a model husband."

"Are you sure?"

"I'm positive of it," Sallie said.

After a while they grew tired of looking at the stars and went below again. I did not go with them. It was quiet on deck after they had left. The boat had been darkened so that the pilot could see his course, and the only light was the red glare from the twin stacks above. Smoke and trails of sparks floated out into the air behind them. We were close to shore again and I could see the dark willows along the banks and the fireflies rising. We would be in Corioli soon.

Captain Dayton came up behind me. I knew he was there before I turned around.

"It's a fine night," he said.

"Yes."

When I looked at him I knew I was in love with him. It was not something new, but it was something I could not lie about to myself any longer. I stood there holding on to the rail.

"Where are the others?" he said.

"They've gone below."

His voice sounded strange and so did my voice, answering him. We could hear people laughing off below, and the sound of music from the cabin. We stood there without talking. All the while the silence seemed to grow tighter and louder around us. I knew I had to get away. I moved from the rail and he moved too and took my hand and then put his arm around me.

"No," I said.

He knew I did not mean it. I tried to speak with conviction but he knew I did not mean it and he kept his arm where it was and drew me closer to him and kissed me. I could feel him shuddering a little as he kissed me and my heart beating and I began to cry.

"No," I said again. "Oh, no. We can't."

"Yes," he said. "We can't. But we do. Don't talk. Don't say anything."

"I have to say it. Now. We can't let it happen."

"It has happened. There's nothing we can do about it."

"Nothing has happened."

"Nothing except that I'm in love with you. And you with me —"

"You weren't ever going to know."

"I knew. You see. You don't have to talk."

"Not for that. I knew too, that first morning on the *Fair Maid*, when you looked at me." Now that it had begun, it was as if all the things we had never said were saying themselves fast, before we could have time to think and time to stop them. I looked up at him then; I had to say it. "Oh, darling, you did love me then, didn't you?" I said.

"I loved you before that. I loved you the first time I saw you."

"You don't have to say that. The first time you saw me you were angry with me. It was afterwards, the next morning. You looked at me and I knew there wasn't going to be anyone else, ever. I've wanted to cry ever since and now I can't stop crying."

I was crying with my face against his shoulder. We stood there in the shadow of the skylight roof. I could hear the steady chuff of the engines and feel the slight motion of the boat beneath my feet. After a little I stopped crying.

"If I died now, this moment, I wouldn't care, " I said. "I think I'd be glad. Because nothing can ever be any better or any worse than it is now."

"Don't talk like that. We're not going to die; we're going to live. We have more reason now to want to live than we ever had before."

"No, we haven't. We haven't, either of us." I looked up at him. "Oh, Jed, we can't do this," I said. "We're not the only people in the world."

"We're the only ones who matter to us."

"We're not. There's Sallie and there's Lorna. You couldn't just go down there to Sallie tonight and tell her you love me."

"Maybe not tonight."

"Not ever. I think she'd lose her mind if that ever happened to her. You don't know how she is."

"I know how she is."

"No, you don't. I don't know how I can face her now. I can't go back to Le Jeune after this."

"It won't make any difference where you go. I'll find you wherever you are."

"No, you won't. You mustn't."

"Because of what people will say?"

"I don't care what they say. They could cut me into little pieces and I wouldn't care as long as I could be with you. But it's not that simple."

"Nothing is simple. You find out what's important and you hold on to that and the hell with all the rest of it."

"No. The rest of it is important too."

I could not talk about it any more. I knew if I did I would go to pieces altogether. I walked away from him to the rail. He followed me.

"Are you trying to tell me this is all?" he said.

"Yes."

"You want me to let you walk off this boat tonight and then forget you're alive?"

"Yes."

"You don't."

I turned away from the rail.

"You don't," he said again.

"No," I said. "I don't. But what good does it do to say it?"

We were standing there together in the shadow of the

roof. I heard voices from around on the side of the boat, where the stairs were that led to the deck below. Jed heard them too, but he did not move. I turned away quickly. Sallie and Mr. Courtney were coming along the deck from the stairs. Sallie saw me first.

"There she is," she said. "I told you we'd find her up here. She has a very romantic disposition; she's been looking at the stars."

She started over to where I was standing, and then she saw Jed and stopped and stood there looking at him. I knew I had to say something at once.

"Were you looking for me?" I said. "I'm sorry. I was just going down, but Captain Dayton came along and we stopped to talk for a moment."

I didn't know whether she believed me or not. Mr. Courtney began to talk to Jed. He did not seem to notice that anything was wrong. I was very glad that he was there. He talked to Jed for a few moments and then Jed excused himself and went off. All the while Sallie hadn't said a word. Mr. Courtney escorted us across the deck and down the stairs and went on talking cheerfully to me. We joined the others on the deck below.

"Oh, you found her," Mrs. Baker said. "We'd all just made up our minds she'd slipped off in a small boat with that handsome young clerk. It's such a perfect night for an elopement."

"I'm sorry to spoil your little romance," Sallie said, "but that young man is already married."

Her voice sounded different from the way it had before. She was trying to act as if nothing was the matter, but her voice was shaking a little and she talked too fast.

"Oh dear," one of the younger ladies said, "nobody cares about that nowadays. People are always running off with other people's husbands; you read it every day in the newspapers."

"Nobody cares," Mr. Courtney said, "except the wife." He laughed; he was really feeling very cheerful. "Or maybe even she doesn't care," he said. "Maybe she's glad to be rid of him."

Mrs. Baker shrieked. "Oh, go away, you dreadful man!" she said. She was about fifty-five, very plump and active. "I'm sure we'd never think such a thing about our husbands. Now would we, Sallie?"

"I wouldn't," Sallie said. She had sat down beside Mrs. Baker. Her eyes looked very brilliant in her pale face. "I'd never let Jed go," she said. "Never. No matter what."

"There," Mrs. Baker said. "Do you hear that, ladies? She's serving notice on you. And I'll do the same for Mr. Baker." She shrieked again. "As if anybody would want him," she said. "He's a splendid husband, but he's not exactly what anybody would call a romantic figure."

I sat there and listened to them talk. They were all having a fine time. All but Sallie. I saw her watching me. She had not been making a joke about it.

CHAPTER XIII   WHEN WE GOT TO CORIOLI I LEFT the boat without having seen Jed alone again. Mr. Fraser, the clerk, went ashore with Sally and me and put us into a carriage. The levee looked strange with the lights from the *Fair Maid* and the other steamboats rippling out over the dark water. It was late, but the landing was full of activity. Under the flaring lights long lines of roustabouts were moving to and from the boats, carrying the sacks and kegs with which they had been loaded, and there was a constant confusion of noise: the crashing of boxes, the rattle of drays, the shouts of the mates and the clerks. Sallie was going to the St. Victor Hotel, but she told the driver to stop at Longmill Street first. I thought she wanted to see where I lived. We moved quickly away from the landing to the dark quiet streets above.

It was only a short drive to Longmill Street. Nora was expecting me; there was a light behind the drawn blinds of the shop. She heard the horse's hoofs on the paving and came out to meet me. I got out of the carriage and she threw her arms about me and kissed me.

"Ah, the darling!" she said. "It's thinner you've got since I saw you last."

Sallie was leaning down from the cab above, watching us. I said to her: "Won't you meet my cousin? Mrs. Mulranny — Mrs. Dayton."

Sallie smiled down intently at Nora.

"Lacey never talks about her people," she said. "I don't know anything about you. I'm so glad I've met you."

Nora stood there, holding on to my arm and looking a little frightened of the carriage and Sallie's fine clothes and the waiting driver.

"I'm sure she's written me how good you've been to her," she said.

"I haven't at all. Everyone's so fond of Lacey. I'm afraid I really must go now."

She did not bother to say good-by. Nora and I stood on the pavement, looking after the carriage.

"She paid a fine penny for that hat," Nora whispered. "Sacred Heart, it had me hypnotized; I couldn't look at anything else. A whole bird on it, is it? There's queer things going these times, and that's a fact."

We went into the house together. Conn was napping back in the bedroom, Nora said; she wouldn't want to waken him.

"He'll be sorry not to be out to welcome you back," she said, "but he's had a desperate hard day of it."

She made me a cup of tea and then sat down to gossip with me in the little kitchen behind the shop. We talked in low voices not to waken Conn. I wondered what sort of hard day it was he had had, for I knew they were still getting their living from the shop. Nora avoided talking about him. She was nervous, and started at every sound.

"Sure who wouldn't be nervous in this town?" she said.

"There's murders going every day in the newspapers; I don't know what's getting into the people at all. Down the street now, old Lindermann, that keeps the livery stable, was knocked on the head the other night only for the money he had in his pocket."

I did not think it was the troubles in the city she was worried about. She had something else on her mind, and I did not have to be very sharp to know that it was Conn. She was afraid to talk about it with him in the next room, but I suspected it would all come out the first time we were really alone. I knew beforehand what it would be. The money, the whisky, the girls on Diamond Street, or perhaps only some one girl who was willing to wait to step into Nora's shoes. I told myself I should have tried to stop her from marrying him. I could not have stopped her; I knew that. I could not stop her even now, with all she knew about him, if she were free again and he were to ask her to marry him.

After she had talked for a while herself, she began asking me questions about Le Jeune. She wanted to hear all about the Daytons' house, and about Sallie's dresses and china and furniture.

"Isn't it lucky you are to fall in with fine rich people like that?" she said. "Maybe they'd find you a sweetheart that would marry you and put you in a grand house the like of that, with nothing to do all day but count how many dresses you'd have hanging in your closets."

I did not say anything. Nora looked at me.

"You're quiet enough," she said, "but I'm thinking there's something behind that. You've the look of a girl that has a man on her mind."

I tried to smile. "Is it mind reading you're doing now?" I said.

"You'll do no good trying to keep it to yourself. You'll have to be talking about it to someone, and I'm the handiest while you're here."

"There's nothing to talk about."

"We'll see. Some nice young man, is it, you met at Mrs. Dayton's house?"

There was a noise in the next room: Conn getting up. Nora stopped talking and looked around. Conn came to the doorway, his great frame almost filling it. He was in trousers and undershirt, his braces hanging about his knees. Apparently he had just waked up; he looked at me sleepily for a moment, as if he were peering through smoke.

"Lacey, is it?" he said. He came over and kissed me on the lips. "A thousand welcomes to you under the roof of the Mulrannys," he said. "Sure you're getting prettier every time I lay eyes on you."

"You needn't eat the face off her, so," Nora said. "Would you like a cup of tea now? The kettle's just on."

He turned around to her.

"Tea would be a poor watery drink to celebrate a home-coming," he said. "It's whisky we'd want at a time like this."

He was being very cordial. I saw that he was quite drunk. He went over to the cupboard and brought out the whisky.

"Haven't you had enough of that and to spare today?" Nora said.

He turned about, facing her again.

"The day I have enough of good whisky will be the day I step into my grave," he said. "And divil a day sooner I'll do that to please you, my good woman, or any of your fancy relations, whoever they may be." He poured some whisky into a tumbler and waved it in the air. "Whether they're pretty schoolteachers in fancy stockings, or fancy lawyers like Tommy Dandy, that belong on the wrong side of the bars they're so clever at getting other people out from behind."

"The Dandys are no relations of mine," Nora said. She was getting her temper up too. "So put that in your pipe and smoke it."

Conn looked at her grandly.

"Smoking," he said, "is a dirty habit, and it's well you know it's a vice I don't indulge in."

"Thank the Lord for it then, for it's the only one," Nora muttered. Then she cried out suddenly, in an unexpectedly passionate voice: "Isn't it ashamed of yourself you are, drinking yourself into a blind sot before this girl? It's different with me, that swore at the altar, the more fool I was, I'd share all your troubles along with small good, but you've a right to keep a respectable face on you in front of a girl that's a guest in your house."

She was ashamed to have me see him in the state he was in. I did not want to make any trouble. I stood up and asked if I could go upstairs to my room.

"I'll take you myself," Nora said.

She got up from her chair. Conn stood in the middle of the kitchen, his legs wide apart for balance and his glass in his hand.

"Too good to stay in the same room with me, is it?" he said. "'Usha, if the truth was in it, I'm a better Christian than many a man walking the streets of this town with a gold chain across his belly and a silk hat on his head." He looked at me. "Tell that to Tommy Dandy when you see him," he said. "Tell him if there's no law in this town there's rope and men who know how to use it."

"Will you whisht with your Tommy Dandy?" Nora said. "What have you got against the poor man?"

"Tell him there's men who don't like the smell of murderers walking their streets," Conn said, "or the smell of the fine clever lawyers who put them there any more." He tried to gesture with his glass, lost his balance slightly, and fell against the table. "And there's talk" — he called after us — "there's talk that it won't be much longer we'll stand by with our hands idle in our pockets —"

"There's talk and little else, I'm thinking," Nora muttered.

She went on before me up the stairs to the third floor. It was directly under the roof, not much more than an attic, with a space partitioned off in front to make a small slant-ceilinged room.

"It's a poor enough place for you," she said, "but I wouldn't know how to do any better."

"It's fine," I said.

I did not look around. All I wanted was to be alone. But Nora stood there looking at me restlessly.

"You see how he is," she said suddenly.

"Yes."

She was ashamed, but it was more than that. She wanted to defend him. I knew that was it.

"There isn't a better man walking on two feet when he's sober," she went on. "You couldn't say he wasn't a good husband to me then. Taking me about like I was a queen itself — It's those wild boyos down at the *Crown of Life* that lead him the way he's going. Talking about a Vigilance Committee when all they care about the laws is the ones that leave a place like that open for them to guzzle themselves into a state where they wouldn't know a city ordinance from one of the Ten Commandments."

"What is it about the city?" I said. "Why is there trouble?"

"How would I know that? It's those fellas down there at City Hall, I suppose — Markey's fellas, they all say. All they're out for in the world is lining their own pockets, and the devil take the rest of us. There's too much money going these days, and more and more people crowding in here all the time to see can they get their hands on a few dollars of it."

She left me soon; she had Conn on her mind, down there alone in the kitchen. I heard her footsteps going down the stairs. It was late; the house was still. I went over to the window and stood looking out — not the river and the quiet Le Jeune levee here, but a narrow cobblestoned city street with chimney pots silhouetted against the summer-night sky. I thought about Jed, wondering where he was. Down on the *Fair Maid* still or, more likely, at the St. Victor with Sallie. I knew I ought not to think about him. I had stopped thinking about him when I had left the *Fair Maid* and I had got along beautifully up to now. I had not really stopped thinking about him; I had only covered it over a little with other things. Now that I was alone I could not cover it over any longer. I stood there at the window and told myself that I had to stop thinking about him.

It wasn't any good. I knew I was going to have to live with it just the way it was. I lay down on the bed and after a little I started to cry, not the way I had cried standing on the deck of the *Fair Maid* with Jed's arms around me, but the kind of crying that makes you feel sick all over when you are done with it. I was done with it after a while, and I got up and undressed and went to bed. I dreamed about Jed after I finally fell asleep. You could not stop it, it seemed, even when you were asleep.

CHAPTER XIV　　　　 THE SUNDAY AFTER THAT I WALKED over to Sevier Street to the Dandys'. I had sent a note to Thomas Dandy asking if I could see him, and in return I had had an invitation to come to tea on Sunday afternoon from Miss Dandy. She said Thomas would be there and I could talk to him then. I would rather have spoken to him alone, but I did not really mind about that now. I did not mind about anything except getting a new school that would take me away from Le Jeune and Jed and Corioli too.

The Dandys' house looked different that afternoon with the trees in full leaf before it now and the cast-iron dog standing in deep shade on the lawn. It was hot: the hall felt cool when the maid opened the door and let me in. Miss Dandy was sitting in the parlor with her white cat on her lap. She said, "Good afternoon," and asked me to sit down. She did not look different. She had on a dark-green silk dress that caught the light and changed color when it did, and there was the same detached expression on her long high-nosed ugly face.

"You came to see Thomas, of course," she said. "He'll be along very soon."

She seemed to expect me to tell her why I had come. She sat there waiting.

"I wanted to ask him about getting another school," I said.

Her eyebrows went up slightly. "Haven't they asked you to come back to Le Jeune?" she said. "I've been talking to Sallie Dayton; I understand that they did."

I did not know what Sallie had told her. I watched her hand moving regularly down the white cat's back. It was impossible to tell what she was thinking.

"I'd like to be closer to Corioli," I said.

If I had to lie, it was the best I could do at the moment. Thomas Dandy would not have asked questions. I had counted on that.

She sat there looking at me, apparently without judgment and without sympathy, continuing to stroke the cat.

"It would be better if you told me the truth," she said. "Sallie isn't a sphinx, you know. Is there something between you and Captain Dayton?"

She was waiting for me to answer her. I knew it would have to be a lie again — if not for my own sake, at least for the other people involved, for Jed and Sallie.

"Sallie makes a good deal out of very little," I said. "There was some gossip in Le Jeune because I happened to meet Captain Dayton one Sunday morning when I was going for a walk, and he came along with me. Sallie knew it wasn't any more than that, but she takes queer ideas; you must know that yourself. The other evening, when we were on the *Fair Maid* coming from Le Jeune, Captain Dayton happened to be talking to me on the hurricane deck when she came up. I don't know what she thought; she acted very strangely afterwards. There was nothing to explain, so I didn't try."

I knew it sounded unconvincing. She stopped stroking the cat, lifted it from her lap to the floor, and poured a cup of tea for me from the silver teapot at her elbow. I took the cup from her.

"So you've decided that the best way for you to stop the gossip is to give up a respectable situation in Le Jeune and hope the director of the next district where you apply for a school will be kind enough to make no inquiries about the reason that you left your last place," she said. "Is that it?"

I could not tell if she had believed me. Whether she had or not, she had put her finger on a weakness in my plan that I myself had never thought of. She was telling me that I could not let Sallie go back to Le Jeune and talk to people there as she had talked to her here in Corioli. She was saying that I had one chance to make them believe me instead of Sallie, and that I was destroying that chance if I ran away. And she was telling me that if I did run away I might very possibly have no place to run to, because what Sallie would say in Le Jeune would go farther than Le Jeune, far enough to reach the ears of anyone interested in finding out if I was a fit person to teach their children.

I sat there holding the cup in my hands. She poured some tea for herself. I could hear the clock ticking in the hall and the dry hot chirping of some sparrows in the trees outside the windows. I waited, and after a while she said: "I've asked Sallie to come here this afternoon."

"Here?" I said. "This afternoon? But why — ?"

"Because it's best to have this out in the open." She poured cream for the white cat into a saucer. He was stretched out under a table; she had to call him: "Puss — puss — puss!" He got up slowly and walked superbly to the dish she held for him. She set it down and looked at me. "Because no matter what you've done," she said, "you can stop her from

talking about it if you tell her in my house that I believe
you've done nothing wrong."

"Do you?" I said.

"I'm not even interested in finding out. You went to Le
Jeune as a connection of the Dandy family; I shouldn't care
to see you involved in anything discreditable. So I'm perfectly willing to give you the benefit of the doubt, and if
you *have* been a fool, I'm relying on you not to be one in
the future. Aren't there enough young men in the world that
you can go walking along the river with and holding con-
versations with on the decks of steamboats without your
having to pick one who is not only married but married to
a flighty, jealous young woman?"

The way she said it, it sounded as simple as deciding to
put your money into one bank instead of another because
the first was safer and would give you better returns. It
might be a fine way to regulate your life if you had no
emotions, but I was in love with Jed, for God knew what
reason except that it certainly was not because it was safer
and would give better returns, and so I could not regulate
my life that way. I had thought I might run away from it,
and now it seemed I could not even do that. I could only sit
there and wait. It was not for long. In a few moments there
was the sound of someone at the outer door.

"That will be Thomas," Miss Dandy said. "He's bringing
Sallie."

Thomas Dandy came into the room, shepherding Sallie.
I saw the startled look that crossed her face as she caught
sight of me sitting there with Miss Dandy.

"Oh — Lacey!" she said. She glanced accusingly at Miss
Dandy. "You didn't tell me —"

"Lacey came to see Thomas," Miss Dandy said. She looked
imperturbably from me to Sallie. "It's about getting another
school; it seems she wants to leave Le Jeune. Won't you
sit down, Sallie? You always look so charming; I do believe
you've got on another new hat."

I tried not to look surprised; she had her own plan, I

could only suppose, that involved her saying one thing to me and five minutes later another to Sallie. But if I did not look surprised, Sallie did.

"Leave?" she said. "Does she want to leave?"

"She thinks it would be better. Don't you want to sit down, Sallie? Thomas, will you give her this cup of tea? I always find tea so refreshing on a hot day."

Sallie sat down and accepted the tea, but she was looking at me.

"Where do you want to go?" she said.

Miss Dandy took it up again before I could answer.

"That isn't important, is it? Just as long as it's anywhere in the world but Le Jeune, and far enough away from the river so there'll be no chance of any more gossip and misunderstanding. Lacey feels that, under the circumstances, it's the only thing she *can* do to prove her good intentions. You see" — she looked composedly at Sallie over her long, clever face — "she's really very fond of you, Sallie."

I sat there listening to her and thinking how, if you didn't have any feelings to worry about, anybody could probably do this well at lying, because lying was only a kind of acting, and you could act any part if you were clever enough and not confused by your own emotions. She was acting well enough to take Sallie in now. I saw how she was looking at me, with the uncertain, guilty air of someone who has begun to doubt the righteousness of her actions.

"I didn't know," she said. She was not drinking her tea. "I hadn't any idea. Do you really want to leave, Lacey?"

"Yes," I said, truly enough.

"I've told her I thought it would be very unwise," Miss Dandy said. "If I were in her place I should certainly stay, if only to prove there was no reason for me to go. But she's afraid that, however innocent she may be of the intention of causing any more trouble, something else may happen to upset you if she stays."

I was so uncomfortable, listening to her, that I was sure

Sallie would see it. But she was looking at Miss Dandy. The guilty expression was even stronger on her face.

"You all think I'm stupid and unreasonable," she said. "I know you do."

"Nobody thinks anything of the kind. Lacey's an attractive young woman; she ought to realize that she has to be more discreet than an old woman like me. If I wanted to walk along the river with a young man, no one would think anything more of it than that I wanted some company and might have found it convenient to have an arm to take to help me over the rough places. Very possibly Lacey had exactly the same motives, but she ought to have been more careful, all the same."

She asked Sallie if she wanted some cake. I saw how careful she was not to press her, or to seem to take my part against her. I knew how it would end. Sallie was being led, in the most tactful manner possible, to believe that she had made a fool of herself over nothing, and she would react to it just as Miss Dandy knew she would, and as I knew, and as Thomas Dandy did. He was sitting on the edge of an ormolu table across the room, eating cake and watching us and not saying a word. His bright-blue eyes had a light in them that was half enjoyment and half admiration. He watched Sallie getting more and more excited and unsure of herself, and Miss Dandy sitting there stroking her white cat again and talking to her in the kind of indulgent tone she might have used to a child, till finally Sallie couldn't do anything but say she'd never taken it seriously about Jed and me and she'd never meant either to drive me away from Le Jeune. Then he stood up and said briskly: "So that's that. I vote we've spent far too much time already on this unpleasant subject for such a hot day. Lacey needn't look for a new school, and Sallie needn't bother her head any longer over what is surely the most needless of all worries — the idea that any man who's lucky enough to call himself her husband is going to forget that fact even for half a minute —"

He flattered her with the soothing, persuasive Celtic flattery I knew so well, taking up the matter where his aunt had left off. I watched Sallie sitting there between the two of them. She had no idea that she was being manipulated like a puppet at the end of a pair of strings. I felt sick and ashamed. I did not want any part of it. I wanted to tell them the truth and then walk out of the house. If I told them the truth it would only make matters worse. There was nothing for me to do but sit there and listen to it.

Sallie did not stay long. She said she was going somewhere for dinner, and the next day she was going back to Le Jeune on the *Sallie Dayton*. She said she had wanted to wait and go back on the *Fair Maid*, but at this time of year the river was undependable and the *Fair Maid* might have to lay up for low water before she could get back to Corioli. She had not mentioned Jed's name before that, and she did not mention it now. I did not think she had quarreled with him about me, but I knew that even the usual strained truce under which they had lived up to this time must have been broken now. She was more bewildered than frightened, like a too-indulged child set down suddenly in strange, indifferent surroundings. I could not bear to look at her.

When she had left, the tension in the room relaxed. Thomas Dandy resumed his seat on the edge of the table. He sat talking brilliantly about a trial just concluded in the courts, in which his client, a doctor accused of buying three bodies from a pair of burkers for fifteen dollars apiece, cutting each body into five pieces, and disposing of the pieces to medical students for five dollars each, had been acquitted.

"Why do you take such dreadful cases?" Miss Dandy said. There was a look of distaste on her face. She lifted the white cat deliberately from her lap and set him on the floor, as if he had served his purpose for the moment. "Do you know what people are saying about you?"

"They're saying I'm the cleverest lawyer in Corioli. And the biggest blackguard, for all I care. The point is that I can juggle them, and they're not keen on being juggled."

"The man wasn't even well-to-do," Miss Dandy said. "He can't have paid you well. Your grandfather never took an unpopular case unless it paid him extremely well."

"I like unpopular cases. There's no point in winning the popular ones; the jury's already convinced itself before you begin."

"You like making people do what you want them to do, whether they like it or not. You may find some day that they'll make *you* do what you don't want to do." She looked at him dispassionately. "You legal Napoleon," she said.

She was not really displeased with him. She understood him too well. She had just finished doing to Sallie, deftly and ruthlessly, what she had accused him of doing to a jury — convincing it against its will, driving it, for no reason except that he had a fancy to try his power on it, to do something that he knew it did not want to do and might even be morally bound not to do.

I did not want to hear any more of it. I was caught in it too; I would go back to Le Jeune now because that was where they had decided I would go, and because there was nowhere else that I could go. I got up and said that I had to leave. They were both quite cordial to me, and asked me to come and see them again before I left for Le Jeune. Miss Dandy said it had been a charming afternoon.

CHAPTER XV   IN AUGUST, ON NORA'S BIRTHDAY, Conn took the two of us up to the Belmont House for the evening. I had not wanted to go with them, but Nora said it would spoil her evening if she had to think of me sitting at home in that hot little room while they were enjoying themselves in the cool, and in the end I had to agree to go. I had never been there before. It was one of the favorite places of resort in Corioli, a restaurant and concert garden built at the top of one of the hills overlooking the city.

We arrived there just after dark, Nora resplendent in her green silk wedding dress, Conn in a derby and flowered vest. He had one of us on each arm, and he insisted on making the full circuit of the promenade around the pavilion with us before he would find a table where we could sit and listen to the music. A band was playing waltzes. There was a splendid view over the city and the river, with the last of the sunset just dying in the sky.

We sat down finally at a table and Conn ordered beer for himself and ginger ale for Nora and me. Nora was happy; she was as giddy as a young girl out in public for the first time with her young man. She wanted to flirt with Conn, and to hold his hand under the table, and he had to tell her crossly to mind the people looking at them before she would stop. I saw that the impression he wanted to give to the people around us was that he was out with me, with Nora along only as chaperone. He had been careful enough before that not to let Nora see any of the overly interested glances he had begun throwing in my direction, but tonight he was irritated by her public possessiveness and less cautious. When he had finished his beer he said that, if Nora's feet were still hurting her in her new shoes, she might sit at the table and have another glass of ginger ale while he and I walked around the pavilion again.

"Sure you wouldn't leave me here alone," Nora said, "with all those boyos walking up and down with their bold eyes out for any bit of female flesh? I wouldn't have an easy moment till you'd be back."

"Ah, you'd be safe enough," Conn said rudely. "They're looking for something a bit younger than you." He glanced at me, getting up. "Now, Lacey — ?" he said.

I shook my head. "It's too hot to walk," I said. "I'd rather sit here with Nora."

Conn argued with me for a while. He was getting sulky. Finally he saw one of his friends in the crowd and went off in a huff to join him. Nora looked at me across the table.

"Now it'll be something stronger than beer he'll be taking with that good-for-nothing," she said. "Why can't they leave the man alone when he's sober for once, and out with his wife for a respectable evening?"

Her pride had been hurt; she was a little stiff with me. I sat there wishing I had not come. There was a family group at the next table: paterfamilias with curled mustaches, stout bonneted mother, two pretty young girls in their teens. They were all having a fine time. The sunset darkened magnificently over the river, but they were too busy with their lady cake and pineapple to notice it. The father made jokes while the two daughters giggled and looked discreetly over their mother's shoulder to see who was watching them.

"Isn't that a grand-looking family?" Nora said. "Those girls will get fine husbands with a father like that to take them about and then stand by to see there's no monkey-business about their young men's intentions. It's a great pity you haven't a father like that, Lacey, for I'm thinking there's plenty of young men you might be encouraging if you could let yourself go a bit like those fillies there. You're too quiet for a young girl, and that's the holy alls of it."

I knew she would have been pleased if I had picked up with one of the young men strolling by and gone off with him for the evening. I wished again that I had not come. When I turned my head I could see Conn inside at the bar with his friend. He looked sullen still. The band finished a waltz and began playing a sentimental popular tune.

Somebody came up behind me and said, "Good evening." It was Jed's voice. I looked up. He was standing there behind me, looking at Nora and me. I knew I had to hold on to myself.

"Good evening," I said. "Are you here with Sallie? I didn't know you were in town." I turned to Nora. "This is Captain Dayton, Nora — my cousin, Mrs. Mulranny."

Jed said, "How do you do?" I could see Nora's eyes going over him as he stood there. She was fluttered and excited at meeting him, as she had been with Sallie a few weeks before.

"Isn't this desperate weather we're having?" she said. "My man brought us up here for a cool evening, but I'll take my word it's as hot as it is below in town."

Jed said something to her. I did not listen to it. I knew he had come there to see me. He was trying to be discreet about it with Nora for my sake. I sat there looking at the table and holding my glass tightly in one hand.

"Is Mrs. Dayton here with you?" Nora was asking. "You didn't say. Ah, it's a grand sight to see her — such an elegant young lady, and she's been kind as a saint itself to Lacey."

"She's in Le Jeune," Jed said. He looked at me. "Can I talk to you?" he said.

I got up.

"You won't mind sitting here alone for a while?" I said to Nora. "There are those nice people across there if anything happens."

Nora shook her head. "Go on with you," she said. She was too impressed with Jed's importance to take in the queerness of his wanting to see me alone. "If Mulranny isn't back here inside of five minutes, I'll go and fetch him back myself."

"I won't be long," I said.

I walked away from the table with Jed. Neither of us said anything till we had turned the corner of the pavilion and were out of sight around the side of the building. I stopped then and looked at Jed. There were people all around; we spoke in low voices.

"How did you know I was here?" I said.

"I went to your house. The people who live upstairs told me where you'd gone."

"You shouldn't have come. We shouldn't see each other."

"I had to come." His face looked bleak under the flaring gaslights. "I tried to stay away. We were laid up for four days at Charleville, and I sat in that damn hotel room all the while and told myself I wouldn't come near you when I got to Corioli. It didn't do any good. I walked straight off the *Maid* tonight and up the hill to Longmill Street to find you."

We stood there looking at each other. It was like trying to hold a private conversation on a stage before an audience. The band was still playing, and the people at the tables sat there listening to the music and watching us, as they watched everyone walking by. Somebody passing jostled Jed. He looked up suddenly.

"We can't talk here," he said. "Isn't there a garden around in back?"

"I don't know. I can't go there with you. Oh, darling, I can't stand seeing you like this."

"Nobody will know. It's only for a few minutes."

"I can't."

"You can. You've got to. You don't know what it's been like. Come on. Please."

People were beginning to look at us. I walked on with him. We went down some steps to the lower level, where the restaurant was, and then down some more steps and around behind the building. There was a rather neglected-looking garden back there — a few trees, some walks laid out between rows of shrubbery, and a fountain playing in a little circle in the center. It seemed almost deserted. We stopped at the end of one of the walks and Jed put his arm around me.

"No," I said. "Someone might come."

"It's dark. They won't see."

"They might. We can't take the chance. Oh, darling, I want to do everything you want, but I can't. You don't know what you'd be risking."

We were standing there facing each other. Our voices

sounded flat and urgent. I could hear the music faintly from the pavilion above.

"I don't care about anything but you," Jed said.

"You do. I don't mind your caring about them, and it's lovely of you to forget them, but you do. You care about a lot of things, about being master of the *Fair Maid,* and about owning your own boats —"

"What has that got to do with it?"

"You see. You don't know what you're getting into. All at once you'd be trapped, and I couldn't bear to do that to you. Don't you see what might happen if Sallie ever found out about this?"

"I don't care what would happen."

"You'd lose everything. You'd have me hung round your neck and nothing else."

"I don't want anything else."

"You would. I'm not very wise, darling, but I lived a long time with men who cared very much about the work they did. You can't just live for me and nothing else."

"If I don't have you, there isn't anything else." He put his arms around me again and kissed me. Our lips were tight together and I could feel us both trembling. "Now do you believe me?" he said.

"I've always believed you. I know you love me. I love you too, darling, and that's why I can't ruin everything for you."

"You can't ruin it. There never was anything to ruin."

"I like you to say that. But it isn't true. You say it because you know I like to hear it."

"It's the truth," he said. All at once I heard the violence in his voice. He took hold of both my wrists, holding me there against him as if he was afraid that if he let me free for an instant I would go away and leave him. "I never cared a damn about anybody before," he said. "They let me alone, I let them alone. Now it's different. I've stopped being alone and I can't go back to it again. You can't make me. You can't send me back to it again."

"I don't want to," I said. "Oh, darling, I don't want to. Don't you know that?"

I was going to say more, but he would not let me; he pulled me closer again. Somebody laughed at a little distance, beyond the trees. I turned my head quickly against his face.

"There's somebody —"

"Let there be."

"No. Please. Please."

He let me go as abruptly as he had drawn me to him.

"Is that all it is to you? Somebody might see? Is that all you care?"

"I told you —"

"You didn't tell me anything I haven't thought of myself. Do you want me to ask you to marry me — is that it? To tell you I'll leave Sallie and tell her I want to be free? What did you think this was all about?"

"I didn't care — I don't care. I wasn't thinking about myself. But I have to think about you, and Sallie, and Lorna —"

"You don't have to think about anything. It's my responsibility, and I'm willing to take it."

"It's mine too." I couldn't even cry; I just stood there looking at him with a weight pressing coldly somewhere inside me. "And I won't take it," I said.

"Won't?"

"I can't. I made up my mind that night on the *Fair Maid* that I wouldn't ever see you again. I even tried to get a school somewhere away from Le Jeune."

I saw his face bleak and incredulous in the darkness.

"You're crazy. You know it won't work. Not any more than it did for me, in that damn hotel in Charleville."

"It has to work." I said it as clearly as I could. "I don't want to see you again."

"You don't want —" he repeated it. "You don't —" I knew he was angry, and he took my wrists again suddenly and drew me close against him till I could feel him breath-

ing and our hearts beating and the two of us like one person standing there. "You're lying," he said then. "You're
alone too; you know it's only the two of us against the rest
of them. You don't want to go back to that hell any more
than I do."

"I can do it," I said.

"You can't."

"Darling, don't make it harder, please don't make it any
harder."

I stopped, growing conscious of footsteps, a voice, Conn's
angry voice somewhere off in the shadows behind me:
"What in the devil's name are you into here? Didn't I tell
that bloody fool of a woman where I'd find you? Let the
girl go now, or I'll stretch you meself —"

"Jed," I said. I only touched his arm; he must have seen
the look on my face. "Don't. It's all right."

"Devil an 'all right' I can see in it," Conn shouted. He
came up, blustering. "A respectable gir-rl, is it, and out
talking love in the dark with a man that can't even
offer to marry her for the ruination of her good reputation?"

"Jed," I said again. With my hand still on his arm I could
feel him move, then control himself, then move again.
"He's drunk," I said. "You can't — Won't you go away?
Please, for my sake, just go away."

"And leave you here with him?"

"I'll go back to Nora. I promise. Please go away. Please.
For my sake."

I knew I had to get him away quickly, before Conn said
any more. There were people appearing from nowhere, at-
tracted by the quarrel. He looked at them, then at me, last
of all at Conn.

"Listen to me," he said to him. I had never heard his
voice like that before. Conn, startled a little out of his
drunkenness, fell suddenly silent. "You can think what you
damn please about me," Jed said, "but if you say a word to
Lacey that you wouldn't have said to her before this, I'll

come back here and kill you myself. Do you understand that?"

"Jed," I said. "He won't. I'm all right. Just *please* go away —"

He looked at me again and walked away. Conn called after him: "And if you show your face around this girl again, it's not all on one side the murdering will be. I'm warning you now —"

"Hush!" I said. Jed did not turn around. I watched him go. Conn stood there staring at me, furious and uncomfortable.

"And you —" he shouted at me suddenly. "What kind of goings-on did you think you were up to out here — ?"

There were people standing at a little distance, in whispering knots. I walked away from them, over toward the stairs leading up to the restaurant and the pavilion. Conn came behind me. At the head of the first flight of stairs I saw Nora waiting anxiously.

"For the love of all the saints, what's the matter now?" she said. "Lacey, you're as white as a sheet —"

"I'm all right," I said.

Conn came up.

"Wasn't it just the way I told you?" he blustered angrily, to Nora. "Down there hiding behind trees with that blackguard — Couldn't you keep a better eye on her than that, your own flesh and blood?"

"I'm going home," I said.

Nora stood there, looking from one to the other of us, amazed and frightened.

"Oh, Lacey, you never did, girl!" she said. "And him a married man, couldn't do you any good at all at all —"

She came trotting after me, lamenting and worrying.

"God help us, who'd ever have thought it of a nice-looking young man like that? Didn't I think all the while you were as safe with him as you'd have been in a church, till Mulranny came asking where you'd gone, and flew off in a great rage when I told him?"

"They're all alike," Conn said. "Mucky little bitches — and they'd have you believing butter wouldn't melt in their mouth."

Nora turned on him suddenly, furious. "Will you shut your great gob, Conn Mulranny?" she said. "Sure if there weren't any of you wicked lying men about, there wouldn't be any troubles for poor girls, and that's a fact. And it's more than one you've led that way yourself, if I can believe half of what I hear, so you needn't go setting yourself up as any marble saint out of a church in front of the rest of us."

She made him keep quiet then till we were back at the shop again, when she shut herself into the kitchen with me and demanded to hear the whole story.

"There's nothing to tell," I said. I had stopped feeling anything. It was like being dead; nothing mattered. "I'm not going to see him again. He's never had anything but me, but I told him I didn't want to see him again."

"Are you in love with him?"

"Yes."

I sat down in a chair beside the kitchen table and leaned my arms on the table and put my head down. It was hot in the room. I sat there without moving.

"Do you want me to make you a cup of tea?" Nora asked, after a little.

"No."

She came over to where I was sitting; I could hear her footsteps.

"Lacey," she said. I did not say anything. "You're not in trouble, girl?" she asked after a minute. Her voice sounded anxious.

"No."

"You're sure?"

"I wish I weren't sure." I lifted my head suddenly and looked at her; I could feel the wildness coming up in me. "I wish I'd stopped thinking about hurting other people and thought about myself. I wish I'd been foolish and wicked and happy instead of wise and miserable. And I've made him miserable too, and I can't bear that. He doesn't even know what it's like to be happy."

I dropped my head on my arms again. I could feel Nora standing there over me.

"That's poor talk for a decent girl," she said after a while. "It's lucky for you it's no worse than it is. You still have the chance so for a home of your own some day, and all this foolishness forgotten."

There was nothing to say. She meant well; she had taken my part against Conn. But there was nothing to say. I sat there with my head lying on my arms while she stood, breathing in anxious expectancy, above me.

CHAPTER XVI   In september i went back to le Jeune. From Jed there had been nothing but a sheet of paper in an envelope mailed from Charleville and with a return direction on it for a hotel there. The sheet of paper had four words on it: *Did you mean that?* I wrote *Yes* on it before I could give myself time to think, and put it into another envelope on which I wrote the address of the Charleville hotel, and took it to the post office myself. It was no harder to add a stroke of the pen to what I already had to live with.

I went down to Le Jeune on the *Sallie Dayton*. It was midafternoon when I arrived, and I walked up from the landing and saw the town the same with the double-galleried houses facing the river, and the locusts and sycamores along the streets, and now the smell of drying tobacco everywhere in the still air. I went straight to the McLeans'. It was a Sunday: Orrin was home, and Mr. Moffat was asked to supper. Ailie took me upstairs so that I could freshen up before Mr. Moffat came. She looked just the same — untidy, reckless, a little worried.

"You look awful, Lacey," she said. "What's happened to you? Is it the heat? I reckon you aren't used to heat like this."

She sat on the bed, watching me take off my hat and the blue challis dress I had worn on the boat and get a fresh dress out of my bag.

"I suppose so," I said.

I went over to the commode and poured water from the pitcher into the washbowl and began to wash my face and neck. I did not want to seem short with her, but I could not tell her what was really the matter. She sat there watching me in silence. After a few moments she began telling me the news of what had happened in Le Jeune while I had been away.

"Old Mrs. Capper's had a stroke," she said, "not a bad one, just bad enough to give her the excuse to spend all her time instead of only half of it sitting looking out her window. And Bessie Collins has married the freight agent over in Belleville and won't be coming back to school, and the Gibbses have twins — that's two more scholars for you if you stay here long enough. I shouldn't think you would, though." She said irrelevantly: "You have such lovely white skin, Lacey; I suppose only Irish girls have skin like that. It's a shame to cover it all up with those schoolteacher's dresses of yours."

I smiled. "What else?" I said.

"Oh — this *is* gossip, Lacey; I really shouldn't say anything about it. But after that talk about you and Jed Dayton — well, I reckon you'd want to know what's going on. He's never been near his house since Sallie came back from Corioli this summer. Even when the *Maid* was laid up for weeks for low water he didn't come here to Le Jeune; he might just as well not have a home. People noticed, of course. I reckon Sallie stood it as long as she could, and then last week, when the *Maid* stopped here on her way down-

river, she went down to the levee herself and went on board.
Nobody knows what happened. She went straight on home
afterward without a word to anybody, and she didn't come
to the Cutlers' for the social club that afternoon — sent
word she had a sick headache. I declare I'd like to shake
them both. There were married people that didn't get along
before they were born, but they didn't act like a spoiled
child or a savage about it, the way the two of them are doing. Did you see Sallie when you were in Corioli?"

"Once," I said.

Ailie hesitated. "I've been beating round and round the
bush," she said. "I might as well come out and say it. I
think Sallie puts the blame on you for the way Jed's been
acting. She's been awfully discreet about it, for Sallie, but
she's let a few things drop. There was a little talk around
here. I'm afraid Mr. Moffat's been feeling uneasy about
asking you back."

"I'll make a fine impression on him tonight," I said. "I
won't talk about anything but Stoddard's *Intellectual Arithmetic*."

I put the towel down on the rack and began getting into
my dress so she could not see my face. She got up from the
bed.

"It's all right if you don't want to talk about it, Lacey,"
she said. "My goodness, I don't want to pry; it's only that
I'm awfully fond of you. I'm just going to give you
one piece of advice and then I'll quit. Don't you go getting
mixed up with Jed Dayton. He's a regular Indian; he
doesn't know how to live like ordinary folks. And I'd as
soon have a herd of buffalo after me as that little Sallie Dayton if she gets roused. Now you take that for what
it's worth, and then forget I ever said it."

She kissed me then, and went on downstairs to see to the
supper. I stood before the mirror and fastened the buttons
on my dress and then did my hair. There was nothing I
could do about Jed or Sallie or Mr. Moffat. I had to get
through it and that was all.

After a little I heard Mr. Moffat come in and I went on downstairs. He and Orrin were sitting in the parlor. In the dining room Ailie had the table laid; above it a spray of asparagus fern, attached to a hook in the ceiling, moved slowly in the late-afternoon breeze. Ailie told me to sit down in the parlor with the men, and I sat answering Mr. Moffat's questions about my trip and the state of my health till we went to supper. He was polite but stiff; I felt him watching me cautiously out of his dark, sharp eyes. I was relieved when Davie was wild at the table and drew Mr. Moffat's attention and disapproval on himself.

After supper Mr. Moffat and Orrin sat talking solemnly for a long while on the front gallery in the soft September darkness while Ailie and I washed up the dishes and then came out to sit quietly together, listening to them. They settled the county business and the next state election and the mistakes that President Arthur was making in Washington, and finally, when Mr. Moffat was leaving, they got around to me.

"We expect to have a fine school this year, Miss Dereen," Mr. Moffat said. He was standing on the front steps then, saying good night. "Strict attention to business — strict attention. You understand me, I'm sure?"

"I understand," I said.

"A young woman in your position —"

"Good night, Mr. Moffat," Ailie said. "We'll hope to see you again very soon. Orrin, aren't you going to walk down to the gate with Mr. Moffat?"

She watched them go off together down the walk.

"The damned old fool," she whispered to me.

I couldn't help laughing. Ailie turned and looked at me.

"That's the first time I've seen you laugh since you've come back," she said. "I'll swear all day long if it'll make you feel any better, Lacey. Papa taught me how to — said a riverman's daughter ought to have at least an elementary idea of what fifty per cent of her menfolks' conversation was about." She looked at Orrin's figure moving toward us again through the darkness. "I reckon if he'd known I was going to marry Orrin he wouldn't have bothered, though," she said.

Orrin came up and stood there clearing his throat and looking at me and Ailie. I said I was going upstairs to my room. It was just as if I had never been away. And the next morning there would be the school again, the children ranged before me in expectant rows, the old black stove in the center of the room, the battered woodbox, the blackboard, the desk. I did not want it, but it was what I had. I had to get used to that idea. At any rate, it was better here than it would ever be again in Corioli, with Nora and Conn.

There was one more thing: I knew I would have to see Sallie again. It was only a question of time in a town as small as Le Jeune. It happened, though, even sooner than I had expected. The second day of school she came instead of Barbara Mason to fetch Lorna home. I was in the schoolhouse, straightening up after the day. I saw her through the window, but I did not think she would come inside. I went on putting things away in my desk, and when I looked up again she was standing in the doorway.

"You're so industrious, Lacey," she said.

She didn't come in; she stood there as if she had come that far on an impulse and wished she hadn't. I got up from the desk and went over to her.

"Am I?" I said. "I hope the school board appreciates it. How are you, Sallie?"

"I'm fine."

She didn't look fine; she looked like a child with a fever. Lorna came to the door and stood there beside her, staring indifferently around the room.

"I want to go home," she said.

"In a minute, honey. You go on outside and wait for me. I have something to say to Miss Dereen."

Lorna shrugged up her plump shoulders and went outside. I stood there waiting, cold. Sallie did not say anything.

I could hear the children's voices outside in the schoolyard. The silence grew longer.

"It's about Lorna," Sallie said suddenly. I didn't think it was; she was saying it too fast, as if it had just occurred to her. "She's had quite a bad summer cold, and I don't want her to have to do too much at school till I'm sure she's perfectly all right again."

"I understand."

"She's never been ill before, you know. She's always been such a healthy child."

"Yes."

"That's why I've been so worried about this. How do you think she looks now?"

"I think she looks splendid. I don't really think you ought to worry about her."

"Yes. Well — you're not the child's mother, of course." She was pleased with that. She stood there with her eyes shining triumphantly, like a child who has just given a clever answer to a grownup. "You'll never understand how I feel till you're married and have children of your own," she said.

"I suppose not."

I knew she had not come there to talk to me about Lorna's health. She was too uncertain of herself, or too impressed by what had happened that Sunday at the Dandys', to say what she really wanted to say. I tried to act as if I did not know anything about that. I could not help being sorry for her. I wanted to feel that she wasn't important, or that it would not be any worse for her if she could not at least keep on pretending for other people that everything was all right between her and Jed, but I couldn't. She was the sort of person who ought to have married a nice young man who looked like a figure off his own wedding cake. Now she was caught in this just as Jed and I were caught.

We were very uncomfortable talking to each other, and it was a relief to both of us when Lorna called her again from outside. She went away quickly then without saying any more. Through the window I watched her go off down the street with Lorna. This was one more time that nothing had happened. I wondered how long it could go on that way.

CHAPTER XVII   THE AUTUMN WENT BY. WE HAD A splendid season, with brilliant days and clear nights sometimes unexpectedly cold and sometimes soft and ripe as August. Before the heavy rains began the river was low and blue, but in November it rose quickly and the flat stretches of beach on either side disappeared. Under the rain the water was gray, and walking along the main street you could see it very near and the current running powerfully in the middle. You could not believe it was the same river that had lain quiet and blue far below when you had walked along that same way in the summer.

I was very quiet, teaching at the school during the day and in the evening going back to the McLeans' and sitting with Orrin and Ailie in the parlor with the clocks ticking and Orrin reading and Ailie sewing or knitting. There was an ingrain carpet on the floor, and on the table an album that Ailie's friends had written verses in when she had been a girl in school. I tried to sew too, but I would be sitting there and all at once I would realize that all I had been doing for the past quarter hour was looking at the red plush and gold clasps of the album or studying the pattern of the carpet on the floor. It was like a kind of hypnosis: you studied the pattern and as long as you did it you did not have to think. I thought that if you were good enough at it you would not even have to remember who you were or anything that had happened to you.

On Saturdays I walked into town with Ailie when she went to do her shopping there. We stood at the counter while the clerk showed us patterns of challis or percale, or stopped at the grocer's for sugar and tea. One morning in November Davie had a sore throat and Ailie stayed at home with him while I went to the shops alone. That was how I saw Jed again. It was a dark morning, with rain coming on, and I walked out of the grocer's and turned toward home and saw him coming along the street toward me. He looked straight at me and walked by without a word. I had stopped, and I stood there holding my parcels till I remembered that people might be looking at me, and then I started on again. It was beginning to rain; I had to hurry to get home. He had looked directly at me, and I had seen his eyes not happy or even angry but only looking straight through me as if I were someone he had never seen before.

The next morning when Ailie came from church she told me that Jed had been home to see Sallie.

"She had to stop everybody coming out of church to show them what he brought Lorna — the finest India shawl you ever saw; goodness knows what he paid for it," she said. "I declare it was embarrassing; Sallie just doesn't realize what people think when they hear her going on that way. She's getting giddier every day. Laura Gibbs says she *ran* after her to be sure she wouldn't miss seeing that shawl. Somebody ought to write to her mother to tell her to come and stay with her for a while."

We were upstairs in my room; the door was open, and I could hear Orrin winding the clocks downstairs. I had to say something.

"Maybe she'll be better now," I said. "If they've made up — whatever it was —"

"Don't you believe it. I'm talking too much again — it's none of my business, but there's that Hendry of hers spreading everything that happened all over town. Says five minutes after Jed walked in the house yesterday he could hear them having words, and Barbara had to go in and stop it because Sallie was getting too upset. They all adore her in that house, you know; why shouldn't they, when she lets them run everything exactly as they like?"

I wished she would not tell me about it. I was standing at the window. It was raining; I saw the drops falling from the bare trees.

"People are saying Jed walked right past you on the street yesterday and didn't even speak to you," Ailie said suddenly. "Of course somebody told that to Sallie too."

"Did they?"

"Yes." Ailie looked at me; she looked worried and embarrassed. "I thought I ought to tell you, Lacey. You know how Sallie is; she's liable to come soothering around you again now. She's got *nice* feelings, along with all those crazy ones of hers, and you never know which kind is going to come uppermost from one minute to the next. Oh, you know, she'll feel she wronged you with that talk of hers — hears that about Jed not speaking to you yesterday, and then his coming home at all, even if they did spend their time quarreling with each other, and jumps to one of those conclusions of hers that everything's going to be all right again —"

She stopped; she did not know how to go on. I stood there looking out the window at the rain.

"You're not angry with me, Lacey?" she said after a minute.

"I'm not angry with anybody."

"It's just that I thought I ought to warn you about Sallie. When she's excited, she's not responsible for what she does. The best thing you can do is just keep away from her."

"I'll keep away from her."

"And you're not angry with me?"

"I'm never angry with you. You're the best friend I have."

"People get angry even with people they love."

"Yes," I said.

I knew all about that; I would have been glad if it had been anger I had seen in Jed's eyes when he had looked at me. It was better this way. I kept telling myself it was bet-

ter this way. It would have been fine if I had been able to
believe it.

Ailie was right about Sallie. She came around the next
day to ask me to come and visit with her some evening, and
I had to give her a not very convincing excuse about being
busy in the evenings now with preparations for the Christmas program the children were going to give. She finally accepted it, with Ailie standing behind it to vouch for its being
true, but a week later she was at the schoolhouse again with
another idea. Lorna was having her birthday party on the following Sunday afternoon, and she wanted me to come too.

"You'll be doing me such a favor, Lacey," she said. "I
don't know what in the world I'm going to do with a houseful of children all afternoon, and Barbara'll be busy looking after things in the kitchen. You're so clever about knowing how to entertain them and keep them in order; now
you've just got to come and help me out."

I knew what it was; she wanted to make some kind of
public amends to me. The trouble was that you could never
be sure how long a mood like that would last with her.
I tried to think quickly of a reason for not coming.

"Ailie's having company for Sunday dinner," I said. "I
promised I'd help her with it."

"That's just fine. You can come right after. It's only one
of Orrin's cousins from over in Belleville — Ailie told me
— and they'll want to be talking family gossip. You'll have
plenty of time to help Ailie and still come to Lorna's party
afterward. The children have only been asked for three."

She went away before I could think of anything to say to
stop her. It looked as if I would have to go. At any rate, a
children's party seemed a safe sort of social occasion for
us to meet. There would be too much noise and excitement
for us to have any time for each other. I told Ailie about it
and she agreed.

"You might as well go and get it over with," she said.
"Sallie never did learn how to take *no* for an answer — might
have been a lot better for her if she had."

I made a dress for one of Lorna's dolls to take to her as
a birthday present, and on Sunday afternoon I walked
over to the Daytons'. The house looked impressive under
the dark mild windy December sky, with its cupola and
white-painted scrollwork and stained-glass windows. Sallie
had had a croquet-ground laid out on the side lawn since I
had seen it last, and there was a peacock strolling in solitary
grandeur behind the iron fence.

I went up to the door and Barbara came to let me in.
The hall was full of children's caps and coats. There were
paper streamers festooned above the doorways and floating
from the newel and the chandelier. The house was hum-
ming like a beehive.

"They're all in the parlor," Barbara said. "You'd better
go right in." She took my cape. "I'm afraid it's going to be
too much excitement for Mrs. Dayton," she said. "I told her
not to bring all those children in here. Listen to that racket
already, and they've hardly got inside the door."

She looked at me as if she wished I would go away myself and take the children with me.

"I'll see what I can do," I said.

I felt her eyes watching me as I opened the folding doors
and went into the parlor. The parlor was decorated like the
hall, and there was a fan of colored paper with *Happy
Birthday* on it in gold letters before the gas grate in the
fireplace. Lorna was sitting on the sofa beside Sallie, opening her presents. She had on a new blue dress and red
stockings, and a huge butterfly bow on her fair hair. She
looked like a queen receiving homage.

Sallie saw me first.

"Oh — Lacey," she said. "Come and look at this." It was
a large dollhouse on a table beside the sofa, completely
furnished even to the tiny set of china on the dining-room
table and the miniature crystal chandeliers. "Isn't it lovely?
I had it sent from New Orleans for Lorna's birthday. I
don't know which of us admires it more."

She looked more excited than Lorna, at any rate, and

less like her mother than an older sister in a blue dress that
was made exactly like Lorna's except for the length. I said,
"Happy birthday," to Lorna, and gave her the present I had
brought her. The children had all hushed a little when I
had come in, as if they had suddenly found themselves in
school. But in a few minutes, when Lorna had torn the last
of the wrappings from her gifts and Sallie suggested "Going
to Jerusalem," they began to chatter again in a subdued way.
They were very curious about the house. Usually Lorna
played in splendid isolation, and most of them had never
been inside it, or seen anything so large and elegantly furnished. While Sallie and I arranged the room for the game
I saw some of the younger ones running their hands over
the huge gilt-framed mirror and reaching up to touch the
Dresden-china shepherd and shepherdess on the table.

Barbara came in to help with the chairs.

"I should think you'd want to stop them doing that, Mrs.
Dayton," she said. "They'll have something broken next, as
sure as fate."

Sallie looked at them helplessly.

"You stop them, Lacey," she said. "They're used to paying attention to you."

I would have suggested something a little quieter than
"Going to Jerusalem" to start the party if I had had the arrangements to make, but there was nothing I could do
about it now. I gathered the children together and got them
into line, and then sat down at the piano and began to play
a reel. Before I had stopped them marching the second time
the doorbell rang. I thought it was only another guest,
but in a moment Barbara opened the hall door and spoke
to Sallie, who was standing beside me.

"It's Captain Dix," she said. There was a careful lack of
expression on her face. "He's brought a present from Captain Dayton for Miss Lorna. He says he doesn't want to
come inside."

Sallie stared at her. "Captain Dix?" she said. "What in

the world is he doing in Le Jeune? I didn't expect — they said there was ice in the river up at Corioli —"

I did not think she quite understood at first the implications of what Barbara had told her. Because if Captain Dix was in Le Jeune, the *Fair Maid* was there too, and so was Jed; and if Jed had sent Captain Dix to the house with Lorna's present, it was very probably because he didn't care to come there himself. I don't know how much of that went through Sallie's mind, but all at once her face changed and she brushed past my chair to the door and went out into the hall.

I went on playing, but she had left the doors open a little behind her, and when I stopped the music to let the children scramble for the chairs I could hear her raised, almost hysterical voice outside: "— never heard anything so unfeeling in my life. He's not that busy that he can't find time to come a few blocks to wish his own child a happy birthday —"

I began playing again quickly. I did not think the children had heard. I played as long as I could without a break, till the children began scuffling among themselves as they marched and the ones who had already been eliminated ran up and down the room looking for some excitement of their own. When I stopped playing at last there was such a rush for the chairs that it covered the sounds from the hall for a moment, but then I heard Sallie's voice again: "— that if he doesn't I'll go down there myself and find out why. I don't *care* any more; I'll make him sorry —"

I started the reel again. A few moments later I heard the front door close. I had no idea what had happened, whether Sallie had really gone down to the *Maid*, or whether it was only Captain Dix who had left, but I thought the best thing I could do would be to keep the children occupied and let Barbara take care of Sallie. In a few minutes Barbara came into the room. She came over to the piano and spoke to me in a low voice.

"Mrs. Dayton says if you'll just go on with the party without her —" she said. "She isn't feeling very well."

She looked tense and angry. I could see it was an effort for her to speak to me civilly. I went on playing.

"Yes," I said. "I'll see to things here."

She went out of the room. I stopped playing, and when I began again Lorna, who had not found a chair, came over to the piano and stood beside me.

"Where is my mother?" she said.

"She's not feeling very well. We'll go on with the party for a while without her — shall we? You can tell me what games you were going to play."

"I don't want to play them if my mother isn't here." She looked around as I stopped playing again and the children scuffled for the chairs. "This is a stupid game. If we can't play another game I'm going upstairs and see my mother."

"We couldn't very well stop it before we finished, could we?" I said. I got up. "Why don't you sit down here and play the piano for the rest of the game? You can play 'London Bridge'; you play that so nicely."

I was willing to tell her she played like Liszt if it would keep her from causing any trouble. Fortunately she was satisfied to be in the limelight at the piano, and we finished the game that way.

After that we sat down to a guessing-game. It wasn't successful; the children had begun to sense somehow that something was wrong. The quieter ones sat without saying a word, looking scared, and the bolder ones, like children in a house where a tragedy is occurring, who are let run wild because nobody can spare the time to look after them, began getting out of hand. When I spoke to them they smiled uncomfortably and defiantly, and as soon as my back was turned went on with what they were doing. One of them was teasing the canary in its huge gilt hoop of a cage, tilting the stand on which it stood, and two of the smaller boys began fighting with each other. I went over to separate them,

and just then I heard someone come in the front door. It
was Jed; I could hear him talking to Barbara for a moment and then his footsteps going rapidly up the stairs.

I didn't know what was going to happen, but I thought
the wisest thing to do now would be to get the party over
as quickly as possible. I went across the room and opened
the door to the hall. Barbara was still there, standing at
the foot of the stairs, listening. She looked around when she
heard the door sliding back.

"I wonder if the children could have their ice cream and
cake now," I said. "Then I can send them home. I'm afraid
they're all getting rather restless."

She nodded and, after another glance upstairs, went on
into the kitchen. I went back to the parlor and began shepherding the children quickly across the hall to the dining
room. There was an elaborately laid table there, with favors
and paper hats at every place, and streamers of colored paper leading from the chandelier to each plate. Barbara
brought in a huge chocolate birthday cake with lighted
candles on it. Lorna looked at it.

"Where is my mother?" she said. "My mother has to cut
my birthday cake."

"Hush," Barbara said. "Your mother's feeling poorly. You
don't want to worry her, do you? Miss Dereen will cut the
cake."

"I don't want Miss Dereen to cut my cake."

"You've got nothing to say about it now. You blow out
the candles and let Miss Dereen cut it."

Barbara went back into the kitchen. Lorna closed her
lips firmly and sat in magnificent disapproval.

"Do you want me to tell the other children to blow out
your candles?" I asked.

I waited. She did not move. I turned to the others.

"All right, children," I said.

The candle flames disappeared in a gusty moment. I cut
the cake quickly and passed it around. Lorna did not begin eating hers, or the ice cream that Barbara brought in

from the kitchen. After a minute she got up and walked over to the folding doors that led out to the hall.

"Lorna," I said.

She glanced back over her shoulder at me.

"It's not polite for the hostess to leave the table before her guests have finished," I said. "I don't think your mother would like that."

"You don't know what my mother likes," Lorna said. She looked at me in majestic defiance. "She doesn't like *you*," she said. "She didn't ask you to come to my birthday party."

She pushed back one of the folding doors and went out into the hall. I got up and followed her.

"Lorna —" I said.

But then I stopped. She was looking up the stairs, and I looked too and saw Sallie coming down, her face absolutely brilliant with excitement and anger, carrying a large flaxen-haired doll, with Jed behind her. She saw Lorna and came quickly down the rest of the stairs and thrust the doll into her arms.

"Take it," she said. Her voice was shaking. "Take the lovely present your father brought you. Wasn't it kind of him to come and say 'Happy birthday' to you? He did try to get out of doing it, of course, but that doesn't matter to us, does it? — as long as he's here. Say 'Thank you' to your father, Lorna —"

"Sallie," I said. I didn't look at Jed; I couldn't. "Stop. The children —"

Sallie turned around and looked at me, still with that brilliant gaze.

"Oh, yes," she said, "we have a houseful of guests, haven't we? It was selfish of us, wasn't it, Lorna, to want your father too? He's really far too busy to be bothered with anything as unimportant as his daughter's birthday party. But now that he's here, he's been so agreeable, and we're all having such a lovely time —"

I glanced around, saw two or three scared, inquisitive faces peering through the doorway, and went over swiftly and closed the door.

"Sallie," I said again, "please think what you're doing. Those children —"

I took her arm and tried to bring her into the parlor, but she pulled away from me.

"I don't care," she said, "I don't *care* who knows." She was laughing and crying at the same time; she rushed over to Lorna again and bent down and put her arms around her. "We're such a happy family," she said, "the three of us, aren't we? I think everybody ought to know. Tell your father how happy you are to see him, Lorna. Tell him how happy he's made us all today."

Jed came over to them. His face was white.

"Will you stop this, Sallie?" he said. "Or shall I — ?"

"Shall you what?" she interrupted him. "Go away? All right, go away. You come here once in months, and then you can't even speak to your own child, or kiss her —"

"I don't want to kiss him," Lorna said. She backed away. For the first time since I had known her, her composure left her; she was terrified at her mother's wild behavior. "I don't like my party; I don't want it to be my birthday."

She threw the doll suddenly on the floor between them. Sallie looked at it.

"Aren't you going to pick it up and give it back to her?" she said to Jed. She put her hand up to her mouth to keep back the laughter that came spilling out. "It's such a beautiful doll," she said; "you must have paid a fabulous price for it. She doesn't even want your presents any more, you see. You can't buy her a father; that's what she really wants." She pressed her hand tightly against her mouth. "You devil," she whispered behind it. "You devil, you devil."

Barbara came out quickly from the kitchen. She gave one look to all of us, took Sallie's arm, and brought her over to the parlor.

"No," Sallie said. "I won't —"

"I'll take care of you now," Barbara said. "Barbara's here now. I'll take care of you."

She spoke to her as if she had been a child. Sallie stopped laughing and began to cry. She flung her arms around Barbara.

"I haven't got anybody," she sobbed. "Nobody cares whether I live or die."

"You oughtn't to talk that way, Mrs. Dayton. You've got a fine daughter, and a loving mother, and scores of friends all over this state. You come along with me now and sit down quiet for a minute." She glanced around over her shoulder at me. "Will you get her aromatic salts?" she said. "You know where they are — the drawer in her dressing table —"

I ran upstairs. As I opened the dressing-table drawer in Sallie's room I heard someone else coming up the steps. It was Jed. Before I could move he came over and took both my arms and held me there, a little away from him, not touching him, his face cold and furious looking down into mine.

"Are you satisfied now?" he said. "Is this what you wanted? Is it?"

"Let me go," I whispered.

"My happy family — you heard her say it. Have you done what you wanted? Are you satisfied with it?"

I could feel his fingers tighten around my arms. There was that same expression on his face that I had seen a few weeks before, on the street — not anger, only the bleak exaltation of absolute not-caring, as if he could have seen the whole world rolled away into an abyss of nothingness without raising a finger to prevent it.

"Jed —" I whispered. "You're out of your mind. Let me go. I've got to get downstairs to Sallie."

"I wish I could let you go," he said bitterly. "I wish I didn't have to carry that damn face of yours up and down the river from Corioli to New Orleans. She thinks it's hell for her; what do you think it is for me? Do you think I set out to make it this way? Nobody's crazy enough to do that."

"No," I said.

There was a noise on the stairs; he jerked around suddenly. I picked up the salts and ran out of the room. On the stairs I met Lorna. She stared at me oddly, with that terrified, shaken composure. I noticed suddenly that she was still wearing her paper hat.

"Why don't you go to your room?" I said to her. "The party's over. You can go and tell Celinda all about the games you played."

She did not move. I went on down the stairs and into the parlor and gave the salts to Barbara. Sallie was crying quietly on the sofa.

"I'll send the children home," I said to Barbara. "Shouldn't I go myself too? Or is there anything that I can do?"

She shook her head, looking at me with an expression between anger and civility. I left the parlor, closed the doors behind me, and went across the hall to the dining room. The room was in chaos: some of the smaller children crying, the bigger ones marching boldly around on the chairs, the cake a crumbled chocolate mass in the center of the table. The children looked at me with bright, frightened eyes, but I was too anxious to get them out of the house to take the time to scold them. I bundled them out into the hall and into their hats and coats. When I had seen the last of them outside I put on my own things and went out quickly into the windy December dusk.

It was only then that I realized that I was shaking all over. I walked slowly; I couldn't go back to the McLeans' till I had got hold of myself again. When I came to the end of the lane I stopped and stood there, leaning against a tree. It was getting dark. I stood there looking at the ragged sky. It would rain soon; the air felt soft and damp. In a few minutes I went on again toward home. I was still shaking inside, but I thought I could face people now.

Ailie looked at me queerly when I came in the door. She was sitting in the parlor, talking to Orrin and his cousin. I went upstairs. In a few minutes I heard her coming up too.

"Lacey," she said. "What's the matter? Didn't the party go off all right?"

I shook my head. I picked up my cape and hung it up so that I would not have to face her directly.

"No," I said. I had to tell her; somebody would. "The *Fair Maid* is in," I said, "and Captain Dayton came up to the house. Sallie made a scene —"

"Not about you, Lacey?"

"No. It didn't have anything to do with me. It was because he didn't want to come up to the house for Lorna's birthday. I'm afraid the children heard most of it." I finished hanging the cape up and turned around. "I don't want to talk about it any more, Ailie."

"All right. We won't talk about it." She looked angry. "I declare I could shake Sallie for getting you mixed up in something like that. You look terrible, Lacey."

"I'm all right. You go on downstairs to your company."

After she had gone I went over to the window and looked out. It was dark, but I could see the lights on the *Fair Maid* down at the levee. She was just leaving the landing, heading downstream. I stood there and watched her till she was out of sight.

CHAPTER XVIII   THE NEXT MORNING LORNA WAS not at school. The other children were subdued and watchful, expecting some reference from me, probably, to what had happened the day before. I could see them whispering to each other at recess, looking over their shoulders to be sure I was not close enough to hear what they were saying. It was raining and they could not go outside. I sat at my desk and pretended to be busy with my work.

It rained all day. When I went home late in the afternoon Ailie said she had not been out, but that Laura Gibbs had stopped by to see if she knew anything about what had happened at Lorna's party.

"I told her I didn't know any more about it than she did," Ailie said. She was in the kitchen, getting supper. "Said you didn't gossip to me about what happened in houses where you were a guest. Then she wanted to know what Sallie was doing this morning down at Moffat's store with Lorna during school hours. Wasn't Lorna at school today?"

"No."

Ailie looked at me. "Well, I reckon it wasn't important," she said. "One of Sallie's ideas. I'll ask Orrin when he comes home to supper if it doesn't slip my mind."

But when Orrin came home he was full of something, his own importance big in him, and he ate his supper with hardly a word to Ailie or me and then went out to the hall at once to get his coat and hat again.

"Where in the world are you going now in this rain?" Ailie said.

"There's a meeting of the school board."

"The school board?" Ailie shot a glance at me. "It's not your regular meeting night."

"No."

"What's it about? Some of Will Moffat's foolishness again?"

Orrin, at the door, turned and looked at her solemnly.

"I hardly think you could call this foolishness, Ailie," he said.

He opened the door and went out. I expected Ailie to say something, but she did not. She went back to the dining room and began clearing the table. I knew she was upset about something. Later, after we had gone back to the parlor, she sat sewing quickly, listening to every sound that might indicate Orrin was coming in again. Finally, around half past nine, there were footsteps outside. She ran to the door. It was Orrin, and Mr. Moffat was with him. I heard them getting out of their wet things in the hall.

"Is Miss Dereen downstairs?" Orrin said. "Mr. Moffat has something to say to her."

I stood up. The two men came into the room. They looked solemn and exalted and a little embarrassed. I said good evening to Mr. Moffat.

"Good evening, Miss Dereen," he said. "I'm afraid I've come on a very delicate — a very painful errand —"

Ailie came into the room behind them.

"Well, you may as well sit down to it," she said. She spoke sharply. "I never saw a man yet who couldn't make a fool of himself just as well sitting in a chair as standing on his legs."

"Ailie — !" Orrin said.

She stood there with her hands on her hips.

"I can't help it," she said. "If the two of you have come here to badger this poor child about some of Sallie Dayton's nonsense —"

"I'm afraid it's more than nonsense, Mrs. McLean," Mr. Moffat said. "It's a very definite and serious accusation that Mrs. Dayton has made. In all fairness to Miss Dereen, we're willing to hear her side of the story before we come to any decision —"

"You're willing to hear her side of it, but you've made up your minds beforehand that you won't believe it," Ailie said. "Is that it?"

The two men stood blinking at her in stubborn discomfort.

"Ailie," I said. "Wouldn't it be best to let them say what they came to say?"

I went over and sat down. My head felt cold and light and quiet. The two men sat down, avoiding my eyes. Mr. Moffat cleared his throat.

"All right, then," Ailie said. "Let's have it. Or are you ashamed to say it out loud yourselves?"

Mr. Moffat looked irritated and began to speak quickly.

"This is a very serious matter, Mrs. McLean," he said. "It's all very well for you to be angry, but what attitude is the board to take when the mother of one of our pupils comes to us and informs us that in her own house her own child saw Miss Dereen behaving improperly with her husband —"

"Improperly?" Ailie said. "Lacey? In Sallie's house? I never heard —"

"The child saw Miss Dereen and Captain Dayton embracing," Mr. Moffat said. His face was red. He took off his glasses and wiped them quickly so that he would not have to look at me. "Lorna has reached the age of reason," he said; "she has been questioned thoroughly, and there is no reason to believe she is telling an untruth. You must be aware yourself, Mrs. McLean, that this is not the first occasion when Miss Dereen's actions have laid her open to this same suspicion —"

I knew what it was — that moment in Sallie's room when Jed had stood there, holding my arms, in an attitude that might very well have looked, to Lorna, like the one she had described. She must have come up the stairs and seen us there and then gone back again to the place where I had found her a few moments later, and of course she had told what she had seen to Sallie.

Ailie came over and put her arm around me.

"I don't care," she said. "I don't believe a word of it. Lacey, you go ahead now and tell them it isn't true. Just go ahead and tell them, honey."

I looked at Mr. Moffat and Orrin. I knew it was no good

trying to deny or explain anything. They had made up their minds, and there would only be my word against Lorna's, and against both Barbara's and Sallie's knowledge that Jed had gone upstairs after me.

"You want me to leave," I said. "Is that it?"

Orrin and Mr. Moffat exchanged glances.

"You admit, then — ?" Mr. Moffat began.

"No," I said. "I don't admit anything. But I know when I'm beaten. I can't prove anything to you. Captain Dayton did come upstairs after me. He was upset about the quarrel he and Sallie had been having, and there was something he wanted to say to me."

There was a moment's silence. Mr. Moffat cleared his throat again.

"Perhaps if you'd tell us what it was that Captain Dayton said to you —" he said. I knew he did not believe me.

"I can't tell you that," I said. "It doesn't matter, does it? No matter what I told you, you'd still want me to go away."

"You're not going anywhere," Ailie said. She turned to Orrin. "Orrin McLean, you ought to be ashamed of yourself," she said. "You know Lacey as well as I do; if Jed Dayton's making a fool of himself over her, it's not her fault. *He*'s the one the two of you ought to be preaching your sermons at — but you wouldn't dare; it's a good deal easier for you just to send Lacey packing. You don't care what sort of reputation you'll be giving her —"

The two men looked at her, uneasy but stubborn.

"We're perfectly willing for Miss Dereen to submit her resignation to the board for whatever reason she wishes to give," Mr. Moffat said. "Family obligations, or health, whatever she likes —"

"Family obligations, fiddlesticks!" Ailie said. "She hasn't got any family, and you know it. And she hasn't been sick a day since she's come here. Don't you think folks in this town are bright enough to put two and two together, especially after a couple of members of that blessed board of yours have talked the whole thing over with their wives?"

"I think you may safely trust the discretion of the board," Mr. Moffat said stiffly. "We're not anxious for this unpleasant business to get out. If Miss Dereen will leave quietly, nothing at all need be said."

"When do you want me to go?" I said.

Mr. Moffat glanced at Orrin. "It will be better — at once —" he said. "I really can't answer for Mrs. Dayton if you don't."

"All right. I'll go over to the schoolhouse now and get my things."

I stood up. Mr. Moffat and Orrin stood up too.

"Of course," Mr. Moffat said awkwardly, "there's the matter of your salary. Under the circumstances, you won't expect us to pay you for the entire term."

"You can pay me for as much of it as I've taught. I hope you won't mind if I say good night now. I'll have a good deal to do if I expect to leave tomorrow."

I went upstairs to get my things. Ailie ran up after me. She closed the door behind her and came over and put her hands on my arms.

"Lacey," she said. "You can't just give up and go away. You've got to go down there right now, before it's too late, and tell them it isn't true and you're going to fight it."

"Do you think it would do any good?" I said. "Tell me honestly now, Ailie."

She looked at me. After a moment she dropped her hands.

"No," she said. And then, furiously: "Oh, *damn* those men! And damn Sallie Dayton! If she hadn't made you come there to her house yesterday, this would never have happened."

"It would have happened some day, somewhere," I said.

It was as if I didn't feel anything at all. It had happened now, and there was nothing I could do but go on making the practical arrangements that had to be made for my leaving. Ailie stood there watching me.

"What are you going to do?" she said.

"Go back to Corioli, to my cousin's, I suppose. I can try to get some kind of work there."

"And Jed? What's he going to do when he hears about this? He's in love with you, isn't he?"

I did not answer.

"You don't have to say it," she said. "And even if he isn't, he's not going to stand for Sallie doing something like this to you. This won't be the end of it."

"I can't help it," I said. "I've done everything I could. I can't help anything now."

I put my cape on and started toward the door. I could see her face as I passed her, looking helpless. There was nothing that she could do either now. Whatever it was that was going to happen, it was out of our hands. I went on down the stairs and out of the house into the rain.

CHAPTER XIX   I LEFT FOR CORIOLI THE NEXT afternoon. There were a few who came to the house beforehand to wish me good-by and good luck; with the school closed that morning, the story had got about, and not everyone was as willing as the school board had been to believe Sallie's story. I was glad that they came, for Ailie's sake. She felt very unhappy about my going. She wanted to go to Sallie herself and see what she could do with her, but I would not let her. I did not want anything more to do with Sallie. Even if she was sorry now for what she had done, I could not trust her not to do the same thing the next time something happened to upset her. It was better for me to go.

There was no boat for Corioli that I could get that day, so Mr. Gibbs took me over to Belleville, where I could take the railway train. It was still raining; it rained all during the night while the train was taking me to Corioli. I slept a little, but I was too worried about what would happen when I got to Corioli to rest very much. I had not worried about that before; all I had thought about was getting away from Le Jeune. I did not know what I would tell Nora and Conn. It would be best to tell the truth to Nora and let her decide what to tell Conn. At any rate, I would not stay with them any longer than I had to. I could get a room somewhere when I had found work.

It was early morning when I got to Corioli. The station was not far from Longmill Street, and I walked over through the streets full of morning traffic — heavy drays and farmers' wagons and the rattle of horsecars carrying people to work. It had stopped raining but the cobblestoned streets were still wet under the gray sky. Nora was just opening the shop when I came up the street. She ran outside to meet me, pulling her apron up over her arms against the raw morning air.

"Lacey," she said. "For the love of heaven, girl, what are you doing here? I couldn't believe my two eyes when I looked out and saw you coming up the street. Sure you've never gone and lost your job?"

"I'm afraid I have."

"Over that young man of yours? Oh, Lacey, child, wouldn't you think what you're doing before you do it, so you wouldn't land yourself in a terrible piece of misfortune like this? You're a Dereen as sure as God ever made any; not a one of them ever had the plain Christian decency to look out for himself first and then for the other fellow. *After* she's a wedding ring on her finger it's time enough for a woman to let a man make trouble for her; they do well enough at it, the dirty twisters, without letting them get a head start at it before."

She brought me into the shop. We stood there in the dull light, the shutters still half-closed as she had left them.

"Don't go on so," I said. "It's not as bad as all that. Sallie made some trouble and the board thought it would be best to ask me to resign. As far as anybody knows, I left because you needed me back here in Corioli."

"*I* needed you?" Nora said. "Holy Mother of God, haven't I enough trouble as it is without needing you to bring me any more? What in the world am I going to tell Mulranny about it now?"

"Tell him I'm not well," I said. I looked around at the shop — the counter, the little glass cases full of odds and ends, trinkets, notions, children's toys. "I won't stay here long," I said. "Just till I can get another job. I can get a room somewhere then."

"You won't do any such class of thing. You might as well go straight into one of those houses over on Diamond Street and be done with it; you wouldn't have a scrap of reputation left in a week if the whisper of that story got about." She put her arms around me. "Don't mind that blathering tongue of mine," she said. "Sure if your own flesh and blood wouldn't stand by you in a time like this, who would? You leave Mulranny to me. I'll manage him."

Conn was sleeping still, she said. I did not see him till noontime, when I came downstairs from my room and found him with Nora in the shop. He looked at me critically.

"Fallen off a bit in flesh," he said, "but divil a bit you look to me that you haven't the strength to sit in a school-house listening to a flock of gossoons saying their A B C's. 'Usha, the younger generation's gone off entirely from the hard-working habits of their elders."

I knew he was suspicious, but there was no way for him to verify his suspicions. So he made the best of it, kissed me, and said I was welcome in the house. He was bored to distraction with Nora by that time, and I suppose he was glad of any diversion. I knew I would have to be care-ful with him. Still it had all gone off better than I had expected. I would see about getting a job in a day or two, and that would keep me out of the house. I did not think it would do any good to go to the Dandys' again. They would be sure to know the reason for my leaving Le Jeune,

and Miss Dandy had made me understand very plainly
when I had seen her during the summer that what she had
been giving me then was a last chance. I thought I would
try the big new department stores in town. It was near
Christmas, and I might be able to get on for a few weeks as
extra help.

Two days later I had a job wrapping packages at
Chatelet's till Christmas, but when I came back to the shop
that evening something else had gone wrong: I found Nora
in tears and Conn in an angry mood. He had met a friend
of his from off the *Sallie Dayton* that afternoon, and the
man had repeated some gossip to him about "the pretty
schoolteacher in Le Jeune that had to leave in a hurry because she'd been caught showing more than the pages of a
book to a man, and to a married man at that."

"What about that now?" Conn shouted at me savagely.

"It's a black lie, that's what it is," Nora cried out. "Sure
a girl can't look crosswise at a man these days without a
lot of dirty little streelers with nothing better to do going
around spreading gossip about her. If she wanted the man,
and him a rich man could buy her silks and satins and fine
houses, would she be coming back to this place and working for a living, like the rest of us that haven't got a handsome face to bring the men running after us?"

Conn hesitated. "Ah, the devil, you're like all the women,"
he said, but a little less certainly now. "You'd stick together
with your lies if you were in the confession box itself. But
I'm warning you," he shouted again suddenly, "if that
blackguard shows his face around here once more, I'll knock
the bloody block off him. I'm not keeping a house for any
bloody rivermen."

I hadn't said a word. Nora motioned me, with a nod of
her head, to go upstairs. It seemed it would blow over after
all. Conn's bluster was always worse than anything he would
really do. It would be all right as long as Jed did not come
to Longmill Street. I did not know whether he would come
or not. I could write to Le Jeune and tell him not to. I did

not think it would make any difference if I did. I felt the
way I had felt that night at the McLeans', when Mr. Moffat had come to ask me to resign. I had done the best I
could, and now it was out of my hands. The only thing I
could do was wait.

CHAPTER XX   THE SATURDAY BEFORE CHRISTMAS IT
stormed all day, the snow beginning early and going on till
after dusk. When I came back to Longmill Street from
Chatelet's there was half a foot of snow in the streets and
more was still falling. During the night it stopped, but the
next day there was a fall of sleet that packed the snow
more tightly and left the whole city glittering with ice. Conn
went out, came back to report that it was getting colder
and there was ice in the river, and then went back to the
kitchen to make himself a whisky toddy. Nora and I could
hear him singing to himself back there —

> *The wran, the wran, the king of all birds,*
> *St. Stephen's Day was caught in the furze.* . . .

"He's in a fine humor, so," Nora whispered to me. "We'll
have a grand Christmas of it if he starts out celebrating it
this way two days before. By tomorrow evening it'll be a
miracle of God's grace if he's able to stand on his two legs.
Still and all, he's better off in his own house than he is down
at the *Crown of Life*. There's little enough mischief he can
get into here."

By evening he was in a happy state, roaring out —

> *Sing holly, sing ivy, sing ivy, sing holly,*
> *A drop just to drink would drown melancholy.* . . .

till the walls shook. I went up to my room to keep out of
his way, and the next morning when I left for Chatelet's

he was still in bed, so I did not see him then. That evening
when I came back to the shop he was not in it either; Nora
was there alone. She was getting ready to close for the
night. She looked up, frightened, it seemed, when I came in.

"Oh, Lacey," she said, "it's you, the saints be praised. He
didn't find you, then?"

"He?" I said.

I knew before she answered me who it was. I stood
there waiting. The shop was quiet. From the room behind I
could hear Conn still muttering his drunken song endlessly
to himself —

> The spit got up like a naked man
> And swore he'd fight with the dripping-pan;
> The pan got up and cock'd his tail
> And swore he'd send them all to jail. . . .

"Captain Dayton," Nora said. "He came round here looking for you this morning after you'd left, and bad luck would
have it that Mulranny'd just come out to the shop when he
came in. Oh, there was like to be the worst class of trouble
between the two of them if I hadn't been there myself to
stop it."

"Did you tell him where I was?" I said.

Nora looked around fearfully at the inner room.

"Divil a bit of it; Mulranny would have cut the tongue
out of me if I had. Sure you know the way he feels about the
man. Said if he came around here again he'd knock him into
the street and you after him, like you was Adam and Eve
itself, and him the archangel at the gates of Paradise."

"What did Captain Dayton do?" I said.

"Do? Nothing at all, after I'd got the two of them calmed
down a bit by letting out a good shriek or two, like I was going to faint. He just stood there listening to Mulranny going
on, and then all of a sudden he slapped both his hands
down, hard, on the counter, like he'd had enough, and
walked out of the door. Mulranny didn't even have the
chance to finish what he was saying."

I stood there. I had no idea what I ought to do. I knew Jed would come back again to the shop to try to see me, but if the *Fair Maid* was scheduled to start down-river that afternoon he might already have left Corioli by now. There was a newspaper lying on the counter, and I picked it up and looked for the column of departure notices. There it was: *For New Orleans. The* Fair Maid, *Jed Dayton, master, and William Fraser, clerk, will depart from the L. and D. wharfboat, foot of Martin Street, at 5 P.M. on Monday.* I put the paper down.

"It's all right," I said. "The *Maid* left at five. He's gone by this time."

I did not know how I felt. It was postponed for another few weeks now; that was all. Nora read the notice nervously.

"*If* there's any boats running on the river at all tonight," she said. "They say there's none of them knows when they'll be leaving this week, with the ice and the storms."

"I think she's gone. It's cold today, but it isn't cold enough to freeze a boat like the *Maid* in."

I was fairly sure I was right. Nora looked a little easier.

"The Lord grant it's so," she said. "I had the heart put crosswise in me once today, and it'd be a poor thing to have it happen a second time, and on Christmas Eve itself." She started back toward the door leading to the rooms behind the shop. "Maybe you wouldn't mind finishing closing up here before you go upstairs," she said. "I'll have a look back at my supper. It'll do Mulranny's temper no good at all if I serve him up burnt food tonight."

I took off my outdoor things and laid them on the counter. It was full dark outside; the gas was on in the shop. I turned it down, and went to cover the cases with the cloth Nora kept for that. I had not locked the door yet. Somebody opened it and came in.

"Lacey," Jed said.

I turned around. He came across the shop. Standing there before me he cursed quietly and with a bleak, impersonal violence.

"Those God-damned self-righteous hypocrites," he said. "Sending you away as if you weren't good enough to breathe the same air they breathed. Why didn't you let me know?"

"It's all right," I said. I stood there holding the folded cloth. "I thought you'd gone," I said. "I thought you'd gone on the *Fair Maid*."

"I've left the *Maid*."

"Left her?"

"The whole thing. The *Maid*, the Dayton Line, Sallie, all of it. I told Sallie yesterday I was through."

I did not say anything.

"Don't stand there as if you didn't believe me," he said. "What did you think I'd do?"

"I don't know. I didn't think. I've tried not to think. Tell me what happened."

"It doesn't matter. It's over, and that's all that counts."

"Jed — tell me what happened."

He shook his head. "It hasn't anything to do with you. You didn't start it; she's the one who wanted it this way. She and that crowd of sanctimonious fools they call a school board —"

He could not talk about them without violence; I heard it there in his voice. We stood there for a moment, only looking at each other. In the silence I could hear Conn stirring in the room behind the shop.

"We can't talk here," I said. "We'll have Conn out on us. Can't I meet you somewhere — ?"

It was already too late. Conn came to the door; I turned around and saw him standing there, half-suspicious, half-bewildered by the sudden dimness of the shop. Then he recognized Jed and started forward furiously.

"Didn't I tell you it was as much as your life was worth to come round this girl again?" he said. "I don't know how much you've got out of her already, but if you want any more of the same you can go over to Diamond Street for it, and her along with you, with her whore's tricks in a decent house —"

He advanced on Jed, flinging his fists wildly, and Jed struck him on the mouth, a blow that drew blood and sent him sprawling back against the counter. At the same moment Nora ran into the room.

"Oh, the Lord have mercy on us!" she cried. "Are they at it again?" She saw the blood on Conn's mouth and shrieked. "Sure you've murdered him, you savage!" she said to Jed. "Look at him bleeding. Can't you see the man's drunk, and doesn't know what he's doing?"

She tried to wipe the blood from Conn's mouth, but he pushed her aside.

"Drunk, is it?" he shouted. "I'm not too drunk to know a whore and her fancy man when I see them. Leave me go now, Nora, and I'll give him more than he came here for —"

Jed turned to me. "Let's get out of here," he said.

"If you go with him, you can go for good," Conn bawled. "You'll not set foot in my house again. And good riddance it'll be —" He flung Nora aside at last and started across the shop toward Jed. "She's been nothing but trouble from first to last."

I looked at Nora, who had run after Conn and was clinging to his arm again.

"Ah, Lacey," she said to me passionately, "wouldn't you get that fella out of here before there's murder done? Sure Mulranny has the right of it; you've no call to let him come around here at all. If you can't keep him away, let you go off yourself and stop troubling decent people that have troubles enough of their own."

I should have known she did not really mean it. She was excited, and frightened for Conn, and so she said more than she would have if she had had time to think. I looked at Jed again.

"Come on," he said. He went over to the counter and picked up my cape. "Isn't this yours?"

"Yes."

He put it around my shoulders. I didn't move. I was still holding the blue cloth Nora used to cover the counter.

"What are you waiting for?" Conn said. "The bit of clothes you have upstairs? 'Usha, even a Diamond Street whore has better than those, and no more than a mate off a lousy scow to buy them for her."

I laid the cloth down on the counter and turned and walked over to the door. Jed opened it for me. I went outside and he followed me. The street was dark and empty. I stood there looking at him.

"You won't be sorry?" I said.

"I don't have to answer that." He was so angry I could see him shaking steadily, as if with the cold. "Come on. I'll get a cab."

"Where are we going?"

"To my hotel first, to pick up my things. I can't take you there; they know me; I don't want any more trouble for you tonight. Then I'm going to get you out of this damned town."

We walked along the street. I felt as if I had stepped into a new world where only wild and impossible things could happen. I don't think I quite realized yet what I had done.

At the end of the street a cab passed. Jed hailed it and we got in. He told the driver to go to the Sheffield House. It was a hotel on Sixth Street. We started off, the horse going slowly up the hill. In the darkness inside Jed drew me to him and kissed me.

"You won't ever be sorry, darling?" I said. "Tell me you won't ever be sorry."

"Don't say that. I've never had anybody but you. It's never been anything but hell without you."

"I want you to be happy. I can't help it if it isn't right. That's all I want for either of us."

"It's as right as anything ever is in this God-damned world." I could feel his arms tighten around me suddenly;

he was still too angry, as I was too dazed, to realize fully what was happening. "I wish I'd killed that rotten scum," he said. "Anyway, you're out of there now."

"It doesn't matter." I looked down at his hand. The knuckles were bleeding slightly, probably where they had struck Conn's teeth. "You've hurt your hand," I said.

"It isn't anything."

He took out a handkerchief and wrapped it around the hand. The carriage stopped at the corner of Sixth Street, then turned and went on again. Jed glanced out the window.

"Listen to me," he said. "I've got to go into the hotel to settle my bill and get my things. I want you to wait for me in the carriage."

"Yes," I said. The carriage went on down the street. "I haven't any things, you know," I said. "It's just like those old stories about runaway brides that you always hear — 'with only the clothes on her back' — only I'm not your bride, am I, darling? We don't even need a justice of the peace."

"Stop it," Jed said. I was trying to laugh, but I was crying instead. "Do you think it's always going to be this way? We'll be married as soon as I'm free."

"It doesn't matter. Really it doesn't." I looked up at him; it was all over in a moment. "Nothing at all seems to matter now. I've tried to do what people thought I ought to do for so long, and now that I've stopped, it doesn't seem to matter at all."

"It doesn't. The only thing that matters is that we're together." The carriage stopped and he glanced out the window again. "Here's the hotel. I won't be long."

He spoke to the driver and got out of the carriage. I saw him go up the steps and into the hotel. It was a long five-story building with Palladian windows. Through the glass doors I could see a Christmas tree with colored ornaments and lighted candles on it in the lobby. It was Christmas Eve; I had forgotten that. With Jed gone I could feel the

excitement going down in me. I felt frightfully alone. I sat
there watching the door. People went in and out. It was
cold; I could hear the horse stamping impatiently as we
waited.

Finally, when it seemed I couldn't bear it another moment, Jed came out. I saw him running down the steps,
looking to make sure the carriage was still there. He spoke
to the driver again and then got in beside me. He had his
bag with him.

"Where are we going now?" I said.

"To the Central Depot. There's a train for Charleville in
twenty minutes. We may as well go there as anywhere else.
Are you all right?"

"Yes," I said. "Oh, darling, I thought you weren't ever
coming back."

"That's one thing you don't have to worry about. I'll come
back, no matter where I have to go."

"I know it. I knew you would. But it seemed like such a
long time."

"It's always a long time when we're not together."

"Yes." The carriage had pulled out from before the hotel
and was going along the street in the direction of the station.
"Darling, when we get to Charleville, where are we going to
go there?" I said.

"To a hotel."

"And after that?"

"I don't know. I'll find someplace for us to live — in
Charleville or wherever else you want."

"It doesn't make any difference, as long as I'm with you."

"Nothing else makes any difference."

"Doesn't it even make a difference that you won't have
the *Fair Maid* and the Dayton Line any more?"

"No."

"You'll have another Dayton Line some day."

"And another *Fair Maid*, only this one will be named
the *Lacey Dayton*."

"That's not my name yet." I shivered a little. "I wish we

could both change our names when I marry you," I said.
"I wish we could be two people who were only born into
our bodies this minute, here together, and who didn't have
to remember anything before that because nothing had ever
happened to them."

"We don't have to remember anything."

"I can't. I can't bear to. You won't let me remember anything, will you, darling?"

He drew me over to him and kissed me, and while the
cab went on over the cobblestoned streets, with the gaslight
flaring and then darkening and then flaring whitely again
over our faces, he held me close to him. The horse's hoofs
sounded steadily outside and we sat there quietly, without
moving. It was not a long time. The cab drew up before
the depot and Jed got out and helped me out. He paid the
driver and we went inside.

"I'll have to get the tickets," he said.

"Yes, I know. I'll wait for you here. We haven't much
time, have we?"

"I think there's enough."

He went over to the ticket window. The station was very
crowded. I remembered again that it was Christmas Eve.
I stood there watching the people passing by, family groups
going to visit relatives for Christmas, a few college boys
looking exuberant, everyone a little more excited than usual.
It was a fine station with marble floors and red-plush seats
and a wide stairway with gleaming brass balustrades.

It was only a few minutes before traintime when Jed
came back.

"We'll have to hurry," he said.

"Yes." I walked along beside him. "Darling, why are we
taking the train?"

"Too many people know me on the river. There might be
some sort of trouble. Don't you want to go by train?"

"I don't care. But you mustn't worry about me. I don't
mind what people say any more. I used to, but I don't
any more. It doesn't seem to make any difference now."

"It does to me."

"You can't make them see the way we feel. All they can see is what we're doing. You mustn't get into any trouble with anybody because of me."

"I'll try not to."

The train was just ready to pull out when we got aboard. It was very crowded, and Jed had only been able to get tickets for the coach because everything else had been sold out. We sat across from a stout woman in black with a baby in her arms who said she was going to Charleville to visit her mother, and there was an ex-Confederate sergeant standing in the aisle who wished everybody a merry Christmas and sang "Good King Wenceslas" over and over in a very hoarse voice till he fell asleep sitting on someone's suitcase in the vestibule.

CHAPTER XXI   WE GOT INTO CHARLEVILLE VERY late, in the early hours of Christmas morning. Jed hired a cab at the station and told the driver to take us to the Grand Hotel. He had never stayed in that hotel when he had been in Charleville, and he did not think anyone would know him there. The streets were deserted as we drove along. It was a raw overcast night, but not so cold as it had been in Corioli.

We sat in the carriage, not talking now, and watched the dark streets fall slowly behind us. It was not far to the hotel. When the cab stopped Jed got out and paid the driver and a porter came out to get the bags. It was a fine hotel and when we went in the big lobby did not look like the middle of the night with its bright chandeliers and polished brass and marble, except that it was too quiet and empty. The clerk at the desk was very polite and he too did not look as if it was the middle of the night. He said he had a splendid room for us on the third floor. It was not the best the hotel had to offer, but they were crowded because of the holidays. He described it to us; he said there was a view of the river from the windows.

"That will be fine," Jed said.

I watched him write the names on the register — *Captain and Mrs. Jed Dayton.* The handkerchief was still around his hand. I saw the clerk looking at it.

"Is there anything you'd like for that hand?" he asked. "A bandage — ?"

"It isn't anything." Jed put the pen down. "Could we have something to eat sent up to the room?"

"What would you like? You could have cold chicken, cold ham, anything cold — I'm afraid not much more just now."

"The cold chicken will be fine."

He ordered some wine and talked with the clerk about it. I had forgotten that I had had nothing to eat since noon, and that Jed probably had not either. I watched the clerk take a key from the rack and hand it to a bellboy. Everything seemed a little unreal; I heard the voices, but they seemed to have nothing to do with me. We followed the bellboy over to the elevator. I noticed that there was a holly wreath over the door.

The elevator stopped at the third floor. We got out and walked along the silent corridor to a room at the end. The bellboy opened the door and lit the gas. It was a big, high-ceilinged room with lace curtains and heavy tasseled draperies at the long windows. The furniture was mahogany, heavy and with a kind of depressing, respectable elegance. I stood looking around. The bellboy said, "Thank you, sir," to Jed and left the room.

The door closed behind him. Jed came over to me.

"Are you tired?" he said.

"I don't know. I suppose I must be. Are they going to bring us something to eat?"

"Yes." He stood there looking at me, not touching me. "Lacey," he said. "You're not sorry?"

"No."

"You look as if you might be."

"No, darling. You don't have to worry about that. You may not be married to me, but it doesn't make any really practical difference, because I'm never going to leave you again. It was just your writing that name on the register that bothered me."

"Mrs. Dayton?"

"Yes. It isn't my name; it's Sallie's. It's always meant Sallie to me. For a minute it was just as if I wasn't there at all and she was."

"You're here," he said. He came closer and put his arms around me. "Oh, Lacey, you don't know how much I love you," he said.

His voice sounded strange. It was perfectly still in the room. We sat down on the bed.

After a little somebody came along the corridor and knocked at the door. Jed got up.

"Come in," he said.

A Negro boy came in with a tray. I stood up and went over and looked into the mirror. I did it automatically, and when I saw myself suddenly in the mirror it was like looking at someone I had known well but had not seen for a long time. I heard Jed talking to the waiter. Then the door opened and closed again.

"Come over here and eat something," Jed said. "I didn't bring you here to starve you to death."

"I don't think I'm hungry."

I came over. The tray was on the table. There was cold chicken and bread and butter and a bottle of wine.

"Our first meal," I said. I looked at Jed. "I'll make you a fine home, darling," I said. "Really I will. I'm very good at that."

"You make me a fine home just by being here."

"It's a very strange home." I looked around at the mahogany furniture and the steel engravings of English cottages and the Swiss Alps on the walls. "So many people must have had it before us. Do you suppose all of them were married? I have a feeling they don't approve of us."

"I don't care if God Almighty and the whole legion of angels don't approve of us."

"Don't say that, darling."

"It's the truth. We haven't got anybody but each other and we don't need anybody."

He had poured the wine, but neither of us had begun to drink it. He stood there looking at me. All at once I went over and put my arms around him.

"Oh, darling," I said, "we are going to be together, aren't we? It's just the same as if we were married? Oh, I wish I knew nothing could happen to keep us apart again."

"Nothing can happen."

"You're so sure of it. I wish I were. I wish I weren't afraid of something."

"What are you afraid of?"

"I don't know. If I knew, it wouldn't be so hard. I think I'm afraid of what other people will do to us."

"They won't do anything."

"Tell me that again. I'll believe it if you tell me often enough."

"They won't do anything. They can't do anything to us as long as we're together."

"And we'll promise to stay together till death do us part."

"Longer," he said. "If there's anything after, I'll find you there."

"If there's anything after, darling, we'll both be in hell. I'm a good enough Catholic to believe that. But it doesn't make any difference. Don't you think God should have known it wouldn't make any difference when He made us the way we are?"

"Don't cry," he said.

"I'm not crying. It's only that I don't think He knows what it's like to love somebody the way I love you."

"Come and drink your wine," he said. "You're tired."

"I'll be all right again in a little while." I looked up and saw a clock on the little shelf across the room. "It's Christmas Day, isn't it? Merry Christmas, darling."

"Merry Christmas."

"You see. I'm fine now. And I'll drink the wine. Oh, darling, tell me we're going to be together forever and ever."

Outside I heard a clock somewhere chiming the hour. It did not feel like Christmas morning in the room.

CHAPTER XXII   LATER, AFTER THE LIGHT HAD BE-gun to come into the room through the open window, we fell asleep, and when I awoke it was full morning and I heard the rain outside. Jed was sleeping. I had never seen him asleep before, and I lay watching him till I knew I would waken him if I did not stop. I did not want to be apart from him, even in sleep. After a while I went to sleep again myself and it was almost noon when I awoke. Jed was sitting on the edge of the bed, looking at me. He had on a dark-blue dressing gown.

"Why didn't you wake me?" I said. "I want to be awake when you are."

"You needed the sleep."

"I think I did at that. I'm fine now." I sat up in bed and he kissed me good morning. "You look so elegant, darling," I said. "I never imagined you in such an elegant dressing gown."

"I'll finish dressing and then you can wear it and we'll have some breakfast."

"All right."

"Tomorrow, as soon as the shops are open, we'll get you some things."

"I don't mind not having any. I'm not the first Irish girl who's slept in her shift."

"You're the most beautiful one."

"I'm afraid you're prejudiced, darling. But I'm glad you are."

"I'm in love with you, if that's what you mean."

"That's exactly what I mean. Let me get up and wash now; then we can have some breakfast, or lunch — whatever they'll give us. You look awfully hungry."

"Not just yet."

"All right. Not just yet."

He put his arms around me.

Afterward we had eggs and fried apples and ham and hot biscuits and coffee in the room, with the rain growing heavier all the while outside. When we had finished I went to the window and looked out and saw the carriages splashing by on the unfamiliar street, with the river, as the clerk had promised, off in the distance behind the veil of rain.

"Do you want to go anywhere?" I said. "Or shall we stay here and celebrate Christmas at home?"

"Whatever you like."

"I think I'd rather stay here. I don't want to see anybody but you."

"It's better here."

"I wish I never had to see anyone but you again. Wouldn't it be lovely if we could be on a boat on the river together and never have to come ashore?"

"We'll do that some day."

"The Flying Dutchman of the Western Rivers. Only this one will have his bride with him. Why do they call them the Western Rivers, darling? I thought California was the West."

"It's an old term. They called them that before the West was part of the United States. It means any river whose waters empty into the Gulf of Mexico."

"I'd like to see the Gulf of Mexico. When you have your own boats again, will you take me down the river on one of them?"

"I'll take you anywhere you want to go."

I turned around from the window. "And you don't really mind it that you won't have the *Fair Maid* any more?" I said.

"No."

"I only want to make you happy, you know. It seems very hard that I can't give you one thing you want very much without making you give up something else you want too."

"I don't want anything else but you. Come away from the window. Come over here."

"All right." I came over. "Who has the *Fair Maid* now?" I asked.

"Captain Dix. I turned her over to him in Le Jeune."

"After you'd found out about my having to leave Le Jeune?"

"Yes."

I didn't say anything for a moment. "Jed," I said then.

"Yes."

"I want to know about Sallie."

"You don't have to know about her."

"I do. It'll be worse if I don't. Was she very upset?"

"It's not your concern."

"She was. I know. She doesn't really care about you, but she cares a great deal what people think about her. She ought to have married someone who would have been very kind to her. You're not really very kind, you know, darling; it's just that I don't mind your not being because I'm you and I know how you are inside."

"I'll be kind to you."

"No, you won't — any more than you'll be to yourself. You'll just live with me, really live with me, the way you do with yourself, and that's all I want."

I was standing there before him and he reached up and took my hand to draw me down beside him.

"No," I said. "Wait. You haven't told me yet. Sallie —"

"She's all right. She'll be all right."

"What did she do?"

"Came up to Corioli after me. I guess even after what I'd told her in Le Jeune she still thought she was going to stop me."

"And you saw her there, in Corioli?"

"Yes. She went to the Phoenix Hotel because she thought I'd be there, and when she found out I was at the Sheffield House she sent a message over to me yesterday afternoon. I had to see her or there might have been more trouble for you. But it's all over now; can't you understand that? I told her to get out of that place and go home; she's probably there now. You don't have to think about it any more."

I shivered. "It makes me feel terrible when I think about her. Oh, darling, why couldn't we have met years ago, before you met her?"

"You were in Ireland then."

"Yes. And I was only a little girl. You wouldn't have looked at me."

"I'd have waited for you."

"I wish you had waited for me. Oh, I wish you had."

"Come here."

I sat down beside him on the bed. He put his arms around me.

"You're shaking," he said.

"I can't help it. Oh, darling, I can't give you up now. I can't lose you now."

"You don't have to. We're never going to have that kind of hell again."

"I want to believe it, but I can't. I know it's only Irish nonsense, but I can't. It's just a feeling I have —"

"Yes," he said. "It doesn't matter. Because I won't let you go."

He held me there against him. I heard the rain outside.

"I'm all right now," I said. "I'm sorry I said those things. It's just that I'm so happy I can't really believe it's true."

"I know. Sometimes I can't believe it either."

"It is true, though. We have this, now, this very moment. Nobody can ever take that away from us."

"We're going to have a lot more."

"Yes." I wanted to believe it. "We'll have tomorrow and all the other tomorrows after that."

"Let's not think about tomorrow. Let's think about now."

"All right, darling. Whatever you want."

"Oh, you're wonderful," he said. "I won't ever let you go. They'd have to kill me to make me let you go."

"Don't talk like that. Please don't talk like that."

"All right. I won't talk. We don't have to talk at all."

Afterwards, when we had had dinner, we left the hotel and walked down toward the river. It had stopped raining, and there was a south wind. We looked at the lighted streets and the carriages going by and they were all different from the way they had been the night before. They all belonged to us now.

"We have everything," I said. "I'm not afraid of anything now."

"It never does any good to be afraid."

"I know. But I'm not as brave as you are, darling."

"You're a brave girl. I told you that a long time ago."

"I remember. But it's much better for me when there's nothing to be brave about."

We went down to the landing and watched a big packet coming in, headed down-river. At the landing she turned around and came in slowly with her bow pointing upstream.

"Why do they do that?" I said.

"Tie up with the bow headed upstream? It's easier to land that way in the current. That's the *Kate Lane*, one of Tom Lorimer's boats."

"You couldn't ever stay away from the river, could you, darling?"

"Would you want me to?"

"No. I only hope you won't go on a boat now that makes such long trips as the *Fair Maid* did."

"I won't. I'll go down to Lorimer's office and talk to him

sometime this week. I hear he has a new boat he's going to put into the Memphis trade soon."

"Do we need money very badly?"

"No. But till the Dayton Line affairs are legally settled I don't want to draw on anything from it. That was all Sallie's money, you know."

"I know that, darling. I didn't want to marry you for your money."

He looked at me. "Why did you want to marry me?"

"You know that."

"Let's go back to the hotel. Then you can tell me all about it."

"I don't have to tell you. You know all about it already."

"You can tell me anyway."

"Not in words. There aren't any words for it."

"No. Not in words."

We walked back the way we had come. It was really a fine night now and we did not hurry. When we went into the hotel the clerk who had been on duty the night before, when we had arrived, was at the desk. I thought he looked at us queerly as he gave Jed the key to our room.

"What was the matter with him?" I said, as we walked to the elevator.

"I didn't notice anything."

"He looked so queer when he saw us — as if he'd swallowed something hot too quickly. Are you sure you were never here before with Sallie?"

"Yes."

"Maybe it's just that he's not used to seeing two people look so happy."

"He'll have to get used to it, as long as we stay here."

The elevator came and we got in. It was like going home to get out at the third floor and walk down the corridor to our room. Jed unlocked the door and we went in.

"It's just the same," I said. "I feel as if we'd been away a long time."

"So do I."

"We'll come back here every Christmas — shall we?"

"Yes."

I turned around. He had closed the door.

"Lacey," he said.

"Yes." I came over to him.

"Lacey. Oh, Lacey."

CHAPTER XXIII   THE NEXT MORNING I WENT OUT
to see about getting the things I needed in the shops in
town. Jed offered to come with me, but I knew he would
not like it, and I said it would be better if I went alone. He
went out with me and showed me where the shops were
and then left me at the door of one of them. He said he
might go down to talk to Mr. Lorimer about the new Memphis packet. We were to meet at the hotel for lunch.

I had a fine time in the shops, picking out things I
thought Jed would like, and then went back to the hotel.
Jed was not back yet when I came in. I thought he had
probably been delayed at Mr. Lorimer's, and I freshened
up for lunch and then sat down to wait for him. At two
o'clock he had still not come. I went downstairs to the
desk to see if there had been any message, but there had
been none, and I came upstairs again. The clerk on duty
was not the same one I had seen the night before, but I
thought he had been nervous too in speaking to me. I had
the feeling that something was wrong, but I did not know
what it could have to do with Jed's not coming.

In the room I sat down again to wait. It was a soft,
cloudy day. The room was very quiet, and I could hear
people going by in the corridor outside, and snatches of
their conversation as doors opened and closed. I began to
think, what if Jed did not come? Of course he would come.
What could possibly make him stay away? I looked at the

clock on the shelf. He would come in five minutes. He had
got into conversation with someone and forgotten about the
time. He wouldn't forget. Yes, but he didn't come. He
would come in five minutes. The five minutes were up. He
would come in the next five. Yes, but what if he didn't
come?

I got up and walked over to the window and stood there,
trying to think what I ought to do. It had begun to rain
again; I could see the sky soft and gray and heavy over the
town. Jed would not like it if I made any sort of fuss. It
had taken him a little longer than he had expected; that
was all. A little longer? It was almost three. He might have
had an accident. Anything might have happened to him. I
had to do something; I couldn't stand there waiting all
afternoon. It might be nothing at all. I tried to keep saying
that to myself. It might be nothing at all. I knew it was not
nothing at all.

Finally I could not bear it any longer and I went downstairs again to the desk. As I got out of the elevator I saw
the clerk talking to a small dark elegant-looking man with
a soft full mustache and large dark eyes. The clerk looked up
as I came over. He said something quickly to the small
man, and the small man turned and looked at me and then
left the desk and came over to me.

"Miss Dereen?" he said. He had a quiet, elegant, slightly
outraged voice. "I am Edgar Lefebre, of Lefebre and Braun,
Attorneys-at-Law. Our firm has represented the Dayton
Line in this city. I've just come from Captain Dayton —
Perhaps we might sit down over here while we talk?"

He gestured toward a settee standing alone in a corner
of the lobby. I started over with him, cold. I knew there
was something terribly wrong. He had not called me Mrs.
Dayton. That made no difference as long as Jed was all
right. I did not care what anyone had found out about me.
Nothing mattered as long as Jed was all right.

"Please —" I said. "Where is he? Where is Captain Dayton? Has there been an accident?"

He looked at me. I was quite certain that he loathed what he was doing.

"Captain Dayton is under arrest," he said.

"Under arrest?" It was so different from anything I had expected to hear that I stopped walking and stood there looking at him. "You can't be serious."

"He is under arrest for the murder of his wife," Mr. Lefebre said. He said it forcibly and a little hysterically. "She was found dead in her room in the Phoenix Hotel in Corioli on the evening before Christmas. It has been in the newspapers —"

"Sallie?" I said. I couldn't take it in; I thought for a moment that he must be playing some sort of monstrous joke on me, standing there with his large mournful dark eyes and his aristocratic hands and his air of being help-lessly enmeshed in some outrageous plot peculiarly con-cocted against himself. "It can't possibly be," I said. "It couldn't possibly —"

"I really think you had better sit down."

"But it's not true! I never heard anything so fantastic in my life."

I sat down; my knees were trembling. Mr. Lefebre sat down delicately beside me, keeping a little distance between us.

"It is certainly true that Mrs. Dayton is dead," he said. "As to Captain Dayton's responsibility in the matter of her death — the Corioli police apparently believed there was a strong enough presumption of it to put out a warrant for him and send a request down here for the Charleville police to hold him."

I sat there trying to understand it. I could feel the fear in the pit of my stomach, and then it was in my chest, and I felt it climbing steadily till at last it was in my throat. I clenched my hands tightly together in my lap.

"What will they do to him?" I said. "It isn't true, you know; he couldn't have done it. He couldn't have."

"If that's true, he can no doubt make a satisfactory explanation to the Corioli police and that will be the end of it. You understand that this state has no direct interest in a crime committed in another state; there will have to be extradition proceedings before he can be returned to Corioli. But I have strongly advised him to waive extradition and allow himself to be brought back to Corioli at once."

I did not understand any of it. I sat there looking at him. It was all unreal: the bright lobby, the people going in and out, the hum of cheerful talk and laughter against which we were holding this incredible conversation.

"But hasn't he explained to them here —?" I said. "Can't they understand that he couldn't have done it?"

Mr. Lefebre shrugged his shoulders. He looked more than ever like a well-brought-up spaniel suddenly thrust into a filthy street.

"Apparently it can be established that Captain Dayton was with his wife at her hotel at about the time the murder was committed," he said, "so there is at least the possibility — which the police can scarcely overlook — that he was responsible for her death."

"But there must be something you can do! You're an attorney; you must be able to arrange some way he can at least be free till all this is explained."

He looked at me as if I had insulted him by drawing his attention to his connection with the matter.

"Murder is a very serious charge, Miss Dereen," he said. "I am not a criminal lawyer, but in my opinion it is highly unlikely that Captain Dayton will be released till he has furnished sufficient proof of his innocence to warrant the charges against him being dropped."

I stood up. "But I can see him, then?" I said. "I can talk to him?"

"That wouldn't be possible just now, even if he wished it. He particularly doesn't; he doesn't want you involved in this in any way. Of course you understand that you will have to leave this hotel at once, and it will be advisable for you to leave the city too if you wish to avoid — unpleasantness. Captain Dayton has authorized me to place the sum of twenty-five hundred dollars at your disposal immediately. I should advise you to go to Corioli. Your testimony may be helpful to him there. There is a time-element involved, it seems. But I advise you, at any rate, to leave Charleville at once. I have used what influence I have, at Captain Dayton's request, to try to prevent your being prosecuted here for any — charges that might be brought against you."

"I understand," I said. I sat down again. "You must have a great deal of influence, Mr. Lefebre. I suppose I really ought to be very grateful to you."

None of it was real. I was going to wake up and Jed would be there and none of it would be real and we would laugh about it together. He would tell me about his morning and I would tell him about mine, and I would say, "Who is Mr. Lefebre, darling?" — and he would say, "He's somebody you dreamed. He isn't real." I looked at Mr. Lefebre.

"You can't be —" I said. "You aren't —"

I saw his face looking alarmed as he got up. He was asking a passing bellboy for a glass of water.

"I'm not —" I said. "Really I'm not —"

I was not going to faint or make a scene. I sat there holding on to myself. In a few moments I knew I was going to be able to do it. The bellboy came up with a glass of water.

"I'm all right," I said.

I drank the water. Mr. Lefebre stood there, still looking alarmed.

CHAPTER XXIV   I GOT BACK TO CORIOLI LATE THAT night and registered at a hotel near the station as Mrs. Moira Fitzgerald. It was my mother's name. On the train I had begun to feel very ill, and as soon as I got up to my room at the hotel everything seemed to give way all at once and I fainted. I was ill for a week; the doctor said it was a kind of bilious disturbance. I couldn't eat, and I was sick all the while. Everyone at the hotel was very kind. They thought I was a young widow who had just lost her husband.

I had them bring me the newspapers, and from them I found out about Jed and about what had happened to Sallie. She had been strangled in her room at the Phoenix Hotel; when they found her, late on Christmas Eve, she had been dead for several hours. Nobody knew of anyone's having seen her or been to her room after Jed had gone up to see her there at about six o'clock that evening. That was just before he had come to Longmill Street to look for me. The clerk at the Phoenix remembered Jed's coming in and asking the number of Sallie's room, and a quarter of an hour afterward a porter had seen him come downstairs and leave the hotel. The only thing that did not fit into the theory that he had killed Sallie was the fact that her jewelry and money were missing. The newspapers said the police believed he might have taken them to make the matter look like a casual robbery and so turn suspicion away from himself. I was frightened by the tone the newspapers took. They all seemed very sure that Jed was guilty. There was a great deal about the case in them, and I saw my name there in the columns and read about myself with the same feeling I had when I read about Jed. It did not seem to have anything to do with us except the names.

The third day I was at the hotel I had a note from Thomas Dandy, asking me to come and see him at his office as soon as I was well enough. I had read in the papers that he had taken Jed's case, but I did not know how he had found out where I was. He wrote that I was to let him know if there was anything he could do for me, and that in the meantime it would be better if I remained Mrs. Fitzgerald and did not leave the hotel except to see him.

The first day I could go out I went to his office. It was on the second floor of an old building down on Levee Street.

A dry-looking elderly clerk asked me to wait, and a moment later came back and said that Mr. Dandy would see me at once. I went into the inner office. Thomas Dandy was there, sitting behind a big walnut desk.

"Well, Lacey," he said. "I was beginning to wonder when you'd turn up." He got up and came over to help me off with my cape. "You look like a ghost, girl," he said. "Don't act as if the world was coming to an end."

"I've been ill," I said. "But I'm fine now. Really. Please tell me — how is Jed? You've seen him? Is he all right?"

"It'll take more than a few days in jail to put a crimp in that young man's style. What did you think was going to happen to him? We don't use the rack and the thumbscrew any more, you know, even here in America." He pulled a chair up close to the desk. "Here, sit down, sit down," he said. "You make me nervous, standing there looking at me with those eyes."

I sat down. It felt very comforting, being with him. He did not look at all serious or worried. I knew that did not mean anything, but it made me feel better all the same. I glanced around the office. There was the desk, and the rows of legal books behind it, and a huge iron safe with a wrought ornamental border and an oil painting of an American Indian chief above it. Everything looked untidy. It did not look like the office of a successful lawyer.

Thomas Dandy had sat down behind his desk.

"Well," he said, "you've got yourself into a fine mess, haven't you?"

"It's all right about me."

"It will be, when we get that young man of yours out of jail. People will forget a lot of things if you can show them a wedding ring on your finger and a husband to go with it who has a quarter of a million dollars or so to his name."

I looked at him across the desk.

"Then you will get him out?" I said. "It's going to be all right?"

"I'll do my best."

"But you're not sure?"

"I'm not sure I'm going to be sitting behind this desk talking to you five seconds from now. That's the fascinating thing about life; when you're dealing with it, you can never be sure of anything. But I've found out that the thing you can rely on most in it is the corruptibility of human nature, so I think you can put Captain Dayton's acquittal down as one of the better risks, if you're inclined to gamble."

"The corruptibility —" I said. "But he didn't kill her. All he needs is for people to know the truth."

"The truth is," Thomas Dandy said, "that he was on very bad terms with his wife, that as a matter of fact he had asked her to divorce him so he could marry you, that he stood to gain a fortune if she left him free by death instead of by divorce, that he visited her at her hotel at about the time of her death, and that he had on his right hand a slight wound of the sort the person who murdered Sallie would very possibly have received in the struggle that led to her death. That's the prosecution's case, and they can prove every part of it. Would you say an honest jury would be a little less than honest if it didn't at least consider it a strong possibility that the truth also included the fact that he strangled his wife?"

He said it all perfectly calmly, in a brisk, matter-of-fact voice.

"And you?" I said. "Do you think it's a strong possibility too?"

"He says it isn't; that's good enough for me. I'm not the judge or the jury; I'm only the defense attorney. My business is to get him off when every other lawyer in town is saying it can't be done, and when every two-bit corner-saloon ruffian who likes to fancy himself on the right side of the law for a change is saying he won't let me do it." He nodded his head. "You may as well have it straight," he said. "What I think, what you think, what the truth really is, doesn't matter. The only thing that does matter is for me to be able to get twelve men together who will

think, or at least say they think, exactly what we want them
to."

I remembered what he had said to me the first time I
had met him — that he hadn't any principles. He was really
a very strange man. I did not believe that, about his having
no principles. I had seen men like him before, men who
were too clever and too fond of excitement, and who were
bored with the legitimate uses of their own cleverness. I
wished Jed had another attorney. That was stupid of me.
Everyone knew that Thomas Dandy was the most successful criminal lawyer in the state. It did not make any difference how he got Jed acquitted as long as he did it. If people
would not believe the truth it would have to be done in a
different way, but it would have to be done. If it was not
done they might hang Jed. I was not going to think about
that. I was never going to think about that.

"If it will make you feel any better," Thomas Dandy
said, "I think personally that the odds are all in favor of
the fact that Captain Dayton is telling the truth. He's not
stupid enough to kill his wife in such a way that it couldn't
help but be traced to him, and then go a few hours'
traveling distance away and register at a hotel under his
own name. Unfortunately that's not proof enough for a jury."

"But somebody must have killed her," I said. "Somebody
killed her and then robbed her. And if the police aren't
even looking for him —"

"I'm looking for him," Thomas Dandy said, "and I'll tell
you frankly that the chances of my finding him, or of anyone else's finding him, are a thousand to one. Sallie Dayton
was murdered because she was a fool, and it's not very hard
to murder a fool. She took a room in a river-front hotel because she knew that was the hotel Captain Dayton usually
stopped at when he came to Corioli alone. She went there
with her expensive clothes and her expensive jewelry and
probably carrying her money in a little net bag dangling
from her wrist, on Christmas Eve, with every room bulging
and the streets outside full of men who could have just walked

in and followed her up to her room — which, if I know
Sallie, she hadn't even locked — and then walked out again.
And by this time the one who did that may be in New
Orleans or Natchez or Pittsburgh or Duluth, for all we
know. Nobody saw him, because there were too many other
people to see, and he didn't ask at the desk for her the way
Captain Dayton did. So he's as safe as he'd be in a church,
unless he's careless enough to get rid of that jewelry in a
way that could be traced to him."

I sat there listening to him spelling it out for me.

"If only he hadn't gone there," I said. "If only she hadn't
come up to Corioli after him and found out where he was
and sent him that message. Do you know how she found
out?"

"She had the hotel detective do it for her. He thought
she was a little crazy, but she said she'd give him fifty
dollars. She was throwing money around there like water;
it'd have been a miracle if somebody hadn't murdered her."

"Jed told her to go home. He told her to get out of
there and go home."

"She never ought to have left there in the first place. She
was the sort of woman that shouldn't have been let loose
on a public street even two yards away from the house she
lived in without somebody to see that she got back there
safely again."

"I know." I couldn't look at him then. "It's my fault, really.
It's all my fault. I knew something would happen. I knew
how Sallie was."

"The chances are something would have happened even
if you'd never set eyes on either of them. It was a poor
marriage from the start. Everybody knew that. And you
can't blame yourself for Sallie's being the sort of hysterical,
reckless person she was."

"I feel so sorry for her. I can't stop thinking about it.
She was always so afraid of any violence."

Thomas Dandy shook his head.

"Don't think about it," he said. His voice sounded serious.

He was in earnest. "I know the kind of girl you are, Lacey," he said. "I know you didn't get into something like this without good cause. You're not God, you know; you couldn't take a situation like that and make it come out so everybody would be happy. You did the best you could, and if you did the wrong thing you'll have hell enough out of all this to pay for it without trying to take on any more."

He stopped. I thought he was a little embarrassed at having talked to me like that. He looked down at a sheet of paper with a notation on it that was lying on his desk.

"Now," he said, "suppose we get down to business here. You're staying at the Market Hotel, name of Mrs. Moira Fitzgerald. That won't do; it's only by the grace of their own stupidity that the district attorney's office or the newspapers haven't found you there yet."

"How did you know I was there?" I said.

"It's my business to know a good many things. And if you'll take my advice you'll get straight out of town before anybody else starts figuring it out that Moira Fitzgerald might be Moira Fitzgerald's daughter. Go to St. Louis, or even farther away than that — anyplace, till the trial is over."

"Mr. Lefebre said it would be better if I came here, to Corioli. He said my testimony might help Jed — something about the time-element —"

"Oh, Lefebre —" Thomas Dandy said. He shrugged his shoulders impatiently. "There are two perfectly competent witnesses — Nora Mulranny and her husband — who can testify as well as you can that Captain Dayton walked into that shop on Longmill Street at half past six on Christmas Eve. And neither they nor you can prove by doing it that he didn't kill his wife, because unfortunately medical science hasn't found a way yet to tell the difference, four hours after death, between a woman who died at a quarter past six in the evening and one who died at half past six. All you'd be doing by getting up on that witness stand

would be giving Jacob Solms a good chance to crucify you
in public, and any effect that would have on the jury
wouldn't do any good to Captain Dayton."

I thought about what he was saying. I knew it would be
better to go, but I could not tell myself to go.

"I couldn't go without seeing him, you know," I said.

"All right," he said. "You want to see him. He wants to
see you too. But he has sense enough to know you ought
to stay away from that jail. Do you think you could keep
that from the newspapers?"

"I wouldn't care."

"Not for yourself, maybe, but what about him? What
good do you think it's going to do that case of his to have
you dragged through the papers all over again? And if you
walk in that jail door just once, you're going to get the
whole treatment. Good Lord, girl, don't you realize the
pair of you have been preached about from pulpits and
threatened in saloons and denounced in the columns of
every newspaper in town? This is more than a murder
trial; it has every sign of turning into a public cause. The
best thing you can do for Captain Dayton is to get out of
town and say your prayers and let people forget you even
exist."

"Yes," I said. "All right. I'll do whatever you say. But I
can write to him?"

"Send the letters to me," he said. "I'll see that he gets
them."

"And tell him —"

"What?"

It wasn't any good. "Nothing," I said. "He'll know. You
won't have to tell him. And you're sure he's all right?"

"He's not very comfortable and he's not very happy, but
he's all right. There isn't anything going to happen to him
in that jail that he can't handle."

I stood up. "Thank you," I said. I put out my hand and
he took it. "I'll be very careful," I said. "I'll leave today.
I'll go to St. Louis."

"Go to the Forrest House. It's a nice quiet hotel, and if anyone asks, you're a widow from Galway who's come over to see about settling an estate. Your older brother's. And use a name that hasn't any connection with you at all. Moira Barry. That will do it. You can get in touch with me if you need anything."

"I'll remember."

He showed me out of the office. He had really been very kind to me. I did not want to go to St. Louis; I wanted to see Jed. All during the week I had been ill I had thought about seeing him and it had been the only thing I had to hold on to. Now I did not even have that. I put my veil down and walked out into the street. It seemed like a long time before the trial would be over.

CHAPTER XXV   I STAYED IN ST. LOUIS FOR TWO months, till the trial began. I had letters from Thomas Dandy telling me how things were going, and I knew, though he did not say it directly, that they were going very badly. Finally I could not bear it any longer, and I wrote to him and asked him if I could come back to Corioli. I was afraid all the while that something might happen at the trial and I might be able to help and I would not be there. He wrote back to me, and I knew he still did not want me to come, but he said he would take some rooms for me in a private house on Martin Street. The owner was a Mrs. Wardman. It would be safer there than at a hotel, he said.

I came back to Corioli early in March. It was the evening of the day the trial had begun. Driving over to Martin Street from the depot I could hear the newsboys calling their headlines — DAYTON GOES ON TRIAL, DAYTON MURDER TRIAL BEGINS. It was just at dusk and the streets were crowded with people going home from work. As we passed Lafayette Park I noticed a large group of them collected around a tall thin man in black who was standing on the pedestal of the statue making a speech. I heard Jed's name and asked the driver to stop the cab for a moment.

"What is it?" I said. "What are they doing?"

He turned his head and spat over the side of his box.

"You don't want to hear nothing about that business, miss," he said. "It's about a dirty scoundrel we've got locked in the jail for murdering his wife. We've had enough murderers here, and to spare; if they let this one off like the others, they'll find there are more ways than one to see that fellas like him get their due." He nodded his head in the direction of the park. "That's old Billy Warfield, the revival preacher, over there," he said. "He's been preaching around the city for a week, telling folks what's going to happen to them if they don't stop the sinning and murdering going on here."

I sat there looking out the cab window at the man on the pedestal. He was talking in a high, hoarse voice, waving one arm repeatedly in the air, and bending a little forward as if he were trying to look into the face of each of his listeners as he addressed him. The wind carried some of his words away from me, but I could catch the hypnotic rhythm of his sentences, the words all on a single monotonous chanting note except when a sudden rhythmic stress marked one out for emphasis. After a few moments I made out more plainly what he was saying: "— and *what* did this thirty-one-year-old man do when he found himself *alone* with the woman who stood in the way of his carnal desires? He *murdered* this woman, my dear friends, he did the foul deed of *murder* with his own hands, on the body of his *wife*, my friends, the woman he had sworn at the *altar* to protect and cherish, and he went *off* on the railroad train with his paramour, my dear friends, and with *blood* on his hands, without *thought* of the Almighty Who see-eth

all things, who *see*-eth and de*test*eth the foulness of man,
oh, he went to *fat*ten himself on his lust and his foulness,
but the *Lord* saw him, my friends, the Lord *saw* him and
de*liv*ered him into the hands of justice —"

I could not listen to any more. It was like something in
a nightmare: the hoarse voice pressing on and on without
a moment's respite, building up gradually to a frenzy of
denunciation, and the crowd standing tense in the spring
dusk, a few women swaying slightly to the rhythm of the
words, all of them rapt and horrified. I could not believe it
had anything to do with Jed and me. I told the cabman to
drive on, and as the horse started on past the statue I heard
the voice rising furiously: "— oh now, my dear friends, now,
now, *now* is the time to put an end to the evil, *now* is the
time for the sinner to quail, *now* is the time for the righteous man to *take* in his hand the *sword* of justice and re-
move from the earth the son of Cain and his foulness —"

We went on past. I heard the voice still for a few moments
behind me, and then it was covered by the sound of the
traffic around me in the street. I sat there trying not to let
it matter. It couldn't matter; Jed was innocent. Thomas
Dandy would prove that to the jury, and the jury would
acquit Jed, and in a few days it would all be over. I looked
out at the buildings as we drove by and tried to concentrate
on them. There were people in all of them, ordinary,
everyday people doing ordinary, everyday things. It was
people like that who would make up the jury, not fanatics
like the man in the park.

The cab came to Martin Street and stopped at the corner,
before a narrow three-story brick-and-stone house with an
iron fence and gate. I got out and went up the stone steps
before the door and pulled the bell. A tall woman with
dark curly graying hair and a still handsome, eager-
looking face opened the door.

"You must be Mrs. Barry," she said.

"Yes."

"I'm so pleased. Such a pretty dress. Are they wearing

those black-and-gray stripes in St. Louis? I'm Mrs. Wardman." She called out to the cabman: "Come along with those
bags. I'm here alone except for that good-for-nothing girl,"
she explained to me in the same breath, "and she's up in her
room reading one of those tracts of hers, I suppose. She has
to *spell* them out, but she *does* insist on getting through
them, like the one-legged man at the dance."

She went on ahead up the stairs. She had a rich, dramatic
voice and a splendid way of carrying herself. Later she
told me she had been on the stage — "with Joseph Jefferson
and *both* the Booths, Edwin and John Wilkes." Now she
lived alone on the ground floor of the house on Martin
Street and let the second floor out to "respectable ladies."
She seemed well enough off; the house was furnished with
lace curtains and heavy draperies and an extravagant lot
of bric-a-brac, including Indian shawls and small Oriental
statues and many photographs of herself in ornate gilt
frames.

I had dinner with her downstairs after I had seen my
rooms. She talked all the while, but she did not ask me
questions except about what I liked to eat and what the
spring fashions were in St. Louis. A tall, flat-faced German
girl called Adelaide served the meal. When she was out of
the room Mrs. Wardman said she was going to give her her
notice at the end of the month because she was ignorant
and sulky and made her uncomfortable with her eternal
tracts.

"I like good people," she said. "I'm good myself; I've
been a good woman all my life, and let me tell you, I've
had plenty of chances not to be. But I don't like people
who moon about over some queer sort of religion that's
supposed to make them a little bit better than the rest of
the human race, and then use that as an excuse for not
doing the work the Lord put them here to do."

She broke off as Adelaide came back into the room. I
understood what Mrs. Wardman meant about her making
her uncomfortable. She looked as if she resented us, or

disapproved of us, or both. I wondered how much either she or Mrs. Wardman knew about me.

After the meal was over I excused myself and said I was going upstairs to my rooms.

"Oh, yes," Mrs. Wardman said. "I believe I forgot to tell you. Mr. Dandy said he would have some business to discuss with you this evening. Shall I send him up when he comes?"

"Please do."

I did not know whether she believed it was business or not, and I did not care. Apparently she was willing to be broad-minded about it, and that was all that mattered. I thought she was a queer person and that she kept a rather queer house. Still I liked her too. She seemed very optimistic and energetic, and though she talked a great deal she was never dull.

Thomas Dandy came to the house about nine o'clock. I heard him downstairs in the hall talking to Mrs. Wardman, and then he came up and knocked at my door. I let him in and took his hat and coat and he sat down.

"How was the trip?" he asked.

He seemed as cheerful as ever. I could not tell anything by looking at him.

"I don't want to talk about the trip," I said. "How is Jed? How is it going for him?"

"Wait a minute. We haven't even got a jury yet, you know."

"But it's all right so far?" I sat down too, in a chair opposite his. "I drove by Lafayette Park on my way from the station; there was a man there preaching to a crowd about Jed. It frightened me."

"It doesn't mean anything. It's only talk."

"But why do they hate him so? He didn't kill Sallie. All of them — the newspapers, the cabman, those people in the park — I can feel how they hate him."

He shrugged his shoulders.

"The newspapers hate him because it sells papers for

them. And a lot of people hate him because it makes them feel a little more righteous to be able to condemn somebody they feel is even worse than they are themselves. He makes a pretty good scapegoat, you know. Apparently he's done all the things they'd like to do themselves — married a rich wife, done away with her when he hadn't any further use for her, and then gone off with a young, pretty woman. If they punish him, they can go home and rest easy that they've done their duty and really aren't such bad fellows after all. Then of course there's your riffraff too, the sort that only wants a little excitement and an excuse for violence —"

"Violence?" I said. "Then you think, even if he gets off —"

"I think, if he gets off, he'd better get out of Corioli as fast as he can and stay out till the next nine-day-wonder comes along." He must have seen how I looked, and stopped himself and smiled. "Don't look so worried," he said. "They've been talking Vigilance Committees around here for two or three years now and nothing's ever come of it. The only thing we have to worry about is that they'll talk loud enough this time to frighten the jury. I can buy a jury, but I can't buy a whole city, and this city happens to be the one where most of that jury has to live and do business."

"But why do you have to buy anybody?" I said. "Jed's innocent; can't you prove that? Can't you find the man who really killed Sallie?"

"I think I've already found him."

"You what?"

"And I can't prove he ever did anything more illegal than take that fifty dollars Sallie gave him to find out what hotel Jed was staying at," he went on. "All I've got is the way it smells to me —"

"The detective at the Phoenix? But if you're sure, there must be some way you can prove —"

He shook his head. "I'm as sure as I can be without any proof," he said, "but he's no amateur, you know. He knows

I haven't anything on him; he knows I never will have unless he does something foolish. And the police aren't even interested in him; they have their own man."

"Have you talked to them about it?"

"I've done what I could. But I've nothing concrete to give them; all I've got is the look of that fellow, the feel you get when you talk to him. Oh, it makes sense all right. He knew how much money Sallie had with her, and he'd have had no trouble getting into her room. Probably he hadn't any idea of killing her; he was only after the money. She may have surprised him, coming back into the room when he didn't expect her, and then he lost his head and strangled her — It's pure theorizing, of course; it might have happened in a dozen different ways. But the point is that, however it happened, I can't prove it ever happened at all. I can tell you one thing: it's going to be a lot easier for me to find twelve men who'll say Jed didn't kill Sallie than to find one who'll say William Barrow did."

I sat there listening to it. It was hard to believe that any-one could stand by and watch another man go in danger of his life for something he himself had done. I had to believe it. If it was not this man, it was someone else. Someone had killed Sallie and now it was Jed who was on trial instead of him.

"You must be able to do something," I said.

"I'll get Jed off. They won't hang him. That's all that matters, isn't it?"

"Yes."

"And you'll stay here like a good girl and not worry?" He got up. "I don't want to come here again till the trial is over."

"Couldn't I go to the trial?"

"You oughtn't to. Don't you care if you get yourself in trouble?" Then he looked at me and smiled and said: "All right. You can go one day. Go with Mrs. Wardman, and try to act like any other curious young woman who wants to see what a real murderer looks like in the flesh."

"Will you tell Jed I'll be there? What day will it be?"

"Make it Friday. The first novelty will have worn off by then; there won't be such a crowd."

"All right." I watched him put his coat on and start toward the door. "What does Mrs. Wardman know about this?" I asked.

"She knows enough. You needn't worry about her. She's a little on the dramatic side, but she's perfectly trustworthy. You should have seen her as Lady Macbeth."

He was trying to joke about it to make me feel better. I looked at him standing there by the door. I knew he was more worried than he wanted me to see. I was not going to think about that. He had said he would get Jed off, and that was enough. I said good night and told him I would be fine. He would see Jed and tell him he had seen me, and I wanted him to tell him I was all right. I did not want either of them to have anything more to worry about just now.

CHAPTER XXVI   Mrs. wardman went to the courthouse with me on Friday morning. It was a fine spring day after rain. The air was soft, and when we left the house we could see the buds beginning to open on the magnolia before the house across the street. It was early, and we walked up to the courthouse and saw on the way caricatures of Thomas Dandy and of the jury hung in the windows of the beer gardens and refreshment houses. On the wall of one building someone had drawn a dangling rope and printed a crude inscription beneath it: *Justice by you or justice from us.* Another wall had the words — *Dayton lives and justice dies* — scrawled boldly across it in white chalk. I tried not to look at them. I knew the sort of people that had put them there, people like Conn and the men he

drank with down at the *Crown of Life*. They were not the
jury, or the police, or the responsible element in the town. It
did not matter what they did.

The courthouse was an impressive-looking three-story
limestone building with Palladian windows and an arched
doorway. There was a crowd in the corridor outside the
courtroom where Jed's trial was being held, and when the
doors were opened we had a hard time getting a place inside. There were quite a number of well-dressed women
there, wearing veils, as we were, so we were not conspicuous.
We found some seats near the side of the room and sat
down. I was waiting for Jed to come in. Now that I was
here I felt worse than I had at any time except when
Mr. Lefebre had first told me about Jed's having been
arrested.

Mrs. Wardman leaned over and spoke to me. "Are you
all right?"

"Yes. It's this waiting —"

"They're coming in now."

I looked. Jed came in by a side door, men all around
him, and went over to sit at a table at the front of the
courtroom. I saw him glance around for me but I knew he
had not seen me in the crowd. He had not wanted to seem
to be looking for anyone because that might have drawn
attention to me. He was thinner and he looked different.
When he sat down at the table he might have been sitting
there alone in an empty room. The people around him were
busy getting ready for the opening of the session, and he could
not stop them, but he had nothing to do with them. They
might have been children playing some sort of game for all
the attention he paid them. I remembered what I had felt
about him when I had first met him, that he was alone because he wanted it that way — not because he was afraid of
people, but because he had seen their stupidity and cruelty
and had no use for them any more. He had tried to cover
over that feeling a little then, but now he was not trying to
cover it any more. I could see that it made people uncom-

fortable and resentful. They wanted him to be afraid, or
ashamed, or to swagger it out somehow so they could
admire him while they sent him to his death. Instead of
that he only sat there and ignored them.

The session began, and the judge asked the prosecuting
attorney to call his first witness. I looked at the judge. He
was a small, carelessly dressed old man with keen little
eyes and long untidy straight hair straggling behind his
ears. His name was Nicholas Dawes; the newspapers called
him Old Nick. Thomas Dandy said he was one of the few
completely honest men on the bench in Jefferson County. He
was not happy about having him on Jed's case.

The clerk called Barbara Mason's name. I saw her come
forward and take the witness stand. She had on a black
dress and hat and looked nervous and determined. I knew
what kind of testimony she would give. The prosecuting
attorney asked her her name and where she lived and how
long she had worked for the Daytons. She answered him in
a low, respectful voice. Her hands were clasped tightly over
her pocketbook in her lap. The prosecuting attorney,
Jacob Solms, a fashionably dressed, handsome man in his
late thirties with his hair parted in the middle and slightly
banged in the English style, spoke to her sympathetically.
I saw Thomas Dandy leaning forward with his arms folded
on the table where he sat beside Jed, watching and listening
with an alert, happy expression in his bright-blue eyes. He
did not seem disturbed as Barbara went on to tell about
the quarrels that Jed and Sallie had had.

"And it was after Captain Dayton met Miss Dereen that
these quarrels began?" Mr. Solms asked her.

"No, sir. Not began; he never treated her properly, as
long as I knew him. But they got much worse."

"Did you ever hear Captain Dayton say that he wished to
be free of his marriage?"

"Yes, sir."

"When was that?"

"The last time he came to Le Jeune, the day before Mrs.

Dayton was killed. I heard him tell Mrs. Dayton that he intended to have no more to do with her, and that she would have to divorce him."

"You were in the room when you heard this?"

"Yes, sir. He was so angry, he didn't seem to care who heard him. I'd come in when I heard him quarreling with Mrs. Dayton. It used to make her ill when they quarreled, and I always tried to take her away out of it if I could."

Jed did not look at her while she was speaking. He did not seem interested in any of it. He looked straight ahead all the while.

"On that same occasion did Captain Dayton tell his wife he was going to Corioli to see the Dereen woman?" the prosecuting attorney went on.

Barbara hesitated. "Not in so many words."

"But she knew that was what he was going to do?"

"Yes."

"And did she tell him nevertheless that, no matter what he did, she would not divorce him?"

"Yes. She did."

"So that Captain Dayton knew when he left Le Jeune that the only way he could be free of his marriage would be if his wife should die?"

"Yes, sir. She told him as plain as she could that she would never divorce him."

The questioning went on. The prosecuting attorney looked pleased with himself. Finally he sat down, wiping his lips with his handkerchief. I looked at the jury. They sat there stolidly in their box, a collection of twelve nondescript faces, ruddy and pale, mustached and clean-shaven. They all looked serious and uncomfortable. It was impossible to tell what they were thinking.

Thomas Dandy got up. He began talking to Barbara in that persuasive voice of his, asking her questions about her feelings toward Sallie. She answered him a little stiffly.

Yes, she said, she had always been fond of Mrs. Dayton.

She might have been fonder of her than a servant usually was of her mistress?

She might have been.

A great deal fonder?

You might say that. Mrs. Dayton had always been so kind, and she needed affection. She had certainly not gotten that from Captain Dayton.

Thomas Dandy considered a moment.

Perhaps, he suggested, Mrs. Dayton expected too much of a man with as many responsibilities as Captain Dayton? A great many busy men did not show their wives as much affection as the wives might wish.

No, she did not think that was it.

Did he neglect her in any other way, then? Fail to furnish her with a fine home, object to her extravagance, her indulgence in all the little luxuries she was fond of?

She couldn't say that.

As a matter of fact, wasn't it common knowledge in Le Jeune that Mrs. Dayton was indulged by her husband in every whim?

She supposed it might be.

She answered him grudgingly; the picture of the Daytons' marriage that he was drawing from her was not at all the one the prosecuting attorney had tried to suggest.

After that he went off on a different tack, bringing up examples of Sallie's notoriously flighty and indecisive behavior that Barbara had to admit were true. By the time he was finished she had acknowledged that Sallie's statement that she would never divorce Jed was hardly one he need have taken at its face value. The prosecuting attorney looked less happy. Barbara looked angry and upset. She had had to say a great many things she had not wanted to say. I was beginning to understand Thomas Dandy's legal reputation a little better. He had twisted Barbara's fondness for Sallie to look like bias, and then had maneuvered her, point by point, into subscribing to the picture he had drawn of Sallie as a spoiled, hysterical young woman. I remembered what he had said to me once, that the truth had nothing to do in a trial. All that was necessary was to make an impression on the jury. After listening to Barbara's testimony I understood what he had meant. Somewhere behind all those conflicting facts was the simple truth that Jed had not killed Sallie. All this other had nothing to do with that, really, and yet it was on that that he would be judged. It was like a terrible game, one of those parlor guessing-games in which all sorts of collateral evidence about an object can be given but the object itself can never be named. If the jury guessed right, Jed would be free. I did not want to think what would happen if they did not guess right.

The clerk was calling the next witness. I heard the name William Barrow and saw a very dark, round-faced, heavyset man of about forty walk up to the witness stand. It was the hotel detective at the Phoenix. He had been called to give testimony about the message Sallie had sent to Jed at the Sheffield House. While he spoke his dark, keen eyes moved knowingly around the courtroom. He spoke in a firm, rather rhetorical way, with an air of exaggerated consideration for both the prosecuting attorney and Thomas Dandy. There was nothing about him that would have made me think of him as a murderer.

The prosecuting attorney asked him if Sallie had seemed upset when she had given him the message for Jed. He cocked his head slightly to look up at the ceiling, as if to consider before he answered.

"Upset? Well, you might say more than that," he said. "She was in a real state. I knew something was real wrong about the whole thing. When I look back at it now, I blame myself for not keeping an eye on her afterward. I've had experience in that sort of thing, you know, the sort of thing that happens between married couples when one of them has a violent disposition —"

"Objection," Thomas Dandy said.

"Sustained," said the judge. "Mr. Solms, will you kindly instruct your witness to confine himself to facts?"

Mr. Solms bowed slightly to the judge and went on with his questions. I looked at William Barrow. It was almost impossible to believe that a man could sit there coolly making damaging insinuations under oath against some-one accused of a crime he himself had committed. There was nothing in his face except a proper seriousness. The eyes were a little too quick and knowing. That might have been it. The eyes were too careful. A few minutes later, when Thomas Dandy got up to cross-examine, I noticed that even more. Thomas Dandy asked him why he had been dismissed from the Pinkerton agency five years before, and while he was explaining it he looked up frequently at the ceiling with that sidewise, bright, considering glance.

It was not a very creditable story. He tried to put a good color on it, but in the end it turned out to have been little better than blackmail. I listened to Thomas Dandy question-ing him, and I realized he was trying to lead him into some statement that would indicate he knew something directly about Sallie's death. It was no good. The man was impudent and humble and wheedling and defiant, but he was never unguarded. All Thomas Dandy could prove was that he had a poor reputation. I watched him leave the stand and pass the table where Jed was sitting. He did not even look at Jed as he went by.

The next person to be called was the clerk at the Sheffield House to whom William Barrow had given Sallie's message. He was a slight, nervous young man who stammered as he told about giving the note to Jed and about Jed's having gone out immediately afterward. He was on the stand only a few minutes and then the clerk at the Phoenix Hotel was called. His testimony placed Jed positively at the Phoe-nix at six o'clock on the evening of Sallie's death, and one of the porters at the hotel was then called to tell of having seen Jed leave there a quarter of an hour later. There was nothing that Thomas Dandy could do against all this.

The men from the Phoenix had known Jed for years and they were positive they had seen him. The porter was not sure of the time he had left, but the clerk was sure of the time he had come because he himself had just been going off duty for supper. When their testimony was finished the prosecuting attorney had proved to the jury beyond doubt that it was possible for Jed to have killed Sallie.

The last witness called that morning was Conn Mulranny. He came up to the stand wearing his best clothes and carrying his derby in his hand, looking very much taken with his importance as a witness. I glanced around and saw Nora sitting over at the other side of the courtroom. She looked nervous, sitting on the edge of the chair. I supposed she would be the next witness to be called. I wanted to go over and speak to her, but I knew it wasn't possible. I was not angry with her any more. She had done the best she could for me, and it was not her fault that things had turned out as they had.

The prosecuting attorney had begun asking Conn about Jed's coming to the shop on Christmas Eve. As Conn told it, the story was quite different from what had really happened. Jed had attacked him without provocation, he said, when he had tried to keep me from going off with him. I knew Thomas Dandy would get the straight of that out, between him and Nora. Conn could not swear to the time; he thought it might have been half past six, or later. He told of Jed's having threatened him at the Belmont House the summer before.

" 'I'll come back and kill you myself'; those were his very words," he said. "As bloodthirsty as a Turk he was, and me only trying to protect a young lady against him. Sure he talked like he'd make no more of murdering me than you'd make of stepping out to your own kitchen for a spot of tea."

He was having a fine time, sitting there with his hat held jauntily in one hand, till Thomas Dandy took over the questioning. After that it was all quite different. He grew more and more uncertain of his answers and shouted them out angrily.

No, he said, he hadn't struck Jed first.

Perhaps he had tried to?

He didn't think he had tried to.

There were other witnesses who might remember it a little differently. He had better think before he answered; he was under oath.

He didn't know; perhaps he had tried to.

Very good. It might be said then that a proper version of the matter was that he had tried to strike Captain Dayton and Captain Dayton had defended himself. Had he any objection to that?

He didn't know that he had.

"Thank you," Thomas Dandy said. "And when he struck you in defending himself, Captain Dayton struck you on the mouth?"

"Yes."

"And in doing so cut his knuckles slightly on your teeth?"

"I don't know that he did."

"But it's quite possible that he might have?"

"I don't say he couldn't."

"The hand wasn't bandaged, wrapped in a handkerchief, anything like that, when he came into the shop?"

"Not that I noticed. It might have been. It might have been cut and not bandaged."

"But you didn't see that it was cut?"

"No."

"And he struck you with his right hand?"

"Yes."

"Don't you think it's likely, Mr. Mulranny, that Captain Dayton, who has been on the river since he was a boy, and knows how to use both hands in his own defense — his left, I understand, is as well thought of in certain circles as his right — would have struck you with his left hand if he had injured his right before coming to the shop?"

"I don't know."

"Oh, come now, Mr. Mulranny! You're not such a peaceable man yourself that you wouldn't have an opinion about a matter like that."

"Objection," Mr. Solms said.

"Sustained," the judge said. "The court is no more interested in this witness's opinions than it is in Mr. Barrow's, Mr. Dandy."

Thomas Dandy looked satisfied. He had made his point, and the jury had heard it. He went on questioning Conn. It was about his having tried to keep me from leaving the shop with Jed. I did not think he really hoped to gain anything in particular for Jed's case from it. As far as most people were concerned, it made no difference why I had gone off with Jed. I had done it, and that was all that mattered to them. But I was beginning to understand that Thomas Dandy never let a witness leave the stand till he had led him or cajoled him or tricked him into saying everything that might conceivably benefit his case. He was like a virtuoso who likes to display all his artistry in public.

He finished with Conn, and the judge decided to recess the court for lunch. It was twelve o'clock. I watched them taking Jed away. I stood up when he glanced around again over the courtroom as he had done when he had come in, and this time I knew he saw me and recognized me. He went on out of the courtroom. I could hear the hoots and groans of the spectators following him. Mrs. Wardman got up and looked at me.

"Shall we go?" she said.

"Yes."

I wanted to come back for the afternoon session, but I knew I should not. I had seen Jed; that was as much as I could hope for now. The trial could not last much longer. Another week, two at the most, and Jed would be free. We could go away and forget that all this had ever happened. I walked out of the courtroom into the spring noon sunshine. I was trying hard not to be afraid.

CHAPTER XXVII   THE TRIAL WENT ON ALL THE next week. I did not go back to the courthouse or see Thomas Dandy again, but the newspapers were carrying long accounts of the trial, so I could keep in touch with what was happening. There was nothing unexpected, only the steady parade of witnesses called by the state to reinforce every point of the case against Jed. When I read their testimony I realized that in spite of everything Thomas Dandy was doing there was still a terrific amount of evidence against Jed. The newspapers speculated openly that he would be hanged. There were scenes outside the courthouse almost every day now. The morning Jed took the stand at the opening of the case for the defense Judge Dawes had to threaten twice to clear the courtroom.

I knew that a great deal of Thomas Dandy's defense would have to rest on the impression Jed made on the witness stand. The newspaper accounts of his testimony frightened me. "Unfeeling," "arrogant," "unrepentant," were only a few of the words they used. The most conservative of them spoke of his "indifference" as showing "contempt for the judge, the jury, and the people of this state." I had nobody to talk to, and I tried to read through the accounts of the trial only once and then not think of them again. Mrs. Wardman never mentioned the trial to me, but once when Adelaide brought the papers in to us she made some remark to us about God's punishment falling on "that murderer they've got there in the jail."

"You go along and mind your own business, like a good girl," Mrs. Wardman said to her. "What do you know about murders? You'd spend your time a good deal better worrying about that burnt roast you served up to us last night."

She had been very kind to me, and I was grateful to her. She sat with me in the afternoons and told me long stories about the stage, and asked my advice about the fashions, and tried obviously to keep my mind off the trial. I was sleeping very badly, and sometimes when she heard me up in the night she would come upstairs and knock at my door and sit with me for a while. She said she had been used to late hours all her life, and that she liked an excuse to keep them now.

The trial ended on a Monday morning. When the evening papers came they carried the closing statements of Thomas Dandy and Mr. Solms, and the news that the jury had not yet reached a verdict. Now that it was over I knew that Jed had not really had a case at all. There was only his word and Thomas Dandy's skill against all the evidence against him. The only possible proof of his innocence would have been in finding real evidence of someone else's guilt.

We had dinner, and afterwards I sat downstairs with Mrs. Wardman. I did not want to be alone to think. Thomas Dandy had said he could buy a jury. He had won more hopeless cases than this before. I did not care how he did it, if only he did it. Oh God, let him do it this time, I prayed. Only this time. Only this once. Jed isn't guilty. Let him do it only this once.

It was raining outside. Mrs. Wardman had a new fashion magazine and was turning it over, commenting to me about the new styles in sleeves and skirts. All at once I heard someone come up the steps and ring the bell. Mrs. Wardman called out to Adelaide, who was in the kitchen, that she would go.

It was Thomas Dandy; I heard his voice in the hall. I got up and went out. He and Mrs. Wardman looked around at me.

"What is it?" I said. "Have they — ?"

He came over to me quickly. He had his handkerchief out, dabbing at his forehead.

"We'd better go upstairs," he said. "There's something

I'd like to talk over with you. You'll excuse us, Adah?" he said to Mrs. Wardman.

I went upstairs with him to my rooms. When I had closed the door behind us I turned around.

"What is it?" I said again.

"You'd better sit down."

He looked grim and angry, now that we were alone.

"Please," I said. "Please. You've got to tell me. It isn't —"

"No, no. Don't look like that; it isn't the worst they could have done. They've found him not guilty of murder in the first degree, but guilty of manslaughter. The pack of frightened fools —"

"Manslaughter?" I said. I didn't know what it would mean. "They won't hang him, then?"

"No. It's a crazy verdict. If they'd had any sense at all, they'd have let him go free or sent him to the gallows, one or the other, but they tried to straddle the fence instead. Something for the public, something for him. Oh, they didn't want to put their hands in their pockets empty, you know, but after they'd made their bargain they didn't have the guts to stick to it — Excuse me; I'm too mad right now to know what I'm saying."

I sat down; I had to. I didn't know how I felt because I didn't know yet how bad it was.

"What will happen to him?" I said.

He stopped pacing the floor and turned around.

"He'll get everything Dawes can give him with that verdict," he said. "The maximum sentence, twenty years. Oh, he hasn't been sentenced yet, of course, but I don't even have to wait to hear what it's going to be. Dawes called that verdict outrageous when the jury handed it to him this evening; he's going to be sitting up nights till he pronounces sentence, trying to find something else he can add to it."

I didn't say anything. I knew I ought to be thankful it wasn't any worse. But it wasn't good enough. You couldn't shut a man up for twenty years for something he hadn't done. I wouldn't believe it. I looked at Thomas Dandy.

"There must be something you can do," I said. "Can't you get him a new trial?"

"A new trial? Listen to me, if he asks for a new trial now he'll be committing suicide, that's what he'll be doing. Do you think I'd be able to put together another jury that wouldn't send him straight to the gallows on that evidence, after what's been happening in this city? Even if I could get a change of venue —" He stopped talking suddenly and sat down too. "I'm sorry, Lacey," he said. "I did the best I could."

I looked over at him, suddenly actually seeing him for the first time, and realized that the handkerchief with which he was dabbing at his forehead was stained with blood.

"What's happened to you?" I said. "Are you hurt?"

"It isn't anything. Somebody threw a rock at me as I came out of the courthouse this evening. One of the dissatisfied upholders of law and decency in this town —"

He spoke with strong irony. I got up and offered to tend to the wound.

"It isn't anything," he repeated. "I'll take care of it when I get home. Sit down. You need somebody to look after you, not the other way around."

I sat down, as he had told me. I suppose I did not believe it yet. I had heard the words, *twenty years,* but I could not take in what they meant.

"I did the best I could," Thomas Dandy said again. "Everything I knew —"

"I know you did. I'm not blaming you. There isn't anybody to blame, I suppose. But I can't bear it. I can't bear it to happen to him." I sat there. I could hear it raining outside. "What did he say?" I asked, after a little.

"Not very much. I don't think he expected anything better. He didn't want to talk about it."

"I've got to see him," I said.

"Not yet. That's one thing I did promise him, and that was to keep you out of this. You can't go to that jail now; I couldn't be responsible for what might happen to you. I'll take him any message you like."

"Tell him it wouldn't make any difference if it was a hundred years."

"I'll tell him."

I sat there. The first numbness was beginning to go off. I was beginning to think again.

"He won't stay there, you know," I said, after a minute.

"Where? In jail?"

"Wherever they send him. He couldn't. He couldn't live that way. They'll kill him or he'll get out. Other people have got out."

He didn't say anything.

"Tell him I'll go anywhere he goes," I said. "Wherever they send him, and after that."

"They'll send him to the state penitentiary at the capital after he's sentenced."

"All right. I'll go there. And anywhere else."

He was silent again.

"Will you tell him that?" I said.

"Yes, if you want me to. But if you want my advice —"

"Don't say it." I knew what he was going to say. "It won't do any good."

"You're a brave girl," he said.

"I'm not. I'm just like everybody else; I want to live. And I can't live without Jed."

"You can."

"I can stay alive. That's not the same."

He got up. "Well, I'm not beaten yet," he said. "As long as there's somebody walking around who did kill Sallie, we've always got a chance. I won't give up."

"Will you tell that to Jed? Tell him not to do anything foolish."

"I'll tell him."

"Tell him to wait. I know how he feels. He won't care about anything now. Tell him to wait, for my sake."

"Don't worry. He knows that right now he's safer in that jail than out of it. He won't do anything." I stood up and he took my hand. "I'll keep in touch with you," he said. "Nothing will happen till after he's sentenced."

"When will that be?"

"Later this week. Let me go home now and try to think this whole damned thing out. Oh, I've botched it this time —"

He was angry with himself still. It was not just for Jed and me; it was because he had not been able to do what he had always done before. I watched him go off down the stairs. In the hall below he spoke to Mrs. Wardman. I stood there, not listening, hearing the voices.

He left, and Mrs. Wardman came up the stairs. She saw me standing there on the upper landing.

"Are you all right?" she said.

"Yes."

I was not going to give way. I couldn't give way now. It was over, but it could never be over while Jed wasn't free, and I knew it, and knew I had to be all right if he should need me. I saw Mrs. Wardman looking at me.

"Let me sit with you," she said. "I promised him I wouldn't speak to you about it, but if you want me to —"

"No," I said. "I don't want to talk about it."

"All right. But you needn't be afraid. Thomas Dandy did a great favor for me once; I'd do anything in the world to pay him back. You wait and see; he'll manage this for you too."

She was being very kind. She had probably been through something like this once herself. It had turned out all right for her, and it would turn out all right for Jed too. I was going to believe that. I said I would come down and sit with her. It was better not to think of anything. I thought I might be able to keep from thinking if I was with somebody else.

CHAPTER XXVIII   THE NEXT DAY I READ ABOUT
the verdict in the papers. Nobody was satisfied. The jurors
had been threatened by a crowd outside the courthouse as
they had left it after reporting their verdict to Judge Dawes,
and had had to run away down back streets and alleys to
escape violence. Thomas Dandy had walked straight through
the crowd to his carriage, and had the mark to show for it
that I had seen the night before. There was talk of holding
a public meeting at the Exhibition Hall to protest the verdict and take steps to reform the jury system in the county.
According to the newspapers, half a dozen of the most prominent men in the city — two of them former mayors and
one a former governor — had agreed to lend their names to
this project. Disbarment proceedings against Thomas Dandy
were also being openly spoken of.

I did not know what was going to happen. Jed was to
be brought into court to be sentenced on Friday, and that
same evening was the time appointed for the public meeting at Exhibition Hall. I asked Thomas Dandy about it
when he came to see me again on Wednesday. He looked as
he had the night he had brought the news of the verdict to
me — energetic and grim. He glanced at the newspaper lying open on the table where I had left it, with its headlines
about the meeting at Exhibition Hall, and brought his hand
down on it angrily.

"The fools," he said. "They're playing with fire, and they
don't even know it. Call a mob together and think they can
satisfy it with pious speeches and civic resolutions — This is
their city; it's been run just the way they let it be run, and
now they've found out that people don't like it, they're trying to do something about it the easy way, standing on a platform and telling the world they don't like murder any more

than the next one. What they don't seem to realize is that
a mob is never satisfied with talk. If they had a sensible
sheriff in this town, he'd have every man jack of them arrested for inciting to riot the minute they set foot in that
hall."

"Riot?" I said. "But you don't think — they can't —"

"Yes," he said, "I do think, and I seem to be the only
man in this town who does. The rest of them won't start
doing it till they've walked over the edge of the cliff and
waked up at the bottom. Because if they call that meeting
there's going to be trouble, and if there's trouble God only
knows where it will end."

He would not sit down; he walked up and down in my
little parlor. I had never seen him so upset before. I sat
there, feeling the fear come.

"You think they'll try to take Jed?" I said.

"It's been done before. You can't tell about a mob. He
oughtn't to be here; they ought to get him out of town."

"But those people — the mayors, the governor — that isn't
what they want —"

"No. It isn't what they want. But it may be what they're
going to get." He struck his hands together suddenly. "Oh,
Christ, how can they be such blind fools!" he said. "As if
they had a town meeting about new water-rates on their
hands —"

I did not say anything. After a little I asked him: "Does
Jed know?"

"Yes. I told him what was going on. He wants you to get
out of town."

"I won't go."

"I didn't expect you would. I told him that too."

"You're not going," I said.

"No, I'm not going. By God, I never knew how
much Irish I had in me till this business began. I thought
I was a sensible man."

He looked at me with that bright, reckless expression in
his eyes. If it had been only for himself, I thought he

would almost have been enjoying it. I had known many men like that in Ireland. I asked him about the talk of his being disbarred.

"Oh, they'll go ahead with the proceedings, for all the good it will do them," he said. "Don't worry about that. I've got two answers for every question they can ask me."

I believed him. It was not that part of it he was worried about; it was Jed. He was going to try to have him moved out of the city before Friday night. I did not think he was hopeful of succeeding.

I did not tell him I was going to the meeting because at the time I myself did not know it. But when Friday evening came, and I sat at dinner with Mrs. Wardman, I knew I could not stay there quietly in the house to wait as I had waited through so many evenings before. Jed was still at the jail; Judge Dawes had sentenced him that morning to be confined in the state penitentiary at hard labor for twenty years, as Thomas Dandy had predicted, but he was not to be taken there till the following day. I sat at dinner, and I knew I could not stay there in the house, and I asked Mrs. Wardman to go with me to the Exhibition Hall.

She looked at me across the table.

"You shouldn't go there," she said. "What good will it do you to go there?"

"I don't know. If you don't want to go with me, I'll go alone."

"You can't do anything there. Stay here with me. I'll send Adelaide out for news later this evening."

"No." I stood up. "It's all right. I'll go alone."

I went upstairs. When I came down a few minutes later she was waiting for me in the hall, in a dark cloak and hat.

"You don't have to go," I said. "Really. I'll be all right."

"No, you won't. You're a very foolish girl, but I promised Mr. Dandy I'd look after you and so I'll go with you."

She looked serious but not angry. She had sent Adelaide out for a cab, and in a few minutes she came back with one and we went outside together. It was a cold overcast spring evening. The cab went slowly up the hill, then turned west in the direction of the Exhibition Hall. I looked out and saw the streets quiet at first, then, as we came nearer the Exhibition Hall, growing thick with men.

We got out before the hall and I glanced around. There was nothing disturbing. People were going quietly into the hall as they might have gone in for a concert or exhibition. Several groups of men in rough jackets and caps stood about at a little distance from the doors, but they looked uncomfortable and uncertain and were not going inside. There were a few women. I saw people looking at Mrs. Wardman and at me.

We went inside and found places at the top of the gallery, where we could see without being conspicuous. The hall was filling rapidly. Once we heard some sort of disturbance below, but the people before us stood up to watch and it was over quickly and we did not see what had gone on. We heard the men in front of us talking after they had sat down.

"What was it?"

"Some fools with a rope. Said we'd be needing it before the night was over."

"That's not the way. More violence, more killing — What we need in this town is a little law and justice."

Somebody laughed. "Can't say it wouldn't be justice, can you, if we gave Dayton a piece of that rope? You're a little particular about your justice, friend."

I knew how they were talking. You talked that way about something you would not do. You talked about it, and flattered yourself with your boldness, and that was all. I looked down at the stage. There was the committee filing out, black-coated, sober, respectable, paunched or spare. You could not associate them with violence of any sort. One of them stood up and began reading a prepared statement about the purpose of the meeting. There were many phrases like "civic virtue" and "corruption of the jury system" and "the responsibility of the law." It was like listening to a not very interesting lecture.

The speeches began. By this time the hall was completely filled and people were standing packed in the aisles. I knew there were seats for over four thousand people in the hall, and with those standing there would be almost twice that number inside. They were all listening quietly but without any appearance of enthusiasm to the speakers. There seemed to be no end of these; one after another of the distinguished citizens on the platform got up and spoke soberly and indignantly on the subject of the abuses of the jury system that had been practiced in the courts, and the necessity for reform. I saw that it was not what the crowd wanted, but still there was no disorder in the hall. When I looked around I saw faces with the strained, bored, uncomfortable look on them that they might have had listening to a dull sermon in a church. There was fidgeting and whispering and crossing and uncrossing of legs, but that was all. I began to breathe a little more easily. I thought that Thomas Dandy had been mistaken, and that there would be no trouble that night.

The speeches came to an end at last, and one of the ex-mayors of the city rose and began reading a series of resolutions to the meeting which he said he would ask it to adopt by a voice vote. The resolutions condemned the jury in the Dayton trial and set forth a number of proposed reforms in the method of the selection of jurors and the operation of the jury system. There was a roar of approval after the reading of each one, but I did not believe that half the people in the hall understood or cared what they were assenting to. They were bored and disappointed with the dullness of the evening and wanted to get it over with. Then the chairman of the committee got up again.

"My friends," he said, "this meeting is now closed. I ask each of you to go quietly to his home. You have come here tonight in the cause of justice. Go back to your homes now and you go in the knowledge that you have done what you could, as law-abiding citizens, to further that cause in our city."

I listened to him say it, and that was when I knew it for the first time. I knew for the first time that it was not over, and that he was afraid, and that I was afraid too. Because they had come for more than this. They had not come to be bored with dull speeches and high-sounding phrases; the very moderation in the tone of the meeting that the committee had counted on to restrain any tendency to violence had defeated its own purpose. I heard the dissatisfied mutterings around me.

"Hell, is this all?"

"Ain't that going to make Dayton sweat, sitting there nice and comfortable in that jail cell? — we went and passed a resolution against him."

"By God, if we had any guts we wouldn't be sitting here listening to no more talk. There's been plenty of talk. It don't need no more talk and just one piece of rope —"

I got up and pushed my way to the door and down the stairs. The stairs and corridors were jammed, people moving slowly, unwilling to leave. There was a low-toned, rather sullen murmur of talk, very slight for such a large crowd. At the foot of the stairs Mrs. Wardman took my arm.

"We'll never be able to get a cab here," she said. "We'll walk over to Chestnut Street —"

I turned my head and looked at her.

"I'm not going yet," I said.

"Don't be a fool." She grasped my arm; I knew that she was frightened too. It was something in the air, something you could almost smell and breathe. "You've seen everything you wanted to see. Nothing else will happen —"

"I can't go yet."

We moved slowly in the crowd to the outer doors of the Exhibition Hall. Standing at the top of the flight of steps leading to the street, I saw that the street itself was full of people who had apparently been waiting outside to hear what had happened in the hall. There were a few cries and jeers as they saw the crowd come filing out, but most of them simply stood there in a waiting silence. They were all waiting for something, standing there almost disinterestedly, like a herd of actors in a mob scene on a stage before the curtain has gone up. I stood beside the door and watched the crowd from the hall slowly merging with the crowd in the street. Nobody was leaving. There were thousands of people now in the street.

Mrs. Wardman took my arm again.

"You *must* come," she said. "We can't stay here; we've got to get away from here."

I looked at her and saw her face with the eyes dark and eager with the fear in them, and the cruelty of fear in them too.

"Go without me," I said.

"No. I promised —"

"Go without me."

I turned to look at the crowd again. At that instant I saw a figure appear suddenly above the crowd across the street, as if it were elevated on the fence railing before one of the houses there, and heard a voice cry thinly over the silent, densely packed street: "To the jail! Come on! We'll hang Dayton!"

The words hung there for a moment in the quiet night air, and then were swept away in a roar that seemed to come from every part of the crowd at once. Somebody went past me quickly, running down the steps to the street. I saw people running in the street. There were only a few at first. They ran south, in the direction of the jail. Then the whole street began to move, the pattern I had been looking down on, made by thousands of people standing there quietly under the gas lamps, suddenly breaking up and flowing like a great river in one direction. I started down the steps, but Mrs. Wardman held my arm still.

"Don't —" she said. "You fool, you fool —"

I pulled myself free and without looking back ran down

the steps. The courthouse and jail were more than half a
dozen blocks distant. There would be time to get Jed away;
there would have to be time. Or at least time to bring more
men to guard the jail. I joined the crowd that filled the
street and went on with them, they not running now because the way was too choked, but all hurrying as if they
would not lose a moment, now they had been told what
they were to do. There was no time to think. If I had stopped
for a moment I would have been pushed on from behind.
It was like being caught in the current of a river. Now and
then I heard cheers above the rush of boots on cobblestones,
and voices repeating faintly in the distance, at the head
of the line of march: "To the jail! To the jail! Give us
Dayton!"

As we turned the corner into Court Street I stumbled
and almost fell. A boy beside me grasped my arm and
jerked me to my feet. I saw him stare at me for a moment.
He was no more than sixteen or seventeen, a healthy-look-
ing, dark-haired boy with a friendly, earnest face.

"This ain't no place for you, miss," he said. "Here, you'd
better get out of this."

He stopped and tried to clear a space for me to reach the
steps of one of the houses along the way, but we were both
pushed on by the crowd, then swept apart by a new rush
from behind us. I heard him shouting something as I lost
sight of him behind a sea of heads. I felt a sudden hope,
and clung to the thought of that friendly, anxious face.
There must be faces like that all through the crowd. Faces
of decent, ordinary people. They would not do it or see it
done. I had to believe that. I had to. They would stop it
somehow. They would not stand by and see it done.

The crowd was stopping somewhere up ahead. There
were shouts and questions. Somebody said that there was a
lumberyard ahead, and that the leaders had stopped to take
some heavy pieces of timber from it so that they could
break down the doors of the jail. The crowd behind us
pushed on impatiently, leaving us so little space to stand

that we could not move. A man beside me swore: "Damn it, let's get on with it."

Nobody looked at anyone else. They pressed forward stubbornly against the crowd before us, and in a minute the block was broken and we were hurrying on again. I could see the courthouse now, up ahead. The jail was at the far side of the square, fronting on Henry Street. When it reached the courthouse the crowd surged around both sides of the building to join again before the jail on Henry Street. By the time I got there some of the leaders were already attacking the doors with the timbers they had taken from the lumberyard. I looked up at the windows of the jail. There was no one in sight. I could hear the heavy thud of the wood against the doors and the shouts from the crowd that was stirring excitedly and uneasily now that it could do nothing but stand waiting before the doors.

"Give us Dayton!"

"We'll give him what the jury wouldn't!"

"You paid the jury, Dayton, but you forgot to pay us."

"Give us Dayton! Give us Dayton!"

Somewhere behind, at the outer edge of the crowd, I could hear the ringing of fire-engine and police-patrol bells, but I knew they would not be able to get through the tightly packed mass of the crowd to the jail. The thousands that had started out from the Exhibition Hall had been joined by more along the way; I could not even guess how many they were now. The only hope I had to hold on to was that most of them seemed curious and uncertain rather than angry. A few had begun to throw bricks and stones at the windows of the jail, but all around me men were standing quietly, in the same strained, mindless sort of excitement and fascination I had seen in animals held near the place where one of their kind was being killed.

All at once a shout went up from the crowd ahead. The doors of the jail were giving way. I felt myself being pushed forward in a sudden rush from behind. I was close to the building now; I saw the tall limestone walls and the barred windows. The leaders were already inside the jail. Then abruptly there was a halt; the shouting continued from the outskirts of the crowd, but near the jail doors a silence came. Then I knew the men inside had met some kind of opposition, something that had brought them at least temporarily to a halt, and my heart began to beat again out of its fear.

We outside heard the explanations after a little, passing in low voices from mouth to mouth. It was the sheriff who had met the leaders inside with his deputies, all of them armed, all of them unwilling to fire, the sheriff said, but bound to fire if the safety of the prisoners upstairs in the cell block was threatened. He had sent for the militia, he went on, and he begged the crowd to disperse before they came. The men who had rushed in hot over the beaten-down doors stood there cold under the stare of a dozen loaded guns. There was muttering, but some of the fainter-hearted began to step back. None of them was sure of himself, or of any plan; none of them wanted, cold, to buy Jed's death at the price of his own. As the sheriff and the guards advanced, the men inside sullenly retreated. Finally the doors were closed again behind them.

"We're not done yet, though!" one of them shouted suddenly, out of the silence. "We'll get that son of a bitch and hang him high enough for Tom Dandy and that jury of his to get a good look at him the way they ought to left him themselves."

There was an answering shout from the crowd behind. The voice had spoken the truth; they were not finished yet. From back in the mob where the police patrols were trying to get through there was a growing confusion, stones flung, once a huge boulder, I heard it said, that had smashed the side of one of the patrol wagons, finally the sound of shots. Someone shouted that a boy had been killed, and I remembered the face of the boy who had spoken to me on the way and felt myself growing sick. But there were hundreds of boys in the crowd; it need not have been he.

And what had any of them bargained for, if they came to kill or to watch killing done?

There were shots being fired near the jail now too, and the rattle of bricks and stones against the walls and windows had become savage and incessant. All at once a burning plank sailed through the air and struck against one of the lower windows. I saw then that a small frame building in the courtyard of the jail had been set on fire; the flames leapt up quickly in the dark. At the same time a plank was being thrust from the pavement to one of the broken second-story windows of the jail, and men began clambering up it to gain entrance in that way. The crowd in front of the doors, taking courage from all this, gathered itself with a wild shout for another assault. Then all at once I knew it was going to happen; I knew it, and I was striking the man beside me with my fists, striking his shoulder, his chest, shouting in a voice that seemed to be torn out of my throat from no volition of my own: "Stop it! Stop it! Make them stop! Stop it! Oh God, make them stop!"

"Here," he said. "Here —" He was looking down at me in astonishment; I saw his slow, heavy, red-cheeked face hanging suspended over me like a face in a dream. "You want to get out of this, that's what you want. Here, Bill," he called, "help me get this young woman out of this."

He and a man near him placed themselves one on each side of me and thrust a way determinedly through the crowd.

"Oh, can't you stop them?" I said. "Can't you please try to stop them? Oh, for God's love, won't you try to stop them?"

I knew it would do no good but I could not stop. People stared at me; I saw their faces hang over me for a moment and then shift and change, always the same face with the mindless, fascinated excitement in it and the eyes that would not meet mine. Then I was over at the side of the street, against a building, bruised and shaken, and the man I had struck was calling to a young woman who stood a few paces away: "Look here now. Here's a young gal havin' hy-sterics. You goin' to look after her — ?"

I stood there, leaning against the wall, my face in my hands. The young woman came over and put her hand on my shoulder.

"I'm all right," I said. "Oh, please, won't somebody stop them? Won't somebody — ? Isn't there somebody who can stop them?"

"You've got yourself all excited," she said. "I wouldn't get that excited if they hanged every one of the bastards. He's got it coming to him, hasn't he?"

"No. No. No. He didn't do anything. He didn't kill her. Oh, my God, isn't there anything I can do to make them believe that?"

I looked at her. I knew what she was, but she was probably several years younger than I, not even out of her teens; she had a pretty, sullen, girlish face and dark-lashed blue eyes.

"Look here, do you know this Dayton?" she asked suddenly.

"Yes."

"Then you take my advice and keep quiet and get out of here." She glanced around. "You're not going to do any good here and you could get yourself in a lot of trouble."

"I don't care about that. I can't go. Oh, can't the police stop them? Can't somebody — ?"

There was a sudden yell from the crowd before us as the doors of the jail were forced open again. The confusion around the jail was so great now that it was hard to take in what was happening. The flames from the small building in the courtyard showed the whole front of the building in a red glare against the night sky, and everywhere the black moving swarms of men about it, hundreds of them, with more uncounted hundreds and thousands behind them, ready to take their places if they should fail. I couldn't watch it. I stood there with my face in my hands, hearing

the savage shouts of anger or satisfaction from the mob as
the advantage turned momentarily for or against them.
There was no way of knowing what was happening inside
the jail. After a little it began to be shouted around us
that the militia had come through the tunnel that led from
the courthouse to the jail, and that they were firing on the
mob inside.

"Oh, Holy Mary," I said, "let them get there in time.
Only let them get there in time. I'll do anything, only let
them get there in time. Oh, God in heaven, won't you let
them get there in time!"

"The dirty sons of bitches," the girl beside me said. "Look
at that now. Look at that. Give us the guns and we'll show
you we can do that too," she screamed suddenly, in a high,
shrill voice.

I looked around. A man was being carried through the
crowd, his bearers pushing a way before them, staggering
and swearing under their burden. I saw the blood that lay
in a great jagged spreading stain on the chest of the un-
conscious man. The bearers went on down the street and
into a drugstore that, after some shouting and delay, was
opened for them.

"Murderers. You're no better than murderers yourselves,"
other voices were shouting off at a distance, where I could
catch a glimpse of a patrol wagon in the midst of the swirl-
ing crowd.

I could feel the temper of the mob changing. It was not
uncertain or passive any more; it was determined and
savage and resentful. Some shots rang out near us, and
the girl beside me pulled me back sharply into the doorway.

"We ought to get out of here," she said.

"No. I've got to know —"

She looked at me. "Listen," she said, "don't make it any
harder for yourself. If you think they're going to let Dayton
sit there in that jail after all this —"

"I've got to know."

"You don't want to see it, do you? Stand here and watch them bring him out and string him up on one of those lamp-posts over there?"

"Don't. Don't."

"All right. But it can happen. Maybe they ought to be doing that to some of those filthy cops instead, but that's not the way they see it. And it's not going to do anybody any good if we get ourselves killed standing here watching it —"

She broke off as another louder shout rose from the crowd near the jail. The jail doors were being closed again, we heard; the militia had succeeded in driving out the mob that for the past half hour had been inside. The girl beside me reached out and stopped a man running by.

"What about Dayton?" she said.

"They got the son of a bitch. Tied a rope round his neck and hanged him out the window of his cell."

Another man, passing, shouted a contradiction: "The hell they did. He wasn't even there when they got in. Sheriff sent him off when he heard the ruckus."

A smaller, older man with a tobacco-stained stubble of beard shrieked furiously: "That's all a packet of lies! Cops passing that word around — want you to think they ain't no reason to keep on trying to get him. He's in there all right. Heard a fella that seen him himself. Sitting inside those jail bars, cool as a cucumber —"

"They got in, I tell you. They hanged him from a beam stuck out the window of his cell."

"Somebody said he got clean away."

"Got away? Hell's fire, how could he get away? There's ten thousand men here."

"And how many of us know what he looks like? Tall, thin, light-haired fella with brown eyes — Hell, there must be a couple of hundred around here tonight that would fit. He could be standing next to you right now and you'd never know it."

They went on, still arguing among themselves. I felt

as if a stone had been lifted from my chest. There was a chance then. He might have got away or been taken away. I had to believe it. I looked across the sea of heads at the walls of the jail, with the light of the burning outbuilding leaping against the sky. If he had got away, where would he go? Down to the river, to Thomas Dandy's house, to Martin Street, to me?

"You heard what they said," the girl beside me said. "You pay your money and you take your choice. Come on, let's get out of here. You're not going to find out anything here."

"All right."

I went with her. If he had got away, he might go to Martin Street. He knew where I was. I had to find out. We pushed our way through the crowd. Half a dozen times we were brought to a halt, or the crowd, surging back, flung us against the walls of a building. I had lost my hat and cape long before, and when we finally reached the edge of the throng I stopped, leaning against a wall, shivering in the cold and trying to get my breath. There was a saloon at the end of the street. All the lights were on, and there was a steady stream of customers going in and out. A pair of them came up to us as we stood there.

"Hello there, girls. Come to see the fun? Nice little hanging, all for free?"

The younger of them put his arm around the girl's waist and peered drunkenly into her face.

"Go on," she said. She pushed him off. "They may be serving fresh meat free up there, but not around here."

"Plenty of money, sister. Plenty of money."

He pulled a handful of coins and bills solemnly out of his pocket and held it out to her. The girl looked at it and then at me.

"Go on," she said. "Get out of here."

"Wha's a matter with your friend? Need 'nother girl for my friend." He clutched at my arm.

"Let her go," the girl said. "She's got troubles enough tonight." She looked at me again. "Good luck," she said.

"Are you sure you're all right?"

"Never better."

"We'll have a little drink first," the drunken man said. "Then we'll go and hang Jed Dayton. Pleasure before business, I always say."

I ran off down the street. A few blocks farther on a crowd of a hundred or so men was trying to break into a gun shop; I heard the crash of breaking glass. They were too busy with what they were doing to notice me, and I turned the corner, hearing the shouts of the mob still behind me and the occasional rattle of gunfire.

Farther on still the street was quiet, all the houses tight-shut, with no lights showing. There was no one in sight. I stopped once and tried to think if I ought to go to Thomas Dandy's house on Sevier Street instead of to my own rooms on Martin Street. There was no way to know. When I stopped I could feel my heart beating heavily and my knees trembling with weariness, and I knew I had to go on or I would be sick in the street. It was not far now; I was almost there. Maybe I did not want to get there because then I would be certain Jed was not there. He might be still at the jail; he might be dead. I was not even going to think about that. If he was not at Martin Street I would go over to Sevier Street at once.

CHAPTER XXIX   COMING DOWN MARTIN STREET toward Mrs. Wardman's house I saw nobody. The street looked perfectly still under the night sky. There was a gas lamp just across the street from the house, but the side of the house I was approaching, which ran along Francis

Street, was in deep shadow. As I crossed Francis Street and came along the walk beside the iron fence I saw something move back there. I opened the gate quickly and went inside and around to the side of the house where I had seen the movement. It was Jed. For a moment I couldn't believe it. The whole earth rocked under me. I put my arms around him and clung to him.

"Oh Jed, darling," I said. "Oh, darling, darling, oh, you're safe, you're here —"

I was laughing and crying at the same time. He held me and kissed me, but I felt him move sharply as I touched him and I knew he was hurt.

"What is it?" I said.

"I don't know. I think I've smashed half my damn ribs. It's all right. Lacey, Lacey —"

"You can't. You're hurt. Oh, darling, are you hurt badly?"

"It's all right. If I had a drink — I can't even breathe with those damn things driving through me."

I looked at him. Even in the dark I could tell I would have to get him inside. He could not go anywhere now.

"I'll take you up to my rooms," I said. I glanced back at the house; it was dark. "I don't think there's anyone up, but I'll go in first and see. Can you go around to the back door? I think it will be safer if you go in the back way."

"Who is in the house?"

"Only Mrs. Wardman and her girl. The girl is on the third floor; Mrs. Wardman lives on the first. She's a friend of Thomas Dandy's; I think she might help us. Oh, darling, you're here, with me; I can't believe it. I've got to get hold of myself —"

"Lacey —"

"Don't, darling. Don't you care that you're hurting yourself? I'll get you inside; I'll take care of you."

"Can you do it without anyone knowing? Because if you can't, I'll have to go on —"

"You can't go on this way. I'll be very careful. Go around to the back, darling, and I'll let you in."

"All right."

He started back. I went quickly to the front door and let myself in as quietly as I could. But I had hardly closed the door behind me when I heard Mrs. Wardman's voice from her bedroom.

"Moira?"

"Yes."

I went to her bedroom door, which gave on the hall.

"Come in," she said.

She was lighting a lamp. I saw her looking at me, at my disheveled hair and torn dress.

"What's happened to you?" she asked.

"I'm all right. I don't want to talk about it."

"Is it over?"

"I don't know. I came away."

She came over to me. "You'd better let me get you something," she said. "There's some brandy in the dining room —"

"No." I was afraid to tell her about Jed. I thought she might help us, but I was afraid. "Go back to bed," I said. "I'm all right."

"You ought to take something. You look terrible. Let me get you a glass of brandy."

"I'll get it myself."

"Let me —"

"No. Please. I'd rather be alone."

I had to get rid of her. I saw her standing there in the doorway looking at me, and for a moment I was sick with the fear that something in my manner had betrayed me. But after that moment she only said good night and gave me the lamp to light my way and went into her room again and closed the door.

I went back to the dining room and got the brandy from the sideboard and then, leaving the lamp there, went very quietly to the kitchen and unlocked and opened the door. Jed moved out of the shadow of the trellis that stood beside it in the back yard.

"Is it all right?"

"Yes. She's awake, but she's in her room. You'll have to be quiet, darling. Come this way, up the back stairs, and I'll go up the front and let you in."

He started up the narrow back stairs in the dark. I went back to the hall, past Mrs. Wardman's door, and upstairs to my own rooms. Jed was in the upper hall when I opened my bedroom door. I let him in and looked at him in the light. His face was gray and he stood there swaying a little, clutching his chest. I helped him over to the bed.

"Oh, darling, you're hurt badly," I said. "What happened? What did they do to you?"

He lay there for a moment without answering, his eyes closed. Then he opened them again and I saw the bleak, absolute hatred in them, he not seeing me now, seeing something else that was there in front of him as if it were happening again at that moment.

"Tommy Dandy told me what they might do," he said. "But I didn't believe it till I saw the first dozen of them come along the corridor with that beam. My God, the thing I thought first was that they were afraid. You could smell it on them — afraid of what they were going to do, and sweating, looking in every cell they passed and thinking maybe they wouldn't find me, somebody else would, and they'd only have to watch what they were afraid to do. Only somebody else there was afraid too — Jerry Burns, in the cell across from mine — and he called out to them that I was their man, they didn't want him, he had nothing to do with it —"

"Don't, darling," I said. "Don't think about it."

"So they had to find me then," he went on, as if I hadn't spoken, "and there were a lot more of them by that time, and they were beginning to enjoy it. They started to work on that cell door, and I sat there and waited for them to get through with it; if I'd had the key I'd have opened the door for them myself. Just to get it over with, just so I wouldn't have had to listen to them and see them and wait for them — And I was glad that when they finally got in they didn't even stop to take breath; they broke out the bars in the window with that beam, and I saw them tying one end of the rope to it, so I knew they weren't going to wait either to take me outside. It's very quick and simple, you see; you tie one end of a rope to a beam and another to a man's neck, and throw the man out the window —"

"Oh, don't," I said. "Don't —"

"Only I didn't wait for them to do it," he said; "I went out that way first myself. They were busy tying the rope to the beam, and half a dozen of them arguing about the knot, and I reckon none of them figured I wouldn't wait for them, with that window three full stories up, even if the bars were out of it then. I just dove through; there wasn't time to get down the best way; it was any way I could. And it was all right; there was some kind of flagpole, something out there that broke my fall, and half my damn ribs too, when I crashed into it, and the crowd was all around at the other side of the jail, so none of them knew what was going on. By the time they did I was in the crowd too, just like anybody else, out to hang Jed Dayton, and then I got through it and out of it and made it down here —"

He stopped, closing his eyes again.

"Don't think about it," I said. "Please, darling, don't ever think about it again. I can't think about it."

"All right. There's no use in thinking about it. I've got to think about getting away. Have you got anything to drink up here?"

"I've brought some brandy. I'll get it for you."

I poured it into a glass. My hand shook so that I spilled half of it as I carried it over to the bed.

"I'll get you some more," I said.

"All right."

I helped him sit up on the bed to drink it.

"What are we going to do?" I said. "You ought to have a doctor. You can't go anywhere like this."

"I can go anywhere I have to go to get away. I'll have to have money, though. Have you any here?"

"Only about fifty dollars. I can get more tomorrow, from Thomas Dandy."

"It would be better if you got it tonight. Could you go there?"

"Yes. But you ought to have a doctor too. You've got to have a doctor."

"Not if it means taking the chance of going back there." I saw the way he looked when he talked about it. "I've had three months of that, locked up like an animal in a cage. If I had to take twenty years of it I'd go crazy and really would kill someone."

"You won't have to go back. I'll go to see Thomas Dandy; he'll know a way you can get out of the country till they find out who really did kill Sallie. But, darling, you have to have a doctor first. I don't know what to do for you; you may be hurt badly —"

"I'm all right. I'm damn lightheaded, that's all. I've got to get out of here in a hurry, before this town settles down again and they really start looking for me. Have you got any more of that brandy?"

"Yes. But maybe you oughtn't to have it —"

"Give it to me. By God, I've got to be able to think straight now. What day is this?"

"Friday the twenty-eighth. Don't you remember? You were in court this morning —"

"That was a couple of weeks ago." He drank the brandy and then said: "All right, it's Friday the twenty-eighth. Tomorrow at five the *Fair Maid* leaves for New Orleans. Tell Tommy to get word to Captain Dix. If he can hold the *Maid* here long enough so it'll be dark when he leaves, he can stop and pick me up somewhere a few miles out of town. They'll be looking for me down at the levee, but if I can get out of town —"

"I'll tell him."

"And tell him I've got to have some money. All the cash he can get his hands on. And somebody he can trust to drive me out of town."

"You keep saying 'me.' I'm going with you."

"No. You can join me afterward. I'll send for you."

"Darling, you can't go anywhere alone this way. I'm going with you. I'm not going to lose you again." He started to say something. "No," I said. "I won't listen. I'm going to see Mr. Dandy now. Will you be all right while I'm gone?"

"Will your landlady come up?"

"I don't think so. If she does, she'll think I'm asleep. I think you'll be safe here, darling. Nobody knows who I am except Mrs. Wardman, and tomorrow I'll say I'm not feeling well and have my meals brought up to my sitting room so we'll have something to eat. I won't let anyone come in here."

I went over to the closet and found a shawl and threw it over my head.

"I don't like your going over there alone," Jed said.

"There isn't anything else to do. It's not far, and the crowd won't be down here."

"You were up there, weren't you? — at the jail?"

"I had to go."

"Were they looking for me when you left?"

"I don't think so. Nobody seemed to know what had happened. They said you'd been taken away, or that you'd got away, or that you were dead —"

"I'm not dead yet."

"Don't joke about it, darling."

"All right." He looked at me. "Come here before you go." I went over to him.

"Darling, don't," I said. "You're hurting yourself."

"I almost went crazy there in that jail without you."

"I know. They wouldn't let me come to see you."

"I didn't want you to come. I didn't want you to be mixed up in this."

"I'm mixed up in anything you're mixed up in."

There was a clock striking somewhere.

"I'll have to go," I said. "Promise me you'll be careful while I'm gone."

"All right."

"I'll go out the back way. I don't want to wake Mrs. Wardman again."

I kissed him again and went out to the hall and down the stairs quietly in the dark. I did not hear anything, and I thought it was all right, but when I opened the door that led into the kitchen I saw that there was a light somewhere in the front of the house. Before I could go back Mrs. Wardman came into the kitchen. She had on a dressing gown and was carrying a lamp. I saw her look at my shawl.

"Where are you going?" she asked.

I made up the lie quickly. "Out for news. I couldn't sleep."

She did not believe me. I looked at her face and I saw the fear and the determination in it, and I knew she did not believe me.

"Don't lie to me," she said. "Is Captain Dayton here, in my house?"

"What do you mean?" I said.

I could feel myself growing cold, but I still believed that I might trust her and that she would help us.

"Don't be a fool," she said strongly. "You can't lie about it so anybody would believe you. I can see it in your face."

"Please —" I said. I knew I had to trust her now. "He's hurt. You've got to let him stay. It's only till we can find a way to get him out of the city. Nobody will know —"

She set the lamp on the table.

"I can't," she said. "Don't you see I can't? It won't be safe for any of us if they find him here."

"They won't find him. Nobody knows I'm here but you

and Thomas Dandy. They'll never think of looking for him here."

She shook her head. "No," she said again. "I told you I'd do anything in the world for Thomas Dandy, but I can't have that man in my house. Suppose somebody out of that mob saw him come in here? And there's Adelaide. Do you think you could keep it from her that he's up there in your rooms?"

"Only for one day," I said. "Only till tomorrow evening."

"No."

I saw the cruelty of fear in her eyes that I had seen there earlier that night, at the Exhibition Hall, and I knew it was no use. I could not blame her. It was not her affair, and she was really terrified of what might happen.

"All right," I said. "But you'll give me time to go to Thomas Dandy and make some arrangement for taking him away? I'm going there now."

"How long will it take?"

"Not more than an hour or so. I'll come back as quickly as I can. He can't go with me; he can't walk through the streets the way he is. I don't know how he ever got down here — Promise me you'll let him stay till I get back."

"I'll let him stay that long. But he must go tonight."

I looked at her. "Will you swear you won't call the police while I'm gone?"

"I won't call them."

"Because I think I could kill you myself if you did," I said. "I won't let anyone hurt him any more."

"I won't call them," she said again.

I had to believe her. There wasn't anything else to do. I opened the kitchen door and went out. It was not far to Thomas Dandy's house. He had to be there and tell me what to do. I began to run down the dark quiet street.

CHAPTER XXX   I DID NOT MEET ANYONE TILL I came to Sevier Street, though I heard distant shouting and the sound of gunfire as I ran, and knew that the trouble at the jail had not yet ended. But when I came near the Dandy house I saw several men standing in the street and two more behind the gate, beside the iron dog on the lawn. For a moment I was afraid that some of the mob had come down here to find Thomas Dandy, but they were only standing quietly about, and then I realized they were his own men whom he had stationed there in case it should happen as I had thought.

I went on up the walk toward the house. One of the men called out to me to ask me what I wanted, and when I said I had to see Mr. Dandy he went to the door with me and knocked and called. Another man opened the door after a moment.

"Who is it?" he said.

"It's a young woman says she wants to see Mr. Dandy."

"Tell her to come in," Thomas Dandy's voice called out from the parlor.

I went inside and crossed the hall to the parlor door. Thomas Dandy was standing before the mantel.

"What is it, Lacey?" he said. "My God, girl, where have you been? You weren't in that mob tonight?"

"Yes," I said. "It's all right. Close the door." He went over and closed it. "It's Jed," I said. "He's at my place, and he's hurt; we've got to get him away —"

"Wait a minute, wait a minute," he said. I saw the light coming into his eyes. "You mean he got away? He actually got away?" I nodded. "Oh, Holy Mother," he said. "That's the best piece of news I've heard in ten years. Oh, he's the jewel of a boy to give them the slip just when they thought they had him, law or no law and lawyers or no lawyers. How did he do it?"

"He jumped out a window," I said, "and I'm afraid he's hurt himself badly. Can't you get a doctor for him? Somebody you can trust? He doesn't want one, but I know he needs one, only he won't take the chance of being sent back to prison."

Thomas Dandy struck his forehead with the palm of his hand. He looked more excited and more cheerful than I had ever seen him.

"Don't worry," he said. "Don't worry. Sit down; leave it to me. If I'm going to be called up before that Bar Association, I might as well add 'aiding a criminal to escape' to the list of the rest of my sins that they're going to have to throw at me. He'll need money first, of course."

"Yes." I told him about Jed's plan. "But he can't stay at Mrs. Wardman's till tomorrow evening," I said. "She knows he's there, and she won't let him stay."

"The hell she won't," he said. "What did you offer her?"

"Offer her?"

"Money, girl, money. When you come to the end of what people will do for you for love, or friendship, or human kindness, or any of the other noble motives, you offer them money, and I'm sorry to say that it usually works. In Adah's case I know it'll work, if Jed's prepared to make the figure high enough."

"Oh, anything," I said. "Anything. It doesn't matter. But if she won't, even with that — ?"

"She will." He went over to a secretary standing at the other side of the room, pulled out some letter paper, and sat down to write, talking to me all the while. "I've known Adah for a good many years," he said; "she's a fine woman, and she's also very fond of money. It's an unfortunate fact that most women are. My aunt Margaret is a splendid example. She wasn't nearly so set against my taking Jed's case when she found out how much I was going to get out of it."

"Where is she now?" I said.

"Don't worry. She won't see you here. She's out of town. I've battened down all the hatches for the storm, if that's the proper nautical terminology."

"Do you think they'll come here?"

"They may." He glanced over his shoulder at me cheerfully. "Since they couldn't hang Jed, they may think of me as an acceptable substitute. But it's beginning to look as if they'd settled for the police and the militia instead." He folded the sheet of paper, put it into an envelope, and handed it to me. "Give that to Adah when you get back," he said. "I think you'll find it will make a marvelous change in her point of view. And now about that doctor — How badly is Jed hurt? Any broken bones?"

"It's his chest — his ribs, he thinks. I don't know what else. He struck against something when he jumped."

"He'll have to travel, you know; there's no way we can keep him hidden here in the city for any length of time. Is he bad enough that he'd be better off settling for twenty years than taking his chances with what might happen to him trying to get away?"

"I don't know. But he won't go back. I know he won't go back. I couldn't make him."

He shrugged his shoulders. "Well, we'll get him a doctor. It won't be one who's in good standing with the Medical Association, you understand, and there'll be another sizable bit of money that'll have to change hands, but I'll do what I can."

"Tonight?"

"Yes. Tell Jed I'll take care of the rest of it too — arranging it for him to meet the *Fair Maid* somewhere out of town. There'll be no problem there. Tell him to be ready to leave the house tomorrow sometime just after dark."

"I'm going with him, you know," I said.

He looked at me. "Does he want you to?"

"No. But he can't travel alone, and there's no one else."

He shook his head. "It's going to be risky," he said.

"There's no guarantee the *Fair Maid* can get down to New Orleans without being searched. And even if he makes it, he still has to get out of the country. Is he going to Mexico?"

"I don't know. Wouldn't that be the best place?"

"It'd probably be the easiest. I suppose he can trust Captain Menary?"

"Yes."

"Well, he may make it. He's got an even chance. If the luck he's had tonight holds, he's got a better than even chance. Tell him I'll take care of everything — clothes, money, the carriage, Captain Menary. I'll let you have as much cash as I can tonight, in case anything comes up, but there'll be more tomorrow." He took a number of bills from his wallet. "It's a lucky thing for Jed he's a rich man," he said. Then he looked at me and said: "I mean rich in more than one way, too."

"He has friends like you and Captain Menary," I said.

"By God, I am his friend. I'm the friend of any man who can get away from a mob like that. Are you going now?"

"Yes. I have to get back."

"I'll have that doctor there inside of an hour. You'd better be on the lookout for him. I'll send one of my men home with you now. I'm all rigged out here with a regular comic-opera army."

"I'd rather go alone. I'd rather nobody knew where I live."

"All right. Then you'd better get some rest. You look as if you'd had hell's own time of it tonight."

"I'll be all right." I stopped beside the door. "I can't thank you, you know," I said. "There aren't enough words."

"You don't need to. I'm doing this for my own satisfaction as much as for you and Jed."

I believed him. He was having a splendid time managing it all, and he was absolutely heedless of any risk there was in it for him. He opened the door for me and I left the house. I knew I had to get back quickly, before Mrs. Wardman began to regret the promise she had made to me.

The house on Martin Street was dark when I let myself in, but as I stood in the hall a lamp was lighted almost immediately in the parlor. I went in. Mrs. Wardman, bending over the lamp on the table, glanced around at me.

"Have you made your arrangements?" she said.

"Yes."

I handed her Thomas Dandy's note and she took it, looking at me distrustfully, and opened it and read it. I watched her face. She was reading it again. Finally she raised her eyes and looked at me.

"Five thousand dollars," she said. She said it as if she did not believe it.

"Yes."

She was silent for a moment, holding the paper in her hand.

"How do I know — ?" she said. "If he leaves town —"

"Mr. Dandy has his power of attorney. Don't you trust his word?"

"I trust Thomas Dandy." She stood there, weighing it, weighing her fear against the money. "All right," she said then. "Till tomorrow evening. I'll risk it. But only till tomorrow evening."

"That's all the time we need. There'll be a carriage to take him away as soon as it's dark."

I was sorry for her. She was ashamed of her terror and ashamed of her greed. She stood there looking at me with that in her eyes.

"I'm sorry," she said. "I wanted to help you —"

Without the money, she wanted to say. But she had taken the money. I did not want to blame her. It did not matter as long as Jed was safe.

"It's all right," I said.

"Is there anything I can do for him while he's here?"

"You can bring our meals upstairs tomorrow. Tell Adelaide I'm ill. We'll be very quiet; we won't do anything to make her suspect. And one thing more. Thomas Dandy is sending a doctor, someone he can trust. He should be here very shortly. Will you watch for him and let him in when he comes?"

"Is he sure he can trust him?"

"Yes, he's sure." *For money,* I could have said, *as he's sure of you.* But I did not say it. I did not care why they helped Jed as long as they did it.

I went upstairs. Jed was up, waiting beside the door.

"You shouldn't be up," I said.

He put his arms around me. "I heard somebody coming. I wasn't sure it was you. Are you all right?"

"Yes. Everything's all right. Come back and lie down again and I'll tell you about it."

We went into the bedroom.

"Mr. Dandy's sending a doctor," I said. "Don't look like that, darling; it's all right. It's someone he knows won't give you away. I'm afraid it's going to cost you a great deal to have him, and to stay here till tomorrow evening, but I think you'll be safe now. Mr. Dandy sent a note offering Mrs. Wardman five thousand dollars in your name to keep you here."

"I don't care if he offered her every cent I've got. It'll be worth it if I can get away."

"That's what I told him. You're to stay here till tomorrow evening, and then he'll send a carriage to take you out of town to someplace where you can meet the *Fair Maid.* He said he'd take care of everything. He was really splendid about it."

"He's all right. I hope it doesn't make any trouble for him."

"I don't think it will. All we all have to do is to be very careful. We mustn't talk so much, you know, darling — even whispering like this. Adelaide is upstairs, and she mustn't know you're here."

"I don't have to talk as long as you're here with me."

"I can't believe it yet."

"Neither can I. I think I went off for a minute, lying here a little while ago, and thought I was back in that damn cell again."

I looked at him. There were big drops of sweat standing out on his forehead from the exertion of getting up and walking to the door and back again. I sat there beside him on the bed and prayed for the doctor to come quickly.

It was almost half an hour before he came. I was listening for the footsteps or I would not have heard them on the stairs. I went to the door and let him in. He was a small man in a dark, threadbare coat and a carefully brushed hat. There was something wooden and frightened and unclean about him, and he had the nervous, unsure movements of a temporarily sober drunkard. I did not like to trust Jed to him, but I knew Thomas Dandy had done the best he could.

He convolved his lips at me, whispering, almost without sound: "Where is he?"

"In there."

I showed him to the bedroom and he tiptoed inside, indicating with a nod of his head that I should remain in the next room. I sat down — I was so tired by now that I could hardly stand — and waited. I did not know how much time passed. Then the doctor was in the room again, without my having heard him come. I stood up.

"How is he?" I said.

He shook his head. "It's hard to say yet. Several of the ribs are badly fractured, and there are possible internal injuries — He should certainly be in bed, and under a doctor's care."

I stood there. "What do you mean?" I said. We were both whispering. There was only a little light that came through the half-open door to the bedroom. "How bad would it be if he had to travel?"

"It would be very dangerous."

"But if it's absolutely necessary?"

He repeated: "It would be dangerous. He should be per-

fectly quiet. I couldn't be responsible." He looked at me
with his nervous eyes that would not meet mine for more
than an instant. "Of course I understand the situation," he
said. "And if the exertion isn't too great, if he is very careful, he may —"

"He'll be very careful. Isn't there something you can do
for him?"

"I'll do what I can."

I was more frightened than I had been since I had been
at the jail. I could try to make Jed stay here, to take his
chances on being discovered and sent back to prison. He
could not stay here, in this house. That was more than Mrs.
Wardman had bargained for — perhaps weeks of having him
here. Once he was on the *Fair Maid* he could be quiet,
and if he could go no farther than New Orleans it would
be infinitely safer for him there than it was here.

"Did you tell him the truth?" I said. "Exactly what you
told me?"

"Yes."

"And he still wants to go?"

"Yes."

I had known he would. The doctor went back into the
bedroom, and I waited again, and after a while he was
back.

"I've given him something for the pain," he said. "He'll
be able to rest now. He ought to rest."

"I'll see that he does."

"And as soon as possible you must get him someplace
where he can see another doctor and remain under care.
In the meantime, he must be quiet."

He went downstairs again, tiptoeing in the dark. I could
see he was very frightened and very glad to get away. I
did not know whether he really had done all that could be
done for Jed, or whether he was right about his condition.
We had to take his word; there was no other way. I went
back into the bedroom. Jed was lying on the bed with his
eyes closed.

"How are you, darling?" I said.

He opened his eyes. "I didn't want that pill peddler to put me out, but I was getting queer in the head anyway with those damn things driving into me every time I breathed. You'd better get some sleep too."

"I will."

He looked at me. "We've had some fine luck, haven't we?" he said.

"Don't think about it, darling. We'll really have some one of these days. We'll go to Mexico or South America and be married and live happily ever after."

"We're married now. We're better than married."

"Yes."

"I used to worry about that in that damn jail," he said. "About you. If we'd known, we could have been married that night in Charleville. Then if anything happened to me you'd be taken care of."

"Nothing is going to happen to you. Don't try to talk any more, darling. The doctor said you ought to rest."

I was crying. All that night I had not cried, but now I could not keep the tears back. I got up from the bed and went over to the dressing table and began to take the pins from my hair. I did not want Jed to see that I was crying.

CHAPTER XXXI   THE NEXT MORNING JED SLEPT late under the sedative the doctor had given him, and all the rest of the day I sat there with him in the still room, we not talking except in whispers, hearing the sounds in the street outside and waiting for the sunlight to fade and gray into darkness. Mrs. Wardman came up at mealtimes with a tray. She brought the newspapers too, and I read about what had happened at the jail. The mob had not dispersed till three o'clock, and before that had happened there had

been five men killed and almost fifty wounded. Even with
Jed gone, there was a general belief that the trouble was
not over. The resentment of the rioters had turned against
the police and the militia, and there had been open threats
of another attack on the jail that night. The governor had
offered to send militia from other parts of the state, and
the sheriff had accepted the offer.

As for Jed, the speculation was that he was still hiding
somewhere in the city. Thomas Dandy's house had been
searched by the police during the morning, and there was
a watch kept on all departing packets and railway trains.
One report said that Jed was thought to have crossed the
river in a small boat during the night, and the towns on the
south side of the river had been alerted in case he should
try to take a boat or a train from there.

Mrs. Wardman took the precaution of letting Adelaide
have the evening off, and as soon as it began to grow dark
she sat downstairs in the parlor to watch for the carriage
that Thomas Dandy was to send. I had packed a bag with
my things; we were all ready to leave. It was a cool night,
with a light mist coming up from the river as it grew dark.
Sitting there waiting in the quiet house, I could hear some
disturbance off in the streets to the north, and I knew that
the mob was gathering again. It seemed to make no difference to them that Jed was not at the jail any more. It
was probably revenge they wanted now because they had
been fired on by the militia and the police. I did not know
where it would end. All I knew was that they must not
find Jed. I sat there watching the darkness fall and waiting
for the sound of the carriage in the street.

It was past eight when it came. I saw it out the window,
and Jed and I started down the stairs and met Mrs. Wardman coming up.

"It's here," she said.

"Yes. We're coming." I said to Jed: "Let me go out first
and see if it's all right."

I went on outside while he waited in the hall. The car-

riage was standing at the curb. I recognized the driver as
one of the men I had seen at Thomas Dandy's house the
night before.

"Is it all right?" I asked him.

"All set, ma'am."

There was nobody in the street. I went back to get Jed.
Mrs. Wardman was still in the hall when I came in. She
stood there looking at me.

"Are you going?" she said.

"Yes."

She wanted to say something to me — perhaps the same
thing she had not been able to say the night before. But
she was afraid; she would not do anything to stop our going.

"Good-by," I said. "And thank you for everything you've
done."

"I've done nothing."

She did not look at Jed. She stood at the door and closed
it behind us as we went down the steps. We got into the
carriage.

"You must drive carefully," I said to the driver. "He's hurt.
Do you understand? You must drive as slowly as you can
and still get there in time."

"I'm all right," Jed said. He asked the driver: "Where are
you taking us?"

"Little place down the river, Newton's Ferry. Know it?"

"Yes."

"The *Maid*'ll pick you up just west of there. There's a
coat and hat on the seat, and a bag on the floor. Mr. Dandy
said you'd find everything you need in there."

I opened the bag. There were clean shirts and linen inside, shaving things, on top an envelope with money in it.

"He's been very thorough," I said. "We should do beautifully with all this, darling."

"We'll be all right."

"When we get out of this we ought to erect a statue to
him somewhere."

"I'll do better than that. I'll name a packet after him."

"I never thought of there being steamboats in South America. Won't it be splendid if you're master of a packet on the Amazon River? It sounds like something out of the Arabian Nights."

"Your geography is a little off, isn't it? Arabia's a few thousand miles from South America."

"Yes, but I never was much good at geography, darling."

I suppose we were both a little lightheaded with the relief of being actually on our way. I turned around to look back at the city we were leaving. There was a red glare in the sky to the north, where the jail and the courthouse were. I remembered the night before and turned away quickly. I did not want to see any more.

"What is it?" Jed asked.

"I don't want to think about it."

He called to the driver: "What's going on at the jail?"

"Looks like they set the courthouse on fire. Barricades been up all day in front of the jail, but I reckon the sheriff never figured they'd start on the courthouse. This town's gone crazy, and that's a fact. I can remember the jail riot here in '48, when I was just a shaver, but it wasn't anything to what's going on now."

I sat there holding Jed's hand in the darkness of the carriage. It was all right; he was here, and we were going away. I wished the carriage did not have to go so slowly. We might miss the *Maid*. We could not miss the *Maid*. Captain Dix would find some excuse to hold her there for us if we were not on time. In a few hours we would be safely on our way down the river.

We drove for what seemed a long time. I knew Jed was in pain with the motion of the carriage, and after a little we did not talk any more but sat in silence, waiting for it to come to an end. Finally we rattled through the streets of a little village that the driver said was Newton's Ferry, and then turned off down a steep rough road that led to the river. At the foot of it the driver stopped the carriage and got down to look for the *Fair Maid*. He came back in a minute to report.

"No sight of her yet."

"What time were we to meet her?" Jed asked.

"Quarter past ten. It's nearly that now. Don't worry; she'll be here."

I sat there and thought what would happen if she did not come. We could get the driver to take us on farther, to the nearest town, and try to get a boat or a train from there. They would probably be watching for Jed there just as they were in Corioli. And he could not go about as if there were nothing the matter with him. The doctor had said he ought to be quiet. I could see how pale he was looking even after the short trip he had had. The minutes went by.

"What if she doesn't come?" I said. I couldn't stop saying it any longer.

"She'll come," Jed said.

"Mister, she better come," the driver said emphatically. "They're looking for you in every town up and down this river. If she doesn't come, you better get you some good ideas about what you're going to do next."

I couldn't sit there in the carriage any longer. I got out and walked down to the river. There was a white, milky fog, but not heavy enough to make a boat lay up. I could hear the lap and suck of the water against the shore. The river was high. All at once I heard something else, and saw the lights of a packet looming through the mist. I ran back to the carriage.

"She's here," I said. "I can't see her, but it must be the *Maid*."

The driver made a flare with a match and a newspaper and waved it slowly, in a wide arc, over his head. I helped Jed out of the carriage. The boat was turning toward the shore; in a matter of minutes she had touched her bow in the willows at the foot of the road and the landing stage was being lowered. The driver brought our bags. I saw a man coming quickly down the gangplank.

"That you, Captain Jed?"

"Hello, Frank."

"I'll take those bags. My God, it's good to see you. You come right along. Captain Dix's got you in Number 14."

The gangplank was already up behind us and the *Fair Maid* was moving slowly away from the shore. We went up the steps to the passenger quarters. Captain Dix met us at the top.

"You all right, Jed?" he said.

"I'm all right."

"Come on. Get inside. We'll talk then."

He went into the stateroom with us and closed the door behind us.

"You look like hell," he said to Jed. "What's the matter with you?"

"Couple of broken ribs."

"It looks like more than that to me. You'd better lay down. You want a drink?"

"I could do with one."

"I told Frank to bring some whisky. Nobody but him and me and Billy knows who we were taking aboard just now. You can trust most of those boys, but one of them might drop the wrong word to a passenger by mistake."

He was uneasy; I saw it in his face. He had hardly noticed me. He had always liked me, but I thought he blamed me now for what had happened to Jed. I did not mind how he felt about me as long as he took care of Jed. Frank came to the door with the whisky and Captain Dix brought it in and poured a drink for Jed.

"Boy, you really look bad," he said. "I could kill those sons of bitches myself. Anybody crazy enough to think you'd murder Sallie —"

"I'm glad somebody didn't believe it," Jed said.

"There isn't anybody on this river that believed it. You're all right as long as you're out here. It's when we hit land that I'm worried about."

"You're worried now," I said. "What is it?"

I had to have it out. I had to know. He looked at me.

"All right," he said. "No use trying to keep it from either one of you. The chances are you'll have to get off this boat tonight. I couldn't get word to you in time or I'd have kept you from coming at all. The *Maid* was searched from engine room to pilothouse before she left Corioli, and the word's around that the same thing's going to happen when we get to Charleville."

I sat down. It was all no use then; we were even worse off than we had been at Mrs. Wardman's.

"What are we going to do?" I said.

"You've got two or three choices. I can transfer you to another boat, but you'd be a hell of a lot less safe there than you'd be here; it only needs one mouth to blab and you're done. And it won't be just on the *Maid* they'll be looking for you tonight; they probably figured you'd try the river. Or I could land you at any town along the way where there's a railroad, and you could try to make it that way, or hole up somewhere in a hotel. That's just about as risky. These are all small towns, and there are people who know Jed in every one of them, all the way up and down the river —"

"We can't hole up anywhere," Jed said. "I'm not going to sit down someplace and wait for them to take me."

"But you can't travel like that either, darling," I said. "Running from one place to another — You know what the doctor said." I looked at Captain Dix. "He's got to be quiet," I said. "He's got to. Isn't there somewhere — ?"

"There's one place," Captain Dix said. "It's a hell of an idea, but I reckon you'd be safer there than you would be anywhere else in the whole damn country." He turned to Jed. "We passed Nate Parraday and half a dozen other shantyboaters laid up around Twinville on our way up-river," he said. "If Nate'd take you in, you could go on down the river with him and we could pick you up wherever we ran into you our next trip down. By that time they

ought to be tired of looking for you on Corioli packets, anyway that far down-river."

"It's an idea all right," Jed said. He was thinking about
it.

"But wouldn't they give you away?" I asked. "Go to the
police — ?"

"Shantyboaters?" Captain Dix said. "You don't need to
worry about that." He said to Jed: "As long as they'd take
you in — Nobody'd look for you there, and you'd be on the
move all the time, so nobody'd have the chance to get curious."

"It's worth trying," Jed said. He glanced over at me. "Not
for you, though, Lacey," he said. "You stay here on the
Maid and go on down to New Orleans. I can meet you
there."

"I'm going with you," I said.

"You're not going to find any staterooms like this on a
shantyboat," Captain Dix said.

"It doesn't make any difference. I'm going with Jed." I
looked at Jed. "You can't stop me," I said, "so please don't
try."

"You don't know what you're getting into."

"I don't care. I'll be with you."

"Do you want to try it, then?" Captain Dix asked Jed.

"Yes. What time is it now? About a quarter to eleven? We
ought to get down around Twinville about five then. It'll
still be dark enough for you to put us off."

"I'll put you off all right. I'll send Frank over first to make
a deal. Have you got enough money?"

"I've got plenty of money. Don't worry."

"I am worrying. I'm worrying plenty."

"It won't do any good," Jed said. "I've got a good chance.
It's a fine idea."

"It might be a fine idea if you weren't in the shape you're
in. You'd better get some sleep now. I'll call you in plenty
of time."

He went out and left us alone. I went over and sat down on the bed beside Jed.

"Will it really be all right, darling?" I asked him.

"Yes, I think so. It won't be very pleasant for you, but I think we'll be safe."

"That's all that matters. But I wish we could stay here, for your sake." He took my hand to draw me toward him and I bent forward and laid my head on the pillow beside his. "Oh, darling, do you think there'll ever be anyplace we can stay?" I said.

"There'll be someplace. There'll have to be someplace."

"On the Amazon River? I wish we were on the Amazon River. I don't think they'd ever find us there."

"They'll never find us."

"I want to believe that."

"They'll never find us."

"I'll pretend we're there now. I'll pretend we're on our own boat on the Amazon River."

CHAPTER XXXII   MUCH LATER, BEFORE THE FIRST dawn had begun to come, Captain Dix returned to tell us that we were near the shantyboats. We left the stateroom and went down with him to the lower deck of the *Maid*. I could hear the water very close beneath us and see the hills beside the river as darker masses looming through the mist. The boat was turning in toward the shore. A few minutes later the landing stage was lowered and Frank, the mate, went ashore alone while we waited. There was a creek or small river that came in here, and the shantyboats, they said, were tied up in the slack water there, but I could not see them in the darkness. We waited in silence. I could hear a dog barking thinly in the distance, but that was all.

In ten minutes or so Frank came back. We went forward with Captain Dix to meet him.

"Is it all right?" Captain Dix asked.

"Yes, I think so." They spoke in low voices so that the sound, which would carry far across the water, would not be heard. "I talked to Nate, promised him two hundred dollars, the way you told me. He said he'd do it for Captain Jed anyway, but you can't ever tell about those sons of bitches. I told him the money was in it too. He's safe enough, I think."

"What about the others?"

"You know what Nate says goes with them. Hell, they got nothing to lose. They're going down-river anyway. And Captain Jed's done them many a favor, towing those shantys of theirs upstream when a lot of pilots just as soon run them down as not."

"All right, then," Jed said. "We'd better get started."

He turned and shook hands with Captain Dix.

"We'll look for you on the up-river run," Captain Dix said. "If everything isn't all right then, give us a hail."

"It'll be all right."

"Is there anything else I can do?"

"I don't think so. Thanks for everything."

Frank was carrying our bags down the gangplank. We said good-by to Captain Dix and followed him. It was too dark to see more than a few steps before us. After a little I saw a light through the willows, and a few minutes later I made out a line of dark objects ahead. It was the shanty-boats. A man came out to meet us, carrying a lantern. In its dim moving light I saw a long, cavernously thin face and a pair of bright dark eyes.

"Mornin', Captain Jed," he said. "You better git right inside. We'll start off down-river soon as it's light."

"You take good care of them now, Nate," Frank said. "If you don't, Captain Dix'll run down every one of your damn boats next time he catches you on the river."

"Don't you worry," the man said. "Long as they got nothin' against catfish and cornshucks, they're goin' to eat and lie like a king."

Frank said good-by, and we went aboard the first shanty-boat in the line. I looked around in the dim light of the lantern. There was a single room, divided in two by a rough burlap curtain, with a wooden table, a stove, and a few boxes that apparently served as chairs, in the nearer part. Beyond the curtain, which was only partly drawn, I saw two children sleeping in a small low bed and a woman who was doing something to a larger bed in the corner.

"That's my old woman," Nate said. "Sukey —" She came out. She was probably not much more than thirty, but she had a passive, weather-beaten face and a frail, overworn figure. "You look after Captain Jed and the lady," Nate said. "I'm goin' to have a little talk with the rest of the boys."

The woman looked at us. I knew when her eyes met mine that she was afraid to have us on the boat, but she said her welcome in a decent way and went back to the far part of the boat to finish preparing a place for us there.

"Nate says you-all can have this room," she said. "I'll git the young ones and their bed out in a minute."

"But where will you sleep?" I said.

"Put a mattress on the floor out yonder."

"Don't wake the children now."

They were girls, the older not five, both reddish-fair like the mother.

"Time they were up anyway. It's near light."

She shook the children awake and they sat up, staring at Jed and me.

"What are their names?" I said.

"Prissy and Allifair. Go on now, you. Get out of there."

She finished tidying the place in a discouraged way. Nate came back.

"We're all ready to start," he said. He grinned at Jed. "She ain't the *Fair Maid*, is she, Cap? But she'll stay afloat and keep the rain off your hide; you can say that much for her."

"That's good enough," Jed said.

He was very pale again after the exertion of coming from the *Fair Maid*. Nate looked at him.

"What those fellas do to you up there in Corioli?" he asked curiously. "You look mighty poorly."

"Just a fall. I got downstairs the quick way instead of the easy way."

Nate grinned again. "With a passel of folks hellin' after you with a rope they didn't git to use?"

"That's about it."

"They'd ought to known better. I seen you near kill a man in a fair fight, eight, ten years ago, when you was still on the *Indian Queen*, but they'd ought to known you wouldn't kill no woman."

"Well, they didn't know."

"You'll git away," Nate said confidently. "If I had a boat like the *Fair Maid*, I wouldn't ever want to lose her, but you'll git away with your skin anyway. And the way I look at it, you can git you another boat, but you can't ever git you another skin."

I didn't know how they could joke about it. Anything might happen still. Somebody on the *Fair Maid* might have seen Jed get off here, and inform the authorities at the next landing. I wanted the boats to begin moving. It was getting light; I could see the dawn coming through the crazy patched glass of the window.

Nate went out again, and the woman went into the other part of the boat to prepare breakfast. Jed lay down on the bed.

"How do you feel, darling?" I said.

"I'm all right. I'd be all right if it wasn't for you. This is a rotten place to bring you."

"I don't mind it at all. I don't mind anything as long as you're safe."

"I'm safe here. I'm just worried about you."

"You mustn't. Really you mustn't. I'm not somebody like Sallie, you know, who doesn't know what it's like not to have everything clean and comfortable around her. I've stayed in cottages in Ireland that were no better than this."

He looked at me. "You've had enough trouble in your life. Now I'm making you more."

"You didn't make it, darling. It's just something that happened to us."

"That's what I used to think. But you sit in a jail cell for three months with nothing to do but try to figure out why you're there, and sometimes you get a different idea. It's like you do one thing wrong in your life and there's something that won't ever let anything come right for you again. Do you know what I mean? If I hadn't married Sallie, none of this would ever have happened."

"If you hadn't married Sallie, I might never have met you. I can't help it, darling; it doesn't seem to matter any more about its being wrong or right. We've done the best we could, and if we've done wrong we've been punished for it. But they can't ever stop me from being glad that we love each other."

There was a sudden lurch of the boat; we had begun to move. I sat there on the bed beside Jed and felt the water take us, the feel of the land left behind and only the small isolated world of the boat remaining.

"You mustn't blame yourself, you know, darling," I said.

"I shouldn't have said anything."

"Yes. You should have. You should have told me before this. I don't want you to worry about anything alone. I don't want anything to happen to you that doesn't happen to me."

"I wasn't really alone. Even in that jail. We're never alone any more."

"I know. They can't make us go away from each other."

We couldn't talk any more; the woman was coming in with some food for us. I got up and looked out the window and saw the river all around us, a sheet of pure light under the gray sky. The boat felt very small. The river was high, and I could see the current running strongly. It was going to be a splendid spring day.

CHAPTER XXXIII   IT WAS A STRANGE WEEK WE lived through after that. We had our small sanctuary behind the burlap curtain, and all day I sat there with Jed and heard the clamor of the children outside and Nate's voice discoursing endlessly with one or another of the shantyboaters and felt the boat rocking clumsily in the current as we drifted slowly downstream. The weather was always marvelous, except for the sudden showers that came up sometimes at morning or evening. I would go out on the little porch of the shantyboat for a breath of air, and it would seem as if the world did not exist except for the small cabin behind me where Jed lay and the river flowing on between the faint new green of the hills. Even the hills and the towns that we passed were not real any more, and I would look at the green mist of the trees reflected in the darker green of the water and think the reflection was no more a dream or an illusion than the actual trees that had given it to me out of their own reality.

At night we lay up somewhere in a cove in the willows, sometimes near a town, and once Nate brought us a day-old newspaper with a piece in it that said the police were working on information that Jed had been seen in a small up-river town, booking passage on a Memphis packet. Corioli was quiet after three days of rioting and the arrival of soldiers from all over the state, but the courthouse had been completely destroyed by fire the night we had left, and before the trouble was over fifty men had been killed and three hundred more wounded.

It all seemed very long ago. I could not believe it had really happened. I would sit in the dim little room and watch Jed lying there with his eyes closed and tell myself it had never happened. I wanted to forget it. I did not want to hate them. It was too much to have to carry around with you for the rest of your life. If Jed was all right and we got away I could forget it. He seemed better; the pain was less now as long as he lay still. I had been frightened by the way he had looked the night we had had to leave the *Fair Maid*, but now that he could be quiet I thought it would be all right till we got to New Orleans and could see another doctor.

We were alone all the time, except when the woman brought us our meals or when Nate came in to talk to Jed about where we were and how far we had come. The first day there had been a steady procession of men, women, and children who had come from the other shantyboats to stare for a moment at us through the half-drawn curtain, the men pausing to say good morning to Jed, the women and children only standing there silently. But after that first morning they had left us alone, and I knew that their aloofness was not consideration, but hostility or fear. I saw it there daily in the woman's eyes, and sometimes at night I could hear her whispering to Nate from the other side of the curtain, remonstrating with him, it seemed, till he turned angrily on the cornshuck mattress and told her to be still.

"Will they go to the police?" I asked Jed once. We were talking in the morning, just after the boats had been set adrift on the river after the night's halt. It was early; the last of the sunrise was still on the water outside. "Captain Dix said, only one mouth —"

"No. They don't want anything to do with the police. We're safe as far as that goes."

"What could they do, then?"

"They won't do anything. They don't want us here, but they won't do anything."

I could hear the voices of the woman and the children outside as they called across the water to someone on one of the other shantyboats.

"We're like lepers," I said. "Nobody wants to come near us."

"It won't always be this way."

"I know that, darling. I wouldn't even mind it, if we were safe. I'm always happiest when we're alone. Only I'm still afraid. You told me once it didn't do any good to be afraid."

"It doesn't."

"I know. But I am. I'm afraid of people."

"You'd better be afraid of the river," Jed said. "In this collection of junk they call a boat —"

"You're not worried about it, are you, darling?"

"I'm not worried, but I'm not happy about it either. They say God looks after fools and children, but I don't know who it is that looks after shantyboaters. By rights they ought all to have been killed off a long time before this. They're so damn careless; everything's too damn much trouble for them."

"They're like the lilies of the field," I said. "I'm beginning to feel a little like that myself. There doesn't seem to be anything to do here but just wait and take what happens to you. Fortunately not much seems to happen except the weather, and it's been such splendid weather."

"It won't last. Not at this time of year."

"It's the time of year we first met each other, darling. I always thought spring was a cruel time until then. It's so lovely, it makes you want things you're afraid can't possibly exist, and then it turns cold and wet again, and you know they don't exist and you're never going to have them. It wasn't till I met you that I found out they really do exist and that we can have them when we're together."

"We haven't had very much," he said.

"We've had everything."

"For two days, there in Charleville. Now with me here in
this bed like this —"

I went over and stood by the window, looking out. The
sun was fully risen now, and I could see the water all glancing light under it.

"Come over here," Jed said after a minute.

I came and sat down beside him on the bed.

"You mustn't pay any attention to what I say," he said.
"I'm just so much in love with you I get a little crazy
sometimes."

"You wouldn't have done it any differently, would you,
darling?" I said. "Even if you'd known?"

"You know better than to ask that. I wouldn't do it any
differently if I had to die for it tomorrow."

"You're not going to die. We're going to have a fine life
together. We'll go to South America, and some day we'll
be able to come back here and you'll have the *Fair Maid*
again and everything will be splendid."

"We always have a fine life when we're together. It
doesn't make any difference where we are."

We were together behind a burlap curtain in a foul little
cabin that smelled of fish and tobacco and kerosene and
the stale ancient emanation of flesh, and it was true, and we
did not ask for more because we knew how much less we
could be given. I sat there beside Jed. We had the whole
long day before us. I was not going to think about anything
after that.

CHAPTER XXXIV   THE NEXT EVENING WE TIED UP
for the night along a sandbar thick with young cottonwoods. We had had another fine warm day, the days suddenly longer now in the coming spring, and I stood at the
window and watched the men making the lines of the boats

fast to the trees outside and seeing the land strangely close and fixed and alien after the endlessly moving panorama of the river. It was just after sunset; there were robins and cardinals calling in the long dusk, and the sky was still rose and green in the west. After a little Nate came in from outside and pushed aside the burlap curtain.

"Snug for the night," he said. He looked at us, surveying the two of us, the room, with his beady dark eyes. "And snug enough in here, too," he said. "Danged if your young lady ain't fixed this place up better'n my old woman ever got round to doin', Captain Jed. Looks like a shame to put in all that work when you'll be goin' back to the *Fair Maid* in such a short time. If you do go back —"

"What does that mean?" Jed said. " '*If* we go back —' "

Nate gestured. "Nothin'. Boys was talkin'. Wondered if you figured it was safe to leave here now. Some of them's gittin' nervous. They're still talkin' about you every place we hit land."

"Don't worry," Jed said. "We're going. They're not going to keep searching packets all the way from Corioli to New Orleans that long." He glanced toward the window. "Where are we now? About two miles above Procter's Landing, isn't it?"

Nate grinned. He looked relieved.

"You been out of that bed, Captain Jed," he said, "or can you just lay there and smell where you are on the river? That's where we are, all right. Current's runnin' mighty good; we'll be down on the Mississip' in another day or so."

"We'll be down there before that if you don't get this boat made fast to something a little solider than a couple of young cottonwoods out there on that bar," Jed said. "This weather's not going to last forever, you know. You and the boys've been snubbing a couple of lines around the first thing handy that looks like it'll still be standing there the next morning, and then you'll wonder what happened when a blow strikes some night and you end up wrong side up in the middle of the river."

Nate shrugged his shoulders. "Ain't ever happened yet," he said.

"It's happened to plenty of other shantyboats. You ought to know that."

"Sure, and plenty other shantyboats got run down by steamboats, and cut down by ice, and ripped down-river in a flood. A man starts worryin' about all them things, and he ends up livin' in his coffin all his life because it's safer'n walkin' around takin' his chances like ordinary folks." He grinned again. "You worry about the *Fair Maid*, Cap," he said, "and let me worry about this yere boat of mine."

It was time for supper, and he went out to the other part of the boat. I went over and sat on the bed beside Jed.

"What is it, darling?" I said.

"It's this damn weather. It's bound to break. It's bad enough trying to ride out a storm in one of these rat-traps if you haven't tied her up like a careless ten-year-old."

"But nothing's happened to them yet. You oughtn't to worry about it. You're not used to being quiet like this, and it makes you worry about things you wouldn't worry about if you were up and around."

"You're damn right I wouldn't worry about them if I was up and around. I'd be out there myself and see that everything was all right." Then he stopped and looked at me and took my hand. "You poor sweet," he said. "You have a rotten enough time without my taking it out on you."

"You weren't. I know just how you feel. You're used to doing everything you want to, or to being able to make other people do it for you."

"I haven't been doing much of that lately."

"You will be. It won't be so long now."

"All I really want is to make you love me."

"You don't have to make me. I do already."

He did not say anything.

"Why do you, really, though?" he said after a while. "Sometimes I get damned afraid you won't."

"I don't know why, darling. It's just the way I am. But you mustn't ever be afraid I'll stop."

"All right. I won't. Come down here now."

"I can't. We're going to have supper. Later I will. Later we'll do anything you want."

The woman brought our meal in. It was stifling that evening in the narrow, almost airless boat, and she drew the curtain aside and left it so while we ate. In the other part of the boat one of the children cried fretfully and Nate and the woman bickered in low, resentful tones over their food. A black mongrel nosed restlessly about the table, waiting for his meal to come. I could hear the voices of some of the other shantyboaters who had already finished their suppers and gone outside to try to find cooler air. After a while Nate and the woman and children went outside too.

"You oughtn't to stay in here either," Jed said. "Go on out for a while and get some fresh air."

"I'd rather stay here with you."

"You see. I can't even make you do a little thing like that."

"You don't really want me to."

"No. I don't want you to, but I'd like you to do it."

"All right. I'll go. But only for a few minutes."

I went outside. It was dark now, but you could still see the last faint color in the sky reflected in the water. The air was very still and the river was calm. I thought Jed had been mistaken about the weather.

Later, inside the boat, after the others had gone to bed, neither of us slept. It was very late when I finally dropped off, and it seemed to me that I had been asleep only a short time when I felt Jed's hand on my shoulder, wakening me.

"Lacey," he said. "Get Nate awake and tell him to get out there and look at those lines. Do you hear me? Now."

I opened my eyes. There was a bright flicker of lightning

in the room, and at the same moment I realized that the boat was swinging rhythmically back and forth, striking the shore with a heavy thud at each forward lurch.

"What is it?" I said.

"Don't talk. Get Nate up."

I stumbled to my feet in the rocking boat. Now that I was a little more awake I could hear the wind and the rain outside. I threw a shawl around me and started toward the curtain, but at the same instant the boat gave a violent lurch beneath me and swung around sharply.

"One of those damn lines gone," Jed said. He shouted: "Nate!"

I pushed aside the curtain; in the wavering glare of the lightning I could see Nate and the woman on the mattress on the floor, both asleep. I bent over and shook him. The boat was swinging wildly now; I could hardly keep my footing on the heaving floor.

"Let be," Nate muttered angrily, half-asleep.

"There's a storm," I said. "Please. You've got to wake up —"

The woman sat up; one of the children began to cry. I heard Jed up now; he came out.

"You crazy fool," he said to Nate. "Get out there to those lines. One of them's ripped loose already —"

In the middle of the sentence there was a sudden violent wrench and the boat lumbered crazily round, free now altogether, it seemed, of the shore. I could feel the current begin to take it. Nate jumped up, suddenly wide awake, and leapt through the door to the small deck outside. The lightning flashed again and I saw Jed following him.

"Jed —" I said. "Don't. You can't —"

The woman had run outside too, leaving the children wailing behind her on the tossing floor. I could feel the boat being carried out into the river, lurching heavily as the waves struck against her. I went to the door and stood there, clutching it for balance and trying to see what was happening. The dark water seemed to be boiling up all around the

boat; I caught a glimpse of trees bending fiercely on the
shore through the driving rain. There was a dark figure
forward and another at the stern of the boat, struggling
with oars.

"Jed," I called again. "You can't — Tell me what to do
and I'll do it —"

"Git back inside, you tarnation fool," Nate shouted at me.
"You want to end up in the river?"

"But he mustn't — He can't —"

"Let him be, I tell you, or we'll all be drowned. You
think one man can get this boat back to shore alone?"

I looked at the frail woman trying desperately to help
steer the boat toward the land with a plank snatched up
from the deck. The wind struck again and the boat went
down sideways into the trough of a wave; I felt the water
pour over my feet. I clung to the door. The younger child,
staggering across the floor inside, was flung against the
door frame and half stunned as her head struck the splin-
tering wood. I carried her inside. There was a sharp cut
on her head that was bleeding profusely. The older child
was crying in terror.

"Hush," I said. "Hush."

I went back and found a towel and tried to stanch the
blood from the wound on the smaller child's head. I sat on
the floor, on the mattress, and held her in my lap and felt
the blood hot and wet through the wad of cloth. Through
the howl of the wind I could hear Jed's voice as he shouted
something to Nate. I knew he ought not to be out there; I
remembered what the doctor had said. If he had not gone
out we might all have been drowned. We might all be
drowned as it was. We had come a long way and now
it might end here, tonight, in the wind and the lightning and the dark water. I could not believe that. It could
not end now. The bleeding was less now, and I bandaged
the child's head as well as I could and set her down on
the mattress. I had to go outside again. There would be
something that I could do.

I reached the door, noticing that the motion of the boat was less violent now, though the wind and rain continued as strong as before. The boat was making headway, edging slowly toward the shore. I saw Nate's strained, desperate face in the glare of the lightning as he bent to his steering-oar. Farther out all I could see was the whitecaps on the river. I started round toward the front of the boat, where Jed was.

"Leave him alone," Nate shouted at me again. "We're makin' it now. Leave him alone, damn you."

He called to the woman, and she came over and pulled me back, clinging to me with all her frail strength.

"You want to drown us all?" she panted. "Me and yourself and those young ones too? You don't know nothin' about boats, and Nate can't do it alone. Leave him be; can't you see we're makin' it now?"

She was frantic with terror; I could feel her body shivering against mine.

"All right," I said. "Let me go. Let me go."

There was nothing else to do. I stood there and watched the boat move with terrific slowness toward the shore, toward the shelter of a small cove downstream in the willows. It was like watching something happen in a dream. The rain had settled down to a steady downpour now, and the lightning was less frequent, so that all I could see for minutes at a time was the darkness and the vague boiling whiteness of the water beyond the boat. I was shuddering with cold, drenched through, but I did not even realize it till Nate, in the calmer water a few feet from land, turned the oar over to the woman and jumped ashore to tie the boat up. Then in a few minutes it was over, the boat secure again, the wind howling harmlessly through the willows above.

Jed came around.

"Are you all right?" I said.

"Yes."

He went into the cabin of the boat, over to the bed, and lay down. I lit a lamp.

"You're not," I said. "Oh, darling, what is it?"

"Leave me alone."

I saw that he could hardly breathe. He lay there with his eyes closed. I crouched down beside the bed and put the lamp on the floor beside me. Nate came in. He looked elated.

"Pretty tidy job —" he began. Then he saw Jed and halted, his certainty fading. "What's the matter?"

"You know what's the matter," I said. "If it hadn't been for you — you stupid, clumsy, careless —"

I was crying; I couldn't go on. I wanted to kill him. Jed opened his eyes.

"I'll be all right," he said. "Give me a minute."

"Sure he'll be all right," Nate said injuredly. "Ain't a little thing like that goin' to hurt anybody like Captain Jed. No need for flyin' off the handle —"

He backed out, behind the curtain. I looked at Jed.

"You ought to get out of those wet clothes," I said. "Let me help you —"

"No."

He lay there without moving. I did not know what to do. I knew he was badly hurt, and I sat there on the floor beside the bed and waited and prayed. I could hear the storm dying away outside. It all seemed like a nightmare I had awakened from, except for Jed lying there, breathing shallowly with his eyes shut, and the cold dampness of my own clothes. After a while I realized I was shuddering with a chill, and I got up and changed to dry things in the lamplight. I dressed completely; I knew I would not sleep any more. Jed opened his eyes as I was finishing.

"How are you now, darling?" I said. "Won't you let me help you out of those clothes? You'll catch a chill."

"It won't make any difference. I'm all smashed to pieces inside. Oh, Lacey, what a rotten mess I've made of it."

I came over and took his hand.

"Don't talk like that," I said. "I won't let you. You're going to be all right. Do you want me to get a doctor, darling? We must be somewhere near a town."

"Don't go away."

"All right. I won't. I'll send Nate. I'll get him in here now and we'll get you into some dry clothes and then I'll send him for a doctor. You'll be all right. Nobody will have to find out who you are."

It did not make any difference now if they found out or not. It was better to take the chance of having him spend twenty years in prison than to take the chance of having him die. He wasn't going to die. It couldn't happen now. We had come all this way, and soon the *Fair Maid* would pick us up again and we would be safe. He couldn't die now. I pushed aside the curtain. The woman was sitting with the smaller child in her lap and Nate was already asleep again on the mattress.

"What do you want?" the woman whispered. She was afraid of waking Nate.

"You've got to wake him," I said. "It's Jed; he hurt himself badly out there. I want to get him into some dry clothes, and then we'll have to get a doctor for him."

The woman stood up, alarmed, still holding the child.

"You can't bring no doctor here," she said. "Don't you know that? They'd run us all in."

"I can't help it. He might die — don't you understand?"

I went over myself and shook Nate awake. He sat up, swearing.

"What in hell you want now?"

"You've got to help me. Jed's hurt."

"He'll be all right. You heard him say it yourself."

"He won't be."

"She wants to bring a doctor here," the woman interrupted. "You ain't goin' to let her do that, Nate?"

"A doctor?" Nate said.

"Oh, can't you understand?" I said. I was almost frantic at their indifference. "He may die if we don't get help."

I stopped; I heard something from behind the curtain. When I ran back Jed was half sitting up in bed, coughing; there were bright splashes of blood on his clothes and on the bed. I went over and put my arms around him and helped him lie down again. His face looked gray-white. He lay there with his eyes closed. I turned my head and looked at Nate and the woman standing there behind me.

"You see," I said. "We've got to get help. We've got to. There isn't any other way."

The woman stood there holding the child.

"Help her get him into some dry things, Nate," she said. "That's what you want, ain't it?" she said to me.

"Yes. Then we'll have to get a doctor. Aren't we near a town?"

"Reckon Procter's Landing is the nearest," Nate said reluctantly.

He came over to help me; the woman disappeared behind the curtain. It was just beginning to get light. I could see the first gray of the dawn through the window.

"He ain't so bad off," Nate said. "Are you, Captain Jed? Take more'n spittin' a little blood to make you cash in your checks."

Jed looked at him. "It's not your fault if I'm not," he said. "You damn crazy fool."

"That ain't no way to talk. It might have happened to anybody. I never see such a wind as that."

"You've seen plenty of them. You just happened to be lucky before."

"Don't try to talk, darling," I said. "You mustn't try to talk." I looked at Nate. "Won't you go now and try to find a doctor?" I said. "If it's money you need, I can give you anything you want."

I went over to Jed's bag and took out the envelope with the money in it and handed Nate some bills. He took them slowly, looking at them as if they were not real.

"Please," I said. "Won't you hurry?"

He went out, without saying anything, behind the curtain. I sat down on the bed beside Jed.

"You'll be all right, darling," I said. "We'll get a doctor now and you'll be all right."

He shook his head. "No," he said. "I'm through. Oh, God damn it, Lacey, I don't want to die."

"You're not going to die. You mustn't talk like that. You couldn't die and leave me."

"I won't leave you."

"You see. You said it yourself. We can't be apart, darling. They can do everything else to us, but they couldn't make us be apart."

"They ought to have given us a chance," Jed said. His face looked bleak. "We never had a chance."

"We have a fine chance now, darling. Say we have a chance." I started to cry. "Oh, darling, please say we have a chance."

"We have a fine chance. I didn't want to sound that way." He put out his hand and took mine. "Don't cry."

"I won't. We'll get you a doctor and you'll be fine. I know you will."

I sat there holding his hand. In a few minutes Nate pushed the curtain aside and looked in at me. He had a hangdog air.

"Can you come here a minute?" he said.

I got up and went out to the other part of the boat with him. The woman was standing there, still holding the child. They both looked at me.

"Tell her," the woman said.

Nate cleared his throat. He handed me the bills I had given him.

"Here's your money," he said. "Ain't no doctor comin' here. We can't take the chance. If you-all want a doctor, we'll have to put you ashore."

I stood there. Neither of them would meet my eyes. I looked at the woman.

"You can't mean that," I said. "If it was someone you loved —"

"I've got these young ones to think of," she said fiercely. "Who's goin' to take care of them if they put Nate and me in jail? You'd never ought to come here in the first place. I kept tellin' Nate —"

I turned to Nate.

"We'll give you anything you like," I said. "As much money as you want. Anything —"

"We don't want your money," the woman answered for him. "'Tain't worth it to us, and then have the police comin' around sayin' we stole it." She looked at me, ruthless in her fear. "He's goin' to die anyway, no matter whether you git a doctor for him or not," she said. "I've seen 'em before, spittin' blood like that —"

"Don't," I said. "He won't." I turned again to Nate. "If you put us ashore here, how far are we from help?" I said.

He gestured vaguely. "There's a house just over the hill up there. Folks live up there, do a little farmin' and fishin'. They'd send over to Procter's Landing for a doctor for you, I reckon."

"Will you stay here with Jed while I go up there and find out?"

Nate looked uncomfortable. "Well now, I reckon if you're set on gittin' a doctor it'd be better for us to git on out of here right away. We don't want no trouble —"

"We'll put a mattress out there for you," the woman said. "He can lay on that. It's turned out to be a right fine mornin'; won't do him no harm to be outside."

There was nothing else to do. I could not argue with them. I went back and told Jed.

"It's all right," he said.

"It isn't all right. It's all their fault that you're this way, and now they're turning you out."

"They didn't make that storm," he said. "It was just the kind of luck we had."

Nate and the woman came in, and together we carried

Jed outside. The sun was coming up over the river; it was a lovely morning. Nate brought our bags off, and then quickly unfastened the lines and pushed the shantyboat away from the shore.

"Good-by," he said. "Good luck, Captain Jed."

I knelt down beside Jed.

"I have to go now, darling," I said to him.

"Not for a minute."

"I don't want to go. But I have to get help."

"There's something I want to tell you."

"What is it, darling?"

He was having a hard time talking. He looked very white.

"I won't leave you," he said. "No matter what happens. They can't make me leave you."

"I know that, darling."

"Not even if I die. They can make me die, but they can't make me leave you."

"You won't die. I love you too much. I won't let you die."

I was crying again. I knew I had to go. I kissed him and got up and ran up the beach toward the hill behind. There was a path that I followed. I could hear the birds singing in the trees all around. I ran as fast as I could, but it seemed a long time before I saw the walls of a cabin through the sycamores. Outside it two old hounds lay sleeping in the early sun. They got up and came over to me with slow, friendly curiosity as I approached. A pair of gamecocks strutted in separate cages beside the front door. I knocked, and in a few minutes a tall man with a drooping mustache, in overalls and muddy knee-boots, opened the door and stood looking at me.

"Please," I said. "My husband is very ill, down at the cove. He needs a doctor. Is there one near here?"

"One over at Procter's Landing." He looked at me, half-suspicious. "What's the matter with him?"

"He had a bad fall. Oh, please, there isn't time to explain;

I've got to get back to him. Can't you send someone for the doctor, or go yourself?"

He turned and went back into the house. A woman's face peered at me through a window, curious. In a few minutes the man came back again.

"Dennison'll ride over and fetch the doctor," he said. "My oldest boy, that is. I'll go on down to the cove with you."

"Oh, will you? But please hurry; we've got to hurry."

We went off together down the path. It was almost full morning now. The two old hounds stretched themselves and followed us. I could see the river glittering off below us. Then I lost sight of it through the trees till we came down to the beach again. I saw Jed there, lying perfectly still.

The man walked on before me. I stood there and watched him bend over Jed. He straightened up and looked at me.

"This fella's dead," he said.

I didn't cry. There was nothing left in me to cry. I went over and knelt down beside Jed.

"Go away," I said.

"You can't stay here with him alone."

"I can. Go away."

"I'll fetch my old woman," the man said. "You can't stay here alone like this."

I heard him go away. It was quiet then except for the birds and the lap of the water on the shore. I sat there on the ground beside Jed. It was a long time before the others came.

So Lacey Dereen went on from the cove near Procter's Landing to become Moira Barry, the admired actress of the New York and London stage, and a dozen years later she left all that to buy the Dayton house in Le Jeune and look down at the river where the Fair Maid had come in for a landing and write in a green copybook: "Jed darling, how long — ?" She died of typhoid fever the following year and was buried beside Captain Dayton in Le Jeune, the two graves close together and lonely in a corner of a cemetery that, in 1921, when the final chapter in the history of the Dayton case was written, had only the silent and private beauty of neglect. That was the year that a vagrant named William Barrow, aged seventy-seven, near death in a charity hospital in Memphis, confessed to the murder of Sallie Denslow Dayton at the Phoenix Hotel in Corioli on the night of December 24, 1883.

The green copybook, along with other material relevant to the Dayton case, found its way to the Historical Society of Corioli when Thomas Dandy died in St. Petersburg, Florida, in 1925. Among the items in the collection is the following curious communication, which Mr. Dandy received at St. Petersburg shortly after the death of Lacey Dereen:

Corioli, March 12, 1897

To Tom Dandy
You think you are safe, but we read in the paper where you live and would like you to know that woman Lacey Dereen has recieved her just punishment now and yours is to come. The mills of the Gods etc. You will have no rest even after that either. The wicked dont lie quiet in their graves. Capt. Jed Dayton the murderer and the woman Lacey Dereen have been seen. Walking together, on a dark windy night. You wont believe this if you can help it, but there are relyable persons that saw them. Look to your own eternal future.
A Citizen